Visit us at www.boldstrokesbooks.com

Visit us at www.hematoncologyassocs.com

FURY'S BRIDGE

by
Brey Willows

2017

FURY'S BRIDGE

ISBN 13: 978-1-62639-841-2

This Trade Paperback Original Is Published By
Bold Strokes Books, Inc.
P.O. Box 249
Valley Falls, NY 12185

First Edition: March 2017

CREDITS
Editor: Cindy Cresap
Production Design: Susan Ramundo
Cover Design By Sheri (graphicartist2020@hotmail.com)

Acknowledgments

Knowing who to thank in your very first book seems like a monumental task. Writing has always been my passion, and to bring it to fruition in a book I'm particularly fond of is an exquisite feeling. Although I'll thank several people here, there are many more who were a part of this amazing journey, and I'm grateful to all of them. Mom—thanks for keeping us above water, for always telling me I could, and for being willing to buy me piles of books whenever I asked. Brett Johnston—your encouragement and reminder that writing is about more than theory put me back on the road to word-passion, and I will be forever grateful. Radclyffe and Sandy—thanks for taking a chance on an oddball story from an oddball author; I've been proud to be a part of BSB for nearly a decade, and it's very cool to be on the other side of the coin. Cindy Cresap—thanks for all you do, and for your insights. I've always looked up to you. And last, but certainly not least, to my partner Nic, who got me to plant my ass on the couch every night until this book was finished, and who stayed enthusiastic and sympathetic in the face of my grumpy imposter syndrome-ness. I couldn't have done this without you by my side.

Dedication

For Nic, who saves me each and every day.

Chapter One

Selene Perkton rested her head against the cold train window, ignoring the drab passing scenery. Winter in California could be lovely, but it could also be grim. Every day, she drove the forty minutes from her mountain cabin to the park and ride in the city and then grabbed the train that took her to Cal State LA. It was a long ride, but worth it. She got the best of both worlds, mountains and city, and only had to drive a portion of it. She used the time to read, or write, or even sleep.

That day, however, she couldn't concentrate on anything but her dreams of the night before. Dark, vivid, sensual dreams that left her in a cold sweat. She couldn't decide, even in the dream, whether she wanted the creature hunting her to find her or not. She would turn to run, then change her mind and turn to face the dark shape coming toward her, only to turn and flee again.

"Hi, Selene. Another day, another dollar?"

Selene looked up, startled from her reverie by the conductor. "Oh, hey, Mark. Sorry, I was miles away. Yeah, another dollar. Do you need to see my ticket?"

Mark laughed, his big belly shaking under the tightly stretched uniform top. "You've been riding this train as long as I have, which is far too long. Like I'd ever need to see your ticket." He hitched up his pants and winked at her. "Better get to the rest, though. Have a good one."

Selene smiled and turned her attention back to the passing scenery. Occasionally, she had intense talks with Mark when it wasn't busy, usually about politics or religion. He was fanatical in his beliefs on both, and since she didn't hold any belief in particular as sacred, she always found his fanaticism interesting. She wondered what he would make of her dark dreams.

The disembodied voice announced their arrival at the Cal State station, and she glanced around. There were about ten other people in her carriage, so she'd wait for them to get off first. She hated the crush of bodies, people invading her personal space. She'd rather wait the extra sixty seconds and be able to move freely. When everyone appeared to be off, she made her way to the door, only to feel someone right behind her. She glanced over her shoulder to apologize, as she'd obviously stepped out right in front of them. But no one was there.

She shivered and rushed out into the crisp morning air. The city was cold in January, and it was just what she needed to drive away the feeling of being watched. She hurried to her office, keeping her face to the weak winter sun.

❖

Alec Graves watched as her target left the train platform. She didn't need to follow her. She knew exactly where the woman's office was, when she would have her mid-morning coffee, where she would have her lunch, and what time she would board the train home. She knew the woman felt her presence, which was surprising in itself, though perhaps it shouldn't be, given the reason Alec was following her in the first place.

What Alec didn't know was how to initiate contact. Generally, she just made her presence known to anyone she needed to talk to, and then made sure they didn't remember the occasion. But this time it was different. She needed to tread carefully, and although she knew the woman's routine inside and out, she didn't know much about her deepest thoughts and needs, and without that knowledge she didn't know how to begin.

She glanced at the screen on her cell phone before she answered. "Hey, Ama. What's up?"

"We've got a double for you, up near Tahoe. Details are sketchy, so you might want to dig before letting loose."

"Got it. Address?"

She memorized the address and hung up. Streams of diluted sunlight created faint shadows on the train platform, and she moved carefully, staying in the dark sections created by the light. The job in Tahoe was a relief, of sorts. The time away from Selene Perkton might give her some clarity and provide a way to get into the woman's life. While they still had some time, she would need a good chunk of it to get Selene's cooperation and understanding, which meant there wasn't all that much left over.

A black Hummer pulled up to the curb, and she jumped into the driver's seat. For now, she could concentrate on the new job. When she got back, she would decide what to do about Selene.

❖

Selene stretched, feeling the muscles popping in her shoulders. Surrounded by concrete, she suddenly felt the need to get out in the open air. The creepy feeling of being watched had disappeared once she'd left the train station, and she put it off to being overtired. Her cell rang and she smiled at the name on the screen.

"Hi, babe. How's things?"

"Great. Running the numbers on that big white-collar case I told you about. I just wanted to be sure we were still on for dinner."

Selene could hear the distraction in Mika's voice, a tone she knew well. "Yeah, of course. If you're sure you can spare the time?"

"For you, anything. I'll see you at seven. Bye for now."

Selene shook her head as she hung up. With Mika, seven meant seven. Not a minute earlier or later. When they'd first started dating, she'd watched from the window as Mika stood at the curb, staring at her watch until it was the time they'd agreed on. Only then had she come to the front door. Although she occasionally found it a bit tedious, she appreciated Mika's steadfast, constant ways. Something she'd had to forgo most of her life. *Although "anything" might be a stretch.* If what they wanted to do differed, it was usually Mika's preference they catered to.

She shook off the melancholy spreading through her. *Time for a walk.* She grabbed her simple, no label purse and headed out, glad she'd worn her sensible shoes instead of the cute heels. Those she'd never worn, but she looked at them almost daily, deciding whether the day was special enough. It never was.

She stepped into the open air and instantly felt a little bit better. She started a slow, steady stroll around the square, stopping here and there to watch students playing Frisbee or acting out plays from their English classes. Selene never got tired of watching humanity, even though she always felt slightly outside it. All her life, she'd been apart from the community around her. In social situations she could chat with other people, making the requisite small talk, but there was always a feeling of awkwardness, of being "other." She had no idea what it was that made her seem that way, or feel that way. When she was young she'd been desperate to figure it out, to understand what it was so she could fix it and be like other people. People who had friends, and went to parties, and had coffee mixed with innuendo and gossip. But no matter how hard she tried, or what she did, it never worked. She wasn't one of "them," whoever "them" was. Even among the other philosophy professors, who were generally considered an odd bunch anyway, she still felt less-than. Logically, she knew how stupid that was, as she was their intellectual equal without question. And yet...

"Heads up!"

She ducked the neon Frisbee that brushed strands of her hair as it whizzed past her head.

"Oh my God, Professor Perkton, I'm so sorry. Are you okay?"

She smiled at one of her most promising students. "I'm fine. I should have been paying attention, and I might have been able to throw it back."

The student gave a little laugh. "Cool. Did you want to play?"

"Thank you, no. I need to head back. I just wanted some air. Have fun."

"Yeah. Um, Professor?" The young woman looked down at her Birkenstocks before glancing back up.

"Yes?"

"Would you…I mean, I know I'm a student and all, but do you think…could we…you know, go for a drink some time?"

Selene felt that familiar flutter in her stomach, the one that reminded her she was still a woman, still desirable, and could feel pleasure at someone else noticing that too. "Thank you, but I'm afraid the ethics here are indisputable. Though it's all semiotics and driven by convention, they're conventions we must live by to continue with our moral laden societies."

The student looked somewhat crestfallen, though it was clear she was also considering the nature of the response.

"Thank you, though. The thought is appreciated. See you in class." Selene wandered back to her office, feeling lighter than she had before. Her course on constructivist philosophy was due to start in half an hour, and she needed a good five minutes to make it to King Hall. On the way, she thought about the student's invitation. She'd been invited out many times over the course of her teaching career, but she'd never been tempted. The age gap had always seemed more significant than a number of years might imply. It was the experience, the knowledge, the craving for ever intensifying questions that captured her interest, and a twenty-year-old didn't quite have that yet. *Neither does Mika.* She brushed the thought away. Perhaps not, but she was passionate about her own area of knowledge. And maybe that was enough.

Chapter Two

Alec watched the trio of people standing on the grass in front of a dilapidated house. Though she couldn't see her, she knew there was also a small girl hiding behind the rusted car sitting on blocks in the driveway.

The two men, both with shaved heads and covered in more tattoos than clothing, were berating the woman for something she'd not done correctly. At least, that was Alec's take on the situation. What she also knew was that all three of them were out of their heads on drugs. The woman pled her case, her attention constantly wandering off until one of the men shouted at her again. Alec had seen enough. She turned away and headed to a local coffee shop to wait for night.

At eleven, when the streets were empty of all but those who had nowhere else to go on a freezing winter's night, she walked up to the house. As usual, she left no footprints even in the fresh snow. The door was locked, but that never mattered. A quick flick of her hand and the lock was undone. The room was strewn with empty beer cans, pizza boxes covered in mold, and various pieces of drug paraphernalia. She had little time for drug users, and even less so for those who forced children into that world. She cocked her head and listened. The child and her mother were sleeping in another room, which was good. Although there was rarely any overflow, working on two people at once was always more risky. She'd decided to leave the woman alone and send someone else from the organization to come fix the woman and child, if such a thing were possible.

She leaned over the two men, who were passed out next to each other on the worn, frayed couch. Holding a hand above each of their mouths, she concentrated and brought out the old magic. She felt it tingle in her palms before the silky black mist began to float around them. She directed it into their mouths, forcing it down their throats. Within a few minutes, both men began to twitch and groan. She released the fog and stepped away, eager to get out of the foul smelling house. The men would have terrible nightmares that would progressively get worse, until they were driven mad, day and night. Had they been wicked enough to warrant a visit from her snakes, the progression would have been quicker, nastier. But as they hadn't killed anyone, yet, they'd have years to live before the madness took them completely. Such was the justice of the furies; death was too quick for those who inflicted a lifetime of abuse on others. For that, they would pay with their sanity.

Just as she was about to step outside, she saw a little head peek around the corner. She put a finger to her lips and motioned the child back to bed. Wide-eyed, she disappeared back into the squalid darkness. *This. This is what happens when people think of nothing but themselves.* Her work wasn't always fun, but she believed in it more now than perhaps she ever had. She got back in the Hummer and headed to L.A. *Time to put Selene into action.*

Selene covered her yawn and tried to look interested, but Mika had been going on about the financial aspects of the case she was working on for nearly an hour. As someone who didn't find numbers appealing, Selene had trouble following the minutia of the conversation, though she grasped the big picture. It was one area of many where she and Mika agreed to disagree. Mika felt it was important for people to work hard, to consume in order to build the economy, and that no one should be given a hand up they hadn't worked for. Selene, on the other hand, believed in achieving all you could, in order to put it back into society to make the world a better place. While both of them were atheists, Mika took a hard line on religion, calling anyone who believed "a superstitious Neanderthal." Whereas Selene found the different religions of the world fascinating and believed in a more live-and-let-live ideology, thanks to the fact that religion and society were value laden constructs anyway.

"Are you even listening to me?"

Selene started and realized her eyes had begun to close. "I'm so sorry. It was a long day at work."

"Oh? Some student question you too hard?"

Selene frowned, as always irritated by Mika's teasing, yet stinging, assertion that teaching was a mediocre profession taught by mediocre people to mediocre students at a mediocre university. "No. I was working on my journal article for *The Philosopher*, between teaching my courses."

Mika stretched, and Selene could see her rib bones through the thin T-shirt. One thing Mika deplored was excess, and that included eating anything she considered unhealthy in any way. Which meant dinner at her place usually consisted of lentils or soy, and never anything that had breathed or had more than one preservative.

"Ah yes, your articles. Really, babe. Your writing is so damn good. I only understand three-quarters of what you write. You should give up the teaching thing and concentrate on your books and conferences. That's what you're good at."

"I'm a damn good teacher, too." Selene stood and took her plate to the kitchen, intentionally leaving Mika's on the table, another pet peeve of hers. *I doubt she understands even three-quarters.* She tried to quash the unkind thought.

"I didn't mean to say you're not. You're just wasted there. I still can't believe you turned down that job at SUNY. New York is a fabulous place, and you'd be working with far more stellar minds."

She scrubbed the plate, trying to let her anger wash down the sink with the beige leftovers. "I told you. I don't like New York. I don't like cities. I don't like cold. L.A. is my home. And the students here need someone to believe in them even more than the students who have the money and family to go to the big schools."

Mika came up behind her and slid her arms around Selene's waist. "Please don't be upset with me. Logically, you know someone of your intelligence and capability should be teaching at the highest level, to achieve the greatest gains. I'm sure there's a philosopher who says something along those lines."

"Sure. Marxists think along those lines. But I'm not one."

Mika kissed a soft line along Selene's neck and shoulder. "Whatever you are, I think you're amazing. I just want to see you reach your potential. Surely that's not so bad?"

Her hands caressed circles so soft they were almost irritating on Selene's stomach. "No, of course not." She threw the hand towel on the counter, knowing it would irk Mika's OCD. "Thanks for the vote of confidence." She turned in Mika's embrace and gave her a quick kiss on the cheek. "I think I'll head home. I'm tired."

Mika rolled her eyes and threw up her hands. "Sure. Head home. I say something you don't like, and you run. Go ahead. Let me know when you want to see me again."

She walked away in a huff and closed the bedroom door behind her. Selene sighed and pinched the bridge of her nose to stop the headache rapidly forming. She hated fighting with Mika, but she really was tired, and the jibes about her not reaching her potential were a hot button, one Mika knew better than to push. She gathered her things and headed for the train station, imagining a nice hot bath and a cup of Sleep Tight tea. *Surely tomorrow will be better.*

CHAPTER THREE

Alec waited at the train station for the Silver Line to arrive. Today was the day she would make contact, and there was so much riding on it she felt like she might be ill. That was a new feeling after so many centuries of knowing exactly what she was doing, and why. Now, although there was no question in her mind about the cause, she had doubts about how to get the one person they needed on their side.

The train arrived, and she watched as Selene was the last to get off, per usual. And, as was the case lately, she clearly felt Alec's presence as she looked around, a sliver of fear showing in her usually calm expression. Alec stepped back into the shadows. *Not yet. She's not ready.* Alec ignored the little voice in her head that said it was she who wasn't ready. Once she took that step, it was acknowledging the plan going into play, something they couldn't pull back from. She decided to head to the office to get an update on other issues before coming back to see Selene during her three o'clock coffee break.

She watched Selene head toward the Engineering and Technology Building, which for some reason also housed the Philosophy Department, and noticed the way Selene's hips swayed just right, and the way her blond hair moved in time with her walk. She thought about her eyes, a rare pale blue. *The color of her mother's eyes.* The thought of Selene's mother made her smile. With a deep sigh, she pushed the memories out of her mind and headed for work.

❖

Selene quickly sorted through the messages on her desk before she checked her email. The first one was from Mika.

Babe, I'm sorry. I know I shouldn't bug you about it. I promise not to say anything ever again. Come over tonight and allow me to make it up to you. M.S.

It wasn't much in the way of an apology, but it was likely genuine, as Mika didn't say things she didn't mean. *Which means she meant exactly what she said last night.* Her fingers hovered over the keyboard before she closed the email and quickly scanned others. She was ambivalent about seeing Mika again tonight, as they normally spent a maximum of three nights a week together so they both got the space they needed. But if she was going to truly accept the apology, then perhaps she should capitulate. She looked up at the knock on her door. There was rarely anyone else around so early in the morning. She liked the silence and the slow ease into her work day.

"Hi, Professor. I'm sorry to bother you, but there's a man at reception asking to see you, and he says it's urgent. A Frey Falconi?"

She tilted her head and studied the student receptionist. "Frey Falconi? Can you tell me what he looks like?"

The student frowned, and her eyes nearly crossed as she considered the question. "Well…he's youngish, like maybe thirty. And he's cute, you know, like in a kind of nerdy, kind of outdoorsy way. His jeans fit him well." The student blushed and smiled. "Is that good enough?"

Selene bit her bottom lip. Yes, that sounded like him. She'd worn her comfortable clothing today, a baggy cream sweater and loose black trousers, with her most sensible shoes. If there was ever a day she would have broken out those heels, this would have been one of them. Frey Falconi was a current philosopher celebrity. He'd been on a number of TV shows discussing the nature of religion as opposed to rational thinking, and had his own YouTube channel discussing philosophy in two-minute spurts. He was a people person. Followers flocked to his charisma and easygoing smile. He put philosophy and logic into layman's terms, and the public was eating it up. When she'd seen him on talk shows or watched his podcasts online, Selene had envied his ability to converse so simply about the subject most students found so difficult, and many philosophers had trouble discussing outside their own profession.

"Okay. Yes. Send him up, please."

The student nodded and scurried off. Selene dug in her desk drawer and found a simple cardigan, balled up and covered in old cookie crumbs. She ripped off her old sweater and pulled the cardigan on over her ribbed tank top, after shaking off the largest of the crumbs. It wasn't much, but it was better.

"Ms. Perkton?" Frey Falconi stood in her doorway, looking for all the world like it wasn't seven a.m. and raining outside.

"Mr. Falconi. What an unexpected pleasure. Please come in." She motioned to the chairs across from her desk, glad she could keep her baggy trousers and shoes hidden away.

"Thank you. I wonder if you'd be so good as to sit with me on this side? I find that the formality of sitting across from someone at a desk creates a sense of hierarchy rather than communal discourse between equals."

She winced inwardly but smiled at his implication they were equals. *Clothes don't make the woman.* She moved to the chair opposite him and waited for him to begin.

"I'm sorry to burst in on you like this, Ms. Perkton—"

"It's Doctor, actually, but please call me Selene."

He nodded, and his eyes crinkled with his smile, which seemed so genuine she couldn't help but smile back.

"Of course. My apologies. I saw on your university profile page that you kept early hours. I hope you don't mind me coming in without an appointment, and I know you're busy, so I'll get right to the point. Selene, I read your paper recently on the transhuman evolutionary parallel with constructivism, and the tie-in with the Deleuzian rhizome. I thought it was absolutely inspired, and I just had to meet you to discuss it."

Selene's shock must have been apparent in her expression, because he started to laugh.

"Did you think no one was paying attention? I admit, I thought the same about my work until I realized it could be put in terms people understand. Taking it out of the ivory tower and feeding it to the masses, so to speak. And then people suddenly started paying attention."

"I've seen the way you discuss objectivism. I don't always agree with what you have to say, but I immensely appreciate the way you communicate it. The videos are always so beautifully shot. I wish I could do that with my students."

He leaned forward, his hands clasped together tightly. "But you can. I've read your work, and I believe you have the same talent. Just as you don't agree with all of my ideas, I don't subscribe to all of yours. But that could create something extraordinary, a new philosophy all its own." He stood up and began to pace, his hands in constant motion as he spoke. "You see, I want to create a movement. I want to write articles, develop TV programs, hell, maybe even do a movie. About the next stage of human evolution. The next stage of the human condition. I know you're a costructivist, so you understand what I'm saying. We both believe humanity has to change. I think, together, we can go to the uneducated, uninformed masses who still pray to some cloud figure in the sky, and get them to understand what their role could be in a new world order."

He stopped and looked at her expectantly, and she found herself dumbstruck. "I'm sorry. You want to change the world. The entire world, and the way it thinks. With philosophy."

He dropped into the chair opposite her and gave her a boyish grin. "Yes! What's so strange about that? Philosophy from the time of Aristotle and Plato has changed the world. We still teach the Socratic Method. You teach it, and teach it well, might I add, because you believe in the power of it to get students to think differently. I've done my research, and I know your students understand philosophy better than any other students I've come across, and that's because of the way you impart the information, and because of your passion."

He leaned forward, breathing hard. "More people are paying attention to the questions of meaning, truth, and existence than ever before. Part of the transhuman issue of technology is making people yearn for information about the next step, to understand what it means to be connected. Did you know that fourteen million people in England alone declared they weren't religious last year? And that there's been a twenty percent decrease over the last decade of people who belong to any religion at all? People are ready for this, and the stats back me up when it comes to my followers. There are likely millions more people ready to take the leap into philosophy and logic, who just need someone to explain things in a way they can understand. I think, together, you and I could give them that. We could take the time to work on a book, and during that time, I'll be discussing the options with agents and such."

"But...I'm not a TV person. I'm not a public person. I like quiet libraries and my house in the woods. I could write with you, of course. I'd be honored, as long as I don't have to put my name on anything I find truly at odds with my own personal philosophy."

He laughed, a big guttural laugh. "Of course, I'd expect nothing less. And I'm aware you're not a public figure." He looked her over. "But with the right people behind the scenes, we could make you into a presentable figure to go on talk shows with me, if that was warranted. And of course, you'd need a new look for the book tour. Perception and semiotics and such, you know."

He grinned conspiratorially, and she gave him a slight smile in return. Between his remarks on her appearance and Mika's on her job choice, she was starting to wonder what exactly she had going for her, if anything. Well, Falconi wouldn't be there if it weren't for her work, so at least she had that.

"Can I take some time to think about it? Obviously, it sounds like an excellent opportunity, but I need to check my schedule and see if I can handle the time commitment you're talking about. I can't just leave my teaching commitments, and I'm in the middle of several articles with deadlines."

He looked deflated, like a child whose balloon has been popped. "Of course. By all means, take the time you need. I'll work with someone else if I need to, but you're my first choice. Shall we give you two weeks?"

She nodded. Two weeks was a good amount of time to seriously consider her options. *Mika won't be able to contain herself.* She held out her hand to indicate their meeting was over, and he looked slightly surprised, and then amused.

"Thank you for coming by. It's been a pleasure, and I'll be in touch within the next two weeks with my decision."

He shook her hand. "I'll be waiting."

❖

Two fifty-five p.m. Alec took a deep breath and waited at the little coffee table by the door of the staff cantina. In a few minutes, Selene would walk in, and there would be no turning back. Her phone vibrated in her pocket and she pulled it out.

"Hey, boss."

"Have you made contact? What's she like?"

"Just about to. I'll come to the office when I'm done."

"I don't need to remind you—"

"Nope. Gotta go."

She hung up just as Selene entered the room. Alec watched her walk to the counter, but this time, instead of noticing her seductive sway, she noticed a strange energy cloud attached to her, dark and thick. She wondered if Selene was even aware of it, and who she'd been with that had such bad energy.

Selene turned away from the counter, and Alec made her move. She got up with her coffee and headed Selene's way while looking down at the phone in her hand.

"Oh my God. I'm so sorry." Alec looked up just as she crashed into Selene and spilled the lukewarm drink on her.

"Oh!" Selene jumped back, but a fair amount was still on the oversized sweater.

"I wasn't watching where I was going. I'm so sorry. Here, let me…" Alec tried to dab at the coffee but just spread it around.

"No, please. That's okay. It happens. Really."

Selene looked more distressed than her words suggested, and Alec felt bad for the clichéd ruse. "Can I get it cleaned for you? Or buy you a new one? A whole new wardrobe?" She relaxed slightly when Selene finally looked directly at her and laughed softly.

"I know it's not the nicest sweater, but I don't think that means I need a whole new wardrobe." She looked at Alec almost speculatively. "But I'll take you up on your offer to get it cleaned."

Bingo. Alec smiled broadly. "Excellent. How shall I get it from you? I assume you don't want to strip down here?" She grinned and wiggled her eyebrows, and the way Selene blushed made her pulse quicken.

"If you want to come back to my office with me, I've got a change in there." She held out her hand. "I'm Selene."

Alec took her hand. "Alec. Lead the way."

They walked the short distance to Selene's office in an awkward silence.

"Do you work here?" Selene asked. "I'm sure I haven't seen you on campus before."

"I was here for an interview. I had only just stopped for a coffee before I decided to share it with you."

"Oh? What position?"

"Theology professor." Alec saw the way Selene tried to mask her distaste.

"That's nice."

Selene opened the door to her office and grabbed the rumpled cardigan she'd thrown on her chair. She held it for a moment, then glanced at Alec and made a vague motion with the sweater.

"Oh, sorry." Alec turned her back and grinned. She somehow always managed to forget how modest people could be. She enjoyed walking around stark naked whenever she could. But then, she had other assets that made her feel less naked than the average human.

"Here you go." Selene held out the stained sweater.

"Thank you. I'll have it back to you tomorrow." Alec took it and folded it neatly before looking at Selene. "I don't suppose I could entice you to have lunch with me? I promise not to make you wear any of it."

Selene looked frozen, and she looked everywhere but at Alec.

"Hey, no worries. You can let me know when I drop your sweater off tomorrow. I promise not to be offended. It would just be nice to have a face I know here, if I get the job."

Selene's expression relaxed. "Great. I'll let you know tomorrow. Thank you."

Alec nodded and took Selene's hand in her own. "Till tomorrow, then."

CHAPTER FOUR

Alec strolled into the office with a box of Krispy Kreme donuts and a tray of Starbucks. Although there were many things about the modern age she didn't like, the junk food was excellent. Thanks to her line of work, she traveled enough to keep her waistline down, but some of the older folks didn't have such luck. Most of them didn't care anymore though. Sitting behind a desk all day seemed to drain away old vanities.

She pushed open her boss's door with her hip.

"About damn time. We've been going batshit waiting for you."

"Sorry. I needed some time to think after I met with her. And I come bearing an edible apology."

"I'll give you an edible apology," he mumbled around a bit of donut.

"I never understand you when you say things like that."

"It's his way of accepting your not-so-humble apology." Ama swept her thick black hair behind her shoulders and snagged a chocolate glazed and a chai latte.

"Being humble doesn't get things done. Or get people to do what you need them to." Raspberry filling oozed over Alec's thumb from the side of her donut, and she licked it off suggestively, making Ama laugh and choke on her drink.

"Disgusting behavior. Report."

She watched Zed wipe the crumbs from his beard. He was one of the few old-timers still working who took pride in his physique, and she knew he'd be in the gym later working off the morning treat. She leaned back in her chair and took a sip of her soy latte before beginning.

"She's what we thought, but more. She's clearly Chandra's daughter—I could feel it when I shook her hand. But she's all…" Alec twisted her hands together, like she was wringing out a cloth. "Bottled up. Seriously closed off. I know she hasn't had an easy life, but it seems like it's really affected her."

"Do you think she'll work with us?" Zed leaned forward, his ancient brow furrowed.

Alec shrugged and pushed away the remnants of her donut, no longer hungry. "I don't know. I'm meeting her for lunch tomorrow, to give back the sweater I spilled coffee on."

Ama moaned and covered her ears. "Please don't tell me you were that obvious. Or that you're really such a walking cliché. I thought you'd progressed beyond that centuries ago."

"Hey, you use what works. And it worked. Hopefully, she'll have lunch with me tomorrow and I can use some of the tricks you taught me." She winked at Ama, who gave her a lascivious grin in return.

Zed tapped the table with his massive hand. "Alec, you know what this means. We have to get her on board. Without her…" The already cavernous wrinkles in his face deepened. "We've had to lay off two more from sector 2-A. Granted, they were already pretty much living on the outside, but still. And I heard the fourth floor has pretty much faded into wraith sector." He took Alec's hand in his. "You're our chance, Alec. She's our chance. We've got to make this happen. In the meantime, I'm taking you off your normal duties. I want your full attention on this. Meg and Tis will cover for you until…well, until things happen one way or the other."

"Have you told Meg and Tis that?" She thought about her temperamental sisters, who already had massive workloads of their own.

"Not yet. I'm about to. I wanted to tell you first, so you're ready for their calls. But make no mistake, I'm not relenting on that. I need you focused. I'll take care of your sisters. You take care of us."

He got up and left, and she noticed a frailty about him she'd never seen before. Ama followed him and shot Alec a sympathetic look before heading back to her own department. She didn't bother saying anything. There was nothing to say.

Alec closed her eyes. "No pressure, then."

Selene woke refreshed and feeling more excited about the day than she had for some time. After the conversation with Frey, and the crash meeting with Alec, she'd been overwhelmed with thoughts and emotions. Needing to sort them out, she'd called Mika and let her know she wasn't angry any longer, but she also wanted to spend some time at home alone, rather than take her up on the offer of an afternoon at the Holocaust Museum. Though she sounded somewhat put out, Mika agreed that they'd be better off keeping to their set routine of seeing each other in the evening, rather than attempting to add a daytime excursion as well.

She debated telling Mika about the conversation with Frey, and what it could mean for her career, for her future. Mika would push her to do it, of that she had no doubt. And she wanted this decision to be her own, one she made with her eyes open and her heart in the right place. Not one she made because other people deemed her current position in life inferior according to their own acquired moral codes.

She pulled some clothes from the closet and thought about Alec. What would a woman like Alec like? She thought about Alec's short, dark hair. It looked soft, like you could spend hours running your fingers through it. She liked the little piece that fell over her eyes, making her look young. But there was something about her that made Selene think she wasn't all that young, though she had a kind of....ageless quality about her. She shook her head as though to dislodge the train of thought. *It doesn't matter what she'd like. It's Mika I should be thinking about.* She pulled out the high-collared dress Mika liked, along with the simple brown flats. Then she tossed them into a corner and pulled out a pencil skirt and simple frosted green blouse. *Better.*

She was tired of feeling frumpy. Tired of feeling older than she was. Tired of…not feeling. *Something has to change.*

❖

By noon, Selene was constantly looking up at the door, the papers on her desk largely ignored. When the knock came, she nearly jumped from her chair. Her pulse pounded and her breathing was labored. *Good God. She's just bringing back a sweater. Don't be ridiculous.*

"Come in."

Alec popped her head around the door. "Hi there. Is this an okay time?"

"Sure. I was just grading papers." *Kind of.*

"Great." Alec held out a tissue paper wrapped bundle. "Nice and clean, no stains."

Selene took it and admired the fine paper. "Thank you. A standard dry-clean would have done."

"You deserved the best, since I nearly ruined it." She leaned against the doorway, her arms crossed casually. "So, can I take you to lunch? We can stay here on campus, if you like? Or I know a great place down the road."

Selene hesitated for a moment before putting the package down on her desk decisively. "Yes, lunch would be good. And it would be nice to get off campus for a while. I don't have class until this afternoon." She ignored the tremble in her hands as she grabbed her bag.

Alec looked genuinely surprised, and then pleased. "Wow, great. I'll drive, since I know where we're going. If that's okay?"

Selene locked her office door and shivered at the slightest touch of Alec's hand against her lower back. She glanced up at her and Alec quickly removed her hand. "Sorry. Old habits."

"Sure, I'm happy for you to drive. I don't have my car here, actually. I take the train in."

They headed to the car, taking the absurd number of stairs down to the lower parking lot. Selene walked behind and noticed the way

Alec moved. She seemed so confident. So sure of herself. Selene had a moment of envy, wishing she felt so at home in her own skin. Hell, even on the planet in general. There was something about the way Alec moved though…something about her physique. If Selene looked right at her, everything was fine. But if she looked from the corner of her eye, in her peripheral, something seemed off, like there was a massive shadow of some kind hovering over Alec's back. She put it off to a trick of the winter sunlight and focused instead on not falling down the steep set of stairs. They got to Alec's Hummer and Selene laughed.

"I always thought men who needed a shot of machismo drove these. Or military personnel. I don't think I've ever seen a woman driving one."

Alec grinned. "First of all, who says I'm not macho? And second, have you really looked at the drivers, or just applied culturally based assumptions?" She held the car door open for Selene.

Selene levered herself into the massive vehicle, using the metal step on the side to climb up. She'd never been in a car so high off the ground. It made her think of being in a double-decker train. The black leather seats were gorgeous, and the inside was immaculate. Alec climbed in the other side.

"You know, now that you say it, I'm not sure. Perhaps I have just assumed." Selene tried to think of other Hummers she'd seen, but couldn't actually think of any drivers. "Are you macho?" she asked with a grin.

"Yes. Maybe. Sometimes? I don't know." Alec laughed. "But I'm certainly not a man." She put the car in gear and headed toward the exit. "Mexican food okay?"

Selene began to salivate. She hadn't had a meal with real flavor in an incredibly long time. "Yes. Most certainly."

They were quiet as Alec negotiated her way onto the 10 Freeway. "So, tell me about yourself, Selene. Who are you?"

Selene groaned. "That's an awful question. How does a person ever know where to start with that kind of thing? The details of a person can seem so…banal."

Alec shook her head and laughed. "If you start with the usual stuff, then that can be true. But if you start with the interesting stuff, and work the other stuff in here and there, it can be way cooler."

"Oh? Okay, smart one. So you start. All I know about you is that you don't pay attention to where you're walking, and you teach theology."

Alec gave her a thoughtful look. "Funny, most people would have said I was religious, rather than I 'teach theology.'"

"Well, you might be religious. But I know creative writing teachers who don't write, and science professors who simply teach out of a book, but never do any actual research. You might teach theology but might not be a believer." Selene wondered if she'd said too much, and steeled herself for an argument, or even an excuse not to have lunch after all.

"Astute. I hadn't thought of it that way. I like it."

Selene breathed a sigh of relief. "So, who are you, then?"

Alec's laugh was infectious, and Selene found herself smiling in return. The little butterflies in her stomach had been away for a very long time.

"I'm a creative. I love pineapple, particularly covered in macadamia nuts and mixed with blueberries. I play guitar, and I love to sing. I'm tone deaf, so you never want to hear me do either of those things. I love to read, and I'm obsessive about gathering knowledge simply because I love to learn." They pulled into the parking lot of Macho's Mexican Food.

Selene laughed at the choice of place. "Had you chosen this before our conversation?"

"No. But it seemed appropriate."

Alec grinned, her cocky one-sided smirk making Selene flush. "I agree."

They sat at a table near the window in the small restaurant with only a few other patrons around them. When Alec didn't pick up the menu, Selene motioned at it.

"Aren't you eating?"

"Most definitely. But I know what I'm having. The chile rellenos here are amazing, and they make the best iced tea in all of Pasadena."

Selene glanced at the menu, but she knew she'd never be able to decide. It all sounded excellent, and she found herself ravenous for flavorful food. "I think I'll have the same."

Alec nodded emphatically. "Good choice." The waiter came up and she ordered for both of them. Selene raised an eyebrow and Alec looked chastened.

"Sorry. Like I said, old habits. It's that old-school chivalry thing I can't seem to shake." She moved her fork over a millimeter and back again. "So, you were going to tell me about yourself. Go for it." She leaned forward and steepled her fingers under her chin.

"Okay. We'll come back to the chivalry thing, at some point. But about me...well...I love pizza, and Guinness—"

"I knew I liked you! Sorry, go on."

Selene laughed again, and the butterflies turned into butterflies on caffeine. "I love all kinds of music. I don't own a TV, I'm allergic to pineapple, and I have a fascination with travel."

"An allergy to pineapple is a travesty. What's your favorite place in the world? And where do you want to go next?"

"Cyprus. And...I don't know, really." Selene leaned back so the waiter could put down the chips and salsa, and took a moment to think about the question. There was a time when she had lived to travel. Every paycheck went toward her next trip, and it was all she could think about. And then she got her tenure, and met Mika. Mika didn't like to travel because of all the germs and the difficulty of eating foods she was unaccustomed to, so Selene had stopped traveling. She hadn't been anywhere in years, and the thought made her feel quite low.

"Selene? I'm sorry, have I said something wrong?"

She took a big bite of chips and salsa and closed her eyes. "No, nothing. This salsa is delicious."

Alec nodded, but she was clearly unconvinced. "It really is. I hope you like the food just as much." She took a bite herself, then asked, "So, why would a transhumanist not own a TV? I thought you were all about technology making humans better. Does TV not qualify?"

Selene frowned. "Not generally. I think some channels had real potential. Like National Geographic and the Discovery

Channel. But even they've gone the way of reality television and pop culture claptrap. It used to be there were shows that expanded your knowledge base. Now they just show you people's over- or underdeveloped bodies and self-esteem issues. Transhumanists, or at least this one, believe that technology can, and should, help the human race evolve. We should use what we've created to overcome our limited human condition in order to create a better world."

Alec continued to munch away on chips as she mulled over Selene's answer. "Why?"

"Why? What do you mean?"

They paused the conversation to let the waiter put their food on the table. Selene became utterly focused on the beautiful smelling meal in front of her. She hadn't seen so much fried food and cheese in far too long.

"I mean," Alec said between bites, "why should we strive to make the world a better place?" She held up her fork to forestall Selene's response. "I don't disagree. I just want to understand why you think so."

Selene relaxed into the seat. She'd nearly jumped out of it at the question, which seemed absurd. "Because we owe it to ourselves as humans, and to our children. We don't have other planets to live on. One day, we might. But we don't know when that will be. So we need to make this one as exceptional as it can be. There's no reason for us to stop evolving simply because we've reached the top of the food chain. We should continue to evolve using the truly astounding technology we have at our fingertips. We shouldn't just rot away, allowing ourselves to only be a percent of what we could be."

Selene stopped talking and started eating, embarrassed at her little tirade. It was an argument she had often, and it was something she felt strongly about. But getting on her soapbox now, with a perfect stranger, wasn't the time.

"I don't know if I agree or not. I'll have to take the time to ruminate on it." Alec looked at Selene over the edge of her iced tea. "But I like your passion."

Selene flushed and put it down to the spice in the food. "Thank you."

They spent the rest of the meal in surface small talk, and Selene was glad they'd left the heavier topics for another time. *Another time?* She hoped so. She had so enjoyed the meal and the light banter. It was energizing, invigorating. Exciting.

They climbed back into Alec's truck and drove the ten minutes in silence. When they got there, Alec turned to her.

"Thank you for lunch. I really enjoyed it. Could we do it again sometime?"

Selene's pulse raced and she thought her heart might beat out of her chest. She saw Alec's gaze move to her mouth, and she flushed somewhere lower.

"I'd like that. But, Alec…" She hated that she felt the need to say the words out loud, but knew she had to. "I'm seeing someone. I've been with her for several years. So, it would only be as friends, right?"

Alec looked slightly surprised, and Selene was mortified at her own presumption. Not only that Alec was also a lesbian, but that she had any interest at all. "I'm so sorry. How stupid of me. I don't mean—"

Alec put a fingertip to Selene's lips. "Stop. Thank you for clarifying, because yes, I would have asked you on a real date. So, if that's not on the table, can we still have coffee? Maybe next week?"

Selene's lips burned where Alec's fingertip lay against them. She moved away from the disturbing sensation. "Of course. I'd like that. Thank you for lunch. And for my sweater."

Alec placed a hand over her heart. "Thank goodness. Otherwise, I'd have to leave a big plate of pineapple outside your door all the time, until you got freaked out enough to go out with me again." She winked, and then reached into the glove box and pulled out a business card holder. She passed a card to Selene. "If you want to get together, as friends, give me a call. Otherwise maybe I'll give you a call sometime next week, for coffee?"

Selene read the business card, but all it had on it was Alec's name and phone number. "This has a clandestine feel to it."

Alec laughed, but there seemed to be some nervousness in it. "Nope. Just an easier way to give my number to people, that's all. Hopefully, I'll get the position here and get new ones. Less mysterious ones."

Selene opened her door and climbed out. "Thanks again."

Alec waved. "Believe me, my pleasure."

She drove away, and Selene turned to watch from the stairs as the Hummer disappeared from sight. Once again, that strange feeling that she couldn't quite see it properly came upon her, and she grimaced. Maybe it was time to see an eye doctor.

As she made her way back to her office, feeling as though she were walking on marshmallows, she decided not to analyze her feelings just yet. She'd hold on to this feeling as long as she could.

Until I get to Mika's tonight, anyway.

CHAPTER FIVE

Itold you, Meg, it's not my choice. Want to trade places? Do you want to be the one everyone is looking to? The one responsible for saving hundreds of jobs and lives? If you do, say so, and I'll gladly switch with you."

Meg rolled her eyes and tossed her fire red hair behind her. When they were young, her hair would constantly be flaming, to match her temper. Now she controlled it, but the reds and oranges of her eyes still showed when she was pissed off. Like now. "You're such a drama queen. We know how important it is, Alec. But I don't see why you can't carry on with your normal work until you have to spend all your time with her. You're not meeting her until next week, right? So why am I doing your job tonight? You know I hate the family disturbance stuff."

"You love the family disturbance stuff. That's your thing."

"Not the kind from tonight's job." She crossed her arms over her chest, and her hair started to snap and crackle.

"Fine. Okay. You're right, I don't have other plans tonight. I'll clear it with Zed and assure him I won't let daily work interfere with the big picture. Okay?"

Meg's hair settled back down, and her eyes returned to their usual jade green. "Better. I promise, once you're in it up to your neck, Tis and I will have your back. But until then..." She fluffed her hair and straightened the low-cut top.

Tis burst into the room. "Alec, we've got to go. The case tonight just changed, and I need to be there too."

Alec sighed. Tis had some of the worst cases, and she was definitely the one with the temperament suited to them. Icy, remote, and controlled, she was rarely affected by what she had to deal with. Meg waved them off. "I'm making dinner for some friends tonight. Feel free to come over if you're done early enough."

Alec waved an acknowledgment without looking back. She saw Tis's brilliant white hair disappear around the corner ahead. If she was in that much of a hurry, it must be serious. She picked up the pace to catch up with her. Whether she liked it or not, this was her job, and one she'd done successfully for years. She wasn't about to let down the company now.

Once in the car, Tis relaxed slightly. She was always happier when she was on her way somewhere. Anywhere. She despised being stationary. Alec knew that of the three of them, Tis had been hardest hit when they'd moved into a real building rather than the caves and forest homes they'd lived in once upon a time.

"Alec?"

"Yeah?"

"Can you do it?" Tis looked straight ahead, her brow furrowed in the way that meant she had something serious on her mind.

"Do what?"

"What Zed wants you to do. What the board has asked you to do. Save us. Save the organization." She looked at Alec and away again. "Jesus. How that sounds. When you think of what we are. What we've been. And it all comes down to you, and a Demi. Like all the rest of us are just...extraneous. And yet we're trying to keep our places."

"Geez, Tis. You sound even more Eeyore than usual. What's up?"

Tis squeezed her eyes shut and rested her head against the side window. "I'm tired, Alec. I'm tired of the nonstop work. When we started, we kept to our little patch of land, and that felt too big at times.

Now we respond to calls all over the world. Sure, there are plenty of other divisions with entities doing what we do, but you know what I mean. Between all of us, we're not keeping up. People are slipping through the cracks. Egregious crimes are going unpunished. And for what?" She shifted to look at Alec, tears running down her face. "For what, Alec? It all just happens again another day. It used to be that what we did mattered, that after we'd done our jobs, people didn't do stupid things anymore." When Alec raised an eyebrow, Tis sighed. "At least, not that particular stupid thing, anyway. But now…" She raised her hands helplessly. "They just do it again, or someone else does it the next moment. It never ends."

Tis looked out the window for a long moment, before she asked softly, "What is it you're trying to save?"

Alec stayed silent, stunned. Tis had always seemed so solid, so resilient. She wasn't prone to flights of temper and narcissism like Meg, or to the black fury and self-doubt that took hold of Alec. If Tis, strong, steady Tis, was feeling this way, how many others in the organization felt the same?

"Would you have me give up? Do you think we should all just…fade?"

Tis shrugged and wiped the tears away with her sleeve. "I don't know. Maybe you're fighting for the ones who want to stick around. But maybe the rest of us should be allowed to make the choice."

Bile rose in the back of Alec's throat. "The rest of *us*? Fuck, Tis. What are you saying?"

Tis didn't respond. She wrapped her arms around herself and rested her head against the side window. They spent the rest of the drive in silence. Alec didn't push. She couldn't, because she didn't have instant answers. She needed to consider her words, her actions. She needed to think and create an answer that made sense. She'd never considered the idea that some of the organization didn't want to be saved. And Tis was right; why, with all the power, knowledge, and ability in the organization, did she have to go it alone? A feeling of unfair despair washed over her.

When they got there, the house was surrounded by yellow crime scene tape. Blue flashing lights cast sickening shadows on the urban middle class houses. The Hummer pulled to a stop in the middle of the chaos, but of course no one saw it. Tis stopped Alec with a hand on her arm before they got out. "I'm sorry. I've had a string of tough cases and it's making me morose. Don't let me get to you. If anyone can do what needs to be done, it's you." She leaned over and kissed Alec on the cheek. "And you know Meg and I are beside you, come what may."

Alec pulled her in for a tight hug. "Don't feel like you have to go it alone either, Tis. You can always talk to me. Talk to someone. Just don't…don't fade on me, okay?"

Tis nestled her head in Alec's neck and nodded, then let go and pulled away. She took a deep breath and visibly pulled herself together. "Let's go do this, shall we? I'd like to get back for Meg's dinner."

They made their way to the house, walking around meandering police staff and crime technicians marking every blade of grass and fallen leaf. Tis sniffed, and Alec saw her eyes change to crimson. She too felt the tang of blood on the back of her tongue, could smell the discharged gunpowder in the air. More than anything, the acrid stench of fear hung thick on the air. They walked inside, and Alec grimaced at the carnage.

She had never gotten used to the damage one human being could inflict on another. Particularly family members. A woman's body lay sprawled on the living room rug, her blood seeping into the simple geometric pattern and creating a grotesque piece of art. A trail of blood indicated where she'd come from, and they followed it to the rear bedroom, where two children lay still, looking as though they were sleeping, if it weren't for the bruises around their necks.

Alec unfurled her wings, the pearlescent black sucking all the light from the room. Her snake tattoos came to life on her arms, and she stalked through the house looking for her quarry as the snakes hissed and writhed around her forearms. Tis let her true self come to the fore as well, her white wings highlighting the horror movie scene surrounding them. Alec followed Tis out the back door. They could smell the coward, his fear and self-loathing, his repugnant sense of entitlement. The authorities searched, but had failed to find the basement shelter located under the shed. Tis and Alec dropped through it without opening the hatch.

He sat with his knees to his chest, blood on his hands and shirt. They could hear his thoughts, and while there was a crumb of remorse, his largest concern was how long he could stay hidden so as not to get caught. Tis held out her hand, and Alec took it. They dropped the magic that kept them hidden and appeared to him in all their terrible glory.

He screamed.

And kept screaming.

They held out their free hands, and Alec's silky black mist twisted around Tis's red one. Entwined into a deadly spear, the combined mists pierced the man's chest, came out the other side, and dove back in. Punishment and retribution were theirs for the giving, and this despicable excuse for a living creature deserved no mercy. They gave none.

He would be plagued with visions of what he'd done, ever increasing in horror, until he lost his mind completely. There would be no relief, no pardon, and no escape from the terrors of his days and nights. Tis punished him for the murders, and Alec punished him for his lack of morality, for caring more about his own desires than about right and wrong.

They finished and left him in the dark hole, still screaming incoherently, which brought the police to the shed.

Back in the truck, they left silently. The job was done, like so many before, and so many yet to come.

Alec pulled her outside world cloak back on, but Tis remained in her true form. There was a time Alec hated pretending to be something she wasn't. But at some point over the years, she'd become just as comfortable in her outside body as she had her true body.

What does that say about me? She didn't know, and that was more terrifying than anything else she could think of.

❖

They pulled up outside the office, both exhausted. The drive back had felt heavy, burdened with unspoken thoughts and fears. Tis turned to her, eyes still their natural red. "Are you coming to Meg's for dinner? I think we can probably still get something. And I think we could both use a drink." She smiled, her razor sharp teeth showing up easily against the black night.

Alec shook her head. "No, I don't think so. You've given me a lot to think about, and I need some sleep. I'll see you at work tomorrow."

"I'm on a job tomorrow, in the East. I won't be back for a few weeks, probably."

Alec gave her a tight hug. "Be careful. And if you need anything, call. I'll come. I promise."

Tis gave her a sad smile and got out. While she and Alec had chosen to live off-site, Meg still lived on campus. She liked being in the center of things, and her dinner parties were always an eclectic gathering of the organization's oldest and elite. The last thing Alec felt like doing was answering the same question she'd been asked too many times over the last few days: "Can you do it?"

She drove the three miles back to her place in Venice Beach. Her home on one of the few canals was her sanctuary. With its view of the water and secluded location, she could let down her guard and just be. Added to that was the same kind of haze that kept it from being noticed, like the Hummer. It was there, but not there. Unless invited inside, no one passing by would notice it. Once, the job and her life had been the same, and she'd lived on campus with everyone else. Her entire existence was meant only to do the work. And she'd been fine with that.

But over time, with the changes of humanity, it had been necessary to change. Adapt or die, as the saying went. She'd needed distance, time to feel like her existence was about more than just evil people doing evil things.

She threw off her clothes and reveled in the feeling of the cool air on her naked skin. She stretched her wings, letting the full length of them fill the width of the living room. While the magic only concealed what they were to the outside world, never actually changing them, it still felt like she was shedding a layer of skin when she dropped the magic and existed just as she was. She poured herself a glass of white wine and let the delicate flavor take her back to a simpler time. When right was right, and wrong was wrong. When wrongdoers understood that their actions had consequences. When people looked out for one another. *Even the old heroes watched one another's backs. War was war, and we rarely had work to do when they were occupied with obtaining glory.*

Was that true, though? She thought about the family dramas they'd been a part of. Epic tales now, but then, a part of life. Yes, life was more black-and-white then, but the machinations of humans hadn't really changed. The difference was that most of them back then believed in the repercussions of a poorly lived life with regard to an afterlife. Now, that was rapidly disappearing, and humanity was living in a cesspool of greed and an ever increasing tornado of consumerism. Nothing was ever enough, and now that included family and friends as well as the material stuff.

She thought about Selene and her belief in humanity and the possibility of humans to better themselves. But she also knew Selene's feelings and views were mixed. While she was a transhumanist who thought the world could be made better through technology, she was also a posthumanist, which meant she thought humans had no special place in the world. They were just another species.

For centuries, Alec had believed in humans. She'd watched them create, build, transform. She watched them save swaths of populations with cures for diseases; she watched them travel to help other countries and even walk on the moon. And then they destroyed. They burned, decimated, blew up entire cities over incoherent moral questions and the desire for more. She and her sisters had been so busy in the 1940s, they'd barely had time to sit down before being called to the next job. At one point, Alec began living in Germany, darting between camps to deliver her particular brand of justice. Humanity had been nothing but a horror. Only later, when they heard tales of heroism, of the underground, of the resistance, did they feel any hope for the race.

She thought about her conversation with Tis and took a deep drink of wine. She needed answers. She needed to understand before she went any further.

And if I don't get the answers I need? What then?

Chapter Six

Selene picked up the phone and put it down again. She walked away. Came back. Picked it up. Put it down. She flipped the strange business card over in her hand. Put it down. Moved it closer to the phone. Picked up the phone.

Oh, for goodness sake. What the hell is wrong with me?

She knew what was wrong, though. Her dreams had taken an unusual turn. If she had dreams, which was rare, they were often about work, or revolved around the theme of being alone. But these new dreams were fraught with tension. Some were sexual, so sensual and filled with need and longing she woke aching and wet. Others were frightening. She was being chased, her pursuer wanting something from her she couldn't fathom. Her dream self knew the price of failure was death. She woke from those covered in sweat, her heart pounding, fear coursing through her wildly.

Somehow, she felt like both of the dreams had to do with Alec. The sexual one she could understand. Alec was attractive, charming, and new. Any rational lesbian would be attracted to her. But the terrifying dream, that made no sense. She thought of the strange feeling she had of not seeing Alec properly, of the blurry effect she'd experienced.

Stupid. The sun this time of year always created superficial auras. She shook off the feeling and picked up the phone.

"Hello?"

She went to speak but nothing came out. She tried again, and this time was mortified at the croaking sound she managed.

"Sorry? I didn't catch that."

"Me. It's me. Selene. From the university. Hi."

"Oh, hey there. I'm glad you called."

Glad. She's glad. That's good. Breathe, stupid. "I was wondering, if you were on campus, if you wanted to have coffee? One I could drink, rather than wear?" She winced. *Excellent. Remind her of her clumsy moment.*

Alec laughed. "Well, that's not as much fun, but I accept. Tomorrow?"

"Today. I mean, are you around today?"

There was a slight hesitation before Alec said, "Yeah. I can do that. Three o'clock?"

Selene finally allowed herself a normal breath. "That sounds great. See you then." She hung up without saying another word, then cursed herself for her rudeness. She plopped down on her sofa. She'd done it. For three days, she'd thought about Alec, dreamt of her, replayed their conversations over and over again, and thought of a trillion more things she wanted to ask, wanted to say. She couldn't help but notice that the feelings she got in her tummy, not to mention between her legs, when she thought of Alec were far different from anything she'd ever felt with Mika. The thought was jarring, and ethically, she knew she was walking in unknown territory by inviting Alec for coffee. She said she wanted a friend. *And I do. There's nothing wrong with that.*

She riffled through her clothes, this time choosing something she liked, rather than what someone else would like. She slid into the fitted pencil skirt and loose sweater, and topped off the outfit with cute flat boots. It wasn't sexy, necessarily, but it made her happy. And she always found happy people more attractive than sad ones. Perhaps because they often seemed her opposite.

She grabbed her keys and headed for work, already wishing the day away. In an effort to focus on something other than Alec, she studied her notes for the day's classes on the train. Mark, the conductor, wasn't there, which was too bad. She would've liked to have spoken to him and gotten his views on theological teaching at the university level. Although he'd not gone far in education, he'd taught himself more than many of her students had learned at college. And he complemented it with the experience that comes with age. She certainly didn't agree with his views on religion, but she appreciated his candor.

When she got to her building, she stopped at reception to sign in, and the young woman jumped up from her chair. "Oh, wait. Something came for you."

She hurried away and came back holding an enormous bouquet of flowers. "Normally, I'd leave them in front of your office door in case I missed you, but they're too big. Someone must really like you. A bouquet like this costs a fortune."

Selene had never bought flowers for anyone, nor could she remember anyone buying her any, so she had no idea what they cost. She sniffed appreciatively at the mix of roses, tulips, and tiger lilies. It was truly gorgeous. "Thank you, I appreciate it." She slung her laptop bag over her shoulder and picked up the heavy vase.

"Aren't you going to open the card?" the student asked, looking hopeful.

"I will. In my office." Selene smiled gently. She didn't let her students know anything about her personal life. She felt it necessary to keep the two completely separate. It was known she was a lesbian, as she often attended the staff and student LGBTQ events, though never with Mika. She'd asked her to attend once or twice, but Mika had made it clear she wasn't about to spend her evening with "smart people wasting their talents on people who didn't appreciate it." *I wonder if Alec would attend something like that?*

She pushed the thought away. No. That would be crossing a boundary. Coffee, during the day, was one thing. She hadn't felt the need to tell Mika about it. She'd just get paranoid and pouty, and given there was no reason for it, Selene decided not to say anything. Guilt niggled at her, though. She wasn't about to mention today's coffee, either, and she knew that once you started keeping secrets like that, it could be a slippery slope. *I'll tell her before dinner tomorrow. That I have a new friend. Then it will be okay.* She was rationalizing, and she knew it. But maybe once it was out in the open, some of the mystique around it would fade.

She barely managed to juggle the flowers and her bag to get her office door open, and when she looked at her sweater, it was covered with yellow pollen smears. She grimaced and opened the card. She knew they wouldn't be from Mika, as she considered flowers a silly waste of money.

Dearest Dr. Selene,

I so enjoyed our chat. I hope these brighten your day the way the thought of working with you has brightened mine. I do hope you're still considering my proposition, and remember, if you have any thoughts or questions, I'd love to discuss them. Even, perhaps, over dinner?

Yours,

Frey

She put the card on her desk and bit her lip. He was likeable, he was direct, and he was passionate. He knew what he was talking about, and people were listening. A lot of people. Maybe that was why she was finding it so difficult to make a decision, something she rarely, if ever, had trouble with. The thought of being in the public eye, with all that responsibility on her shoulders, made her stomach ache. Although she often gave things serious thought, and she never went anywhere or did anything without thinking it through, she could also think things through quickly, and could be quite decisive when pushed. She felt pushed now, and she didn't like it. It was too big a decision to take lightly.

She looked at the pollen dust on her sweater and thought back. One of her foster parents had loved gardening, and was often covered in the stuff. Selene locked her office door and shrugged carefully out of the sweater. She snapped it several times and watched the pollen dust fly off. When she was done shaking it out, there was only a bit left. She grabbed her tape dispenser and pulled off a long piece. Then she carefully went over the various pieces of the sweater still slightly yellow, lifting it off bit by bit. Who knew that kind of knowledge would come in useful? She certainly hadn't, when she was ten and living with the gardening family. *At least they were kind.* The elderly woman had seemed to enjoy having company and had taught Selene about all kinds of flowers and herbs. But then, she'd had a heart attack, and the woman's husband decided to move to Toronto to live with his son. After a year away, Selene was sent back to the children's home to wait for the next set of foster parents.

Turning to put the sweater back on, she caught sight of herself in the mirror. The black lace bra she wore showed a hint of her nipples. Her one concession to extravagance was her lingerie. Granted, no one saw it, and yes, it was certainly at odds with her often somber, utilitarian clothing choices, but it made her feel pretty, sexy, even when she was on her own. Like now. She ran her hands over the soft, expensive lace and felt her nipples harden under her palms. She closed her eyes and reveled in the sensation. Just for a minute. When she allowed images to come, it wasn't Mika she saw.

Alec. Alec's bright eyes, her kissable lips. She felt her panties grow wet, and she pressed her lips together to keep from moaning out loud. Instantly guilty, she tugged the sweater back on and placed the flowers far from her desk. They left a mess of pollen on her papers, and she shook it off. Selene wondered if there was a symbolic aspect, philosophically, of something from Frey changing what it touched. Once again, she chose to ignore the thought. She pushed Alec's image from her mind and settled down to grade papers. She needed to refocus. She'd learned as a child the only way to get ahead was to take control. She'd never give it up again.

Alec pulled onto the campus at two forty-five. She wanted plenty of time to make her way up the ridiculously long staircase to the buildings. Since their conversation that morning, she'd been pondering the next step with Selene. Granted, she'd wanted her attention, and Alec needed to build a relationship with her. Zed had told her "by any means necessary," and he meant it.

But if there was one thing she wasn't, it was a player. Leading Selene on would be morally problematic, and it could also jeopardize the entire operation. Sure, there was an attraction, she could admit that to herself. But her many years on the planet had taught her that not every attraction had to, or should be, acted on. This was certainly one of them. What she needed to do was get Selene's trust. Her friendship. She needed Selene to see her as an intelligent peer and confidant. Then, when she explained what they needed, what Selene, and only Selene, could do, it wouldn't come as such a shock.

Right. Sure. Of course not. Nothing like telling someone the monsters are real.

She shook the thoughts off and headed for the cantina. She sat by the door, as she had the last time, after ordering both their coffees. When Selene came in, she ignored the flutter of desire between her legs and waved her over.

Selene smiled and gestured at the coffee. "For me? Unless you're particularly thirsty."

"One to throw on someone, one to drink. Seemed only right to continue the pattern."

"That seems wasteful. Why don't I drink one, and if you really feel the need later, we can get you some water to throw instead? That way you don't have a dry cleaning bill."

Alec grinned. "Well, when you put it that way, I suppose that sounds reasonable." She tilted her head at the coffee. "I wasn't sure if you take anything in it." She was, of course. She knew very well Selene took two sweeteners in a large coffee, but she wasn't about to let on she was a stalker. *A stalker with good reason, but still.*

"I do, thanks. I'll grab some—"

"I've actually already got a selection." Alec pulled a napkin off a pile of sugar and sweeteners. "I'm a bit OCD that way." She liked the way Selene looked at her appreciatively.

"That's lovely, thank you." Selene took a moment to fix her coffee.

Alec cleared her throat. "So, I was surprised to get your call."

Selene folded her napkin in half, then half again, before reopening it and smoothing out the creases. "You said you could use a friend, and I enjoyed our lunch the other day. Since we made it clear where our boundaries lay, I thought it made sense…" She shrugged, looking embarrassed.

"I'm really glad you did. I've been at a loss about what to do with my time while I'm waiting for this job decision."

"Have they said when they'll get back to you? I don't know many people in the theology section, but I might be able to have a word?"

Alec shook her head quickly. "No, no. Please don't. I don't want to look desperate or like I'm having a friend jump in on my behalf. I just have to be patient, which isn't one of my strong suits. And it's not like there isn't plenty to do in L.A."

Selene nodded, looking serious. "It's a wonderful place. Not the city itself, obviously, but the outlier cities are great. Are you from here?"

Alec struggled to keep a poker face. "Kind of. I've lived here for a while. But I've traveled extensively, so I don't really have a certain place I call home." *All true. Not lying to her. Yet.*

"Where have you traveled to? Was it for work? Or pleasure?" Selene's eyes lit up with interest.

Alec hesitated. There wasn't a part of the world she hadn't been to, but that wasn't really anything she could say without revealing too much, too soon. "God, it seems like I've been everywhere. I think Europe is my favorite, particularly around the Med. Mostly teaching lessons of various sorts, for work. Though I gladly travel for pleasure, when I have the time. You?"

Selene looked wistful as she sipped her coffee. "I love Europe too. Particularly Greece. It's the philosopher in me. I can't seem to get enough."

Alec's heart skipped a beat, and she steadied her hands by holding on to her coffee. "Yeah, I know what you mean. Do you have any plans to travel this year?"

"No. I haven't been in a while. My partner isn't very travel friendly. So I tend to stay Stateside. Well, in California, really. Denver, occasionally."

Selene looked so sad, and as though her thoughts were a million miles away.

"Could you not travel alone?"

"Alone?" Selene looked vaguely surprised at the suggestion. "Without Mika?"

Alec shrugged. "Yeah. I mean, I know some couples are joined at the hip, but I know plenty who go on vacations with friends or family instead of their partners. Or alone, even. I've never understood the expectation some people have that they should give up their hopes and dreams for someone else." She gave Selene what she hoped was a convincing smile. "Seems to me, being with someone should help you fulfill those dreams, not make them impossible."

"I hadn't thought of it that way." Selene started folding, refolding, and unfolding the napkin again, this time with more concentration. "I guess I've been alone so much, the thought of going somewhere wonderful without someone seems depressing."

Now it begins. "Alone a lot? Were you an only child?"

Selene tensed visibly, the tiny few lines around her eyes deepening. "Kind of. In a manner of speaking."

"Vague, much?" Alec laughed, and Selene laughed with her.

"Let's talk about something else. Tell me about theology."

Retreating to the mind. Okay. I can do that. "What do you want to know?"

"Why would you choose religion? What drew you to that?"

Alec turned the coffee cup around and around in her hands. *Focus. Careful.* "Well, my mother and father were both religious leaders, in their time. I saw a lot of good come from it. It gave people hope, something to hold on to in their darkest times."

Selene nodded. "Okay. Go on."

Alec grinned. "I assume you're mentally poking holes in everything I say as I say it?"

"Of course. But I'd still like to hear it. I'm fairly open-minded, I think."

You have no idea. "But I decided to study religion as a way to understand humanity. As a way to get into the social and cultural minds of humans as a whole. The way they understand deities and afterlife, the way they function in the world according to the spiritual laws they work under—"

"They? Do you consider yourself something other than human?" Selene laughed.

Alec winced internally. *Rookie mistake.* "Not at all. Just using the royal we, so to speak. Anyway, I find that fascinating, and anthropologically, it tells us so much about our existence." Selene was studying her intently as she spoke, and she felt that same flutter again. "So you see, it's not that I subscribe to any one religion. I'm just fascinated by them all. And I think understanding them can help us understand ourselves as humans."

Selene leaned back in her chair as though just having ingested a large meal. "That's an interesting reason to teach it. And what about all the arguments against religion? Do you create discourse around those too?"

"Indeed. What's learning without asking the difficult questions?" Selene's eyes lit up again, and Alec winced inwardly at the slight trickery. She knew, from eavesdropping on Selene's lectures, that she used that exact phrase in her own classes. "However, I have to bring up the issue of faith. A primary tenet of most religions is that you have faith. Belief that things are the way you say they are, the way you believe them to be, even if you can't see them or have no evidence of their existence. And, as such, you have to believe that the things we judge as 'bad' things are all part of a plan we don't fully understand."

Selene shook her head, but she was smiling. "Now that's where I have a problem. Belief in something you can't see, in the hopes that an articulated desire for something to happen will make it so, seems ludicrous to me." She raised her hands in a placating gesture. "But I'm sure the study of the world's religions must be truly fascinating."

"Well, you believe in the mind. In the state of being, right? Or do you think we all cease to exist when we fall asleep because we're no longer conscious of our surroundings?"

Selene smiled. "I think therefore I am? And if I'm not thinking, I don't exist?"

Alec nodded.

"No. I don't follow that blindly."

"And you believe in the mind as a concept? In semiotics and semantics? So in that sense, you believe we construct much of our world through meaning and words." She watched as Selene was clearly already formulating an argument. "In that way, you believe in things the same way a religious person does. You just ascribe those things to people and behavior instead of to a deity."

Selene frowned for a moment, and Alec wanted to trace the crease between her eyebrows with her thumb.

"I need to ponder a proper response to that, I think."

Alec grinned. "Good. I like that you do. It means we can have a real conversation about it."

"You won't be offended if I argue with you?"

"Are you kidding? As long as we can have a genuine discussion." Alec felt like she was being watched, and the hairs on the back of her neck bristled. She tried to subtly glance around, but couldn't see anyone. *Or anything.* "I've had more than one discussion where the other person just blew me off because of the religious aspect, and to me, that's not truly engaging."

Selene nodded, still looking thoughtful. She glanced up when a student stopped by their table.

"Hi, Professor. I'm really sorry, but do you have a minute?"

The girl had obviously been crying, and her cheeks still glistened slightly from her tears. Her hair was in disarray, and her clothes looked oddly askew.

Selene looked at Alec apologetically, and Alec just gave her an understanding nod and smile. "By all means. Maybe we could finish our discussion later?"

Selene quickly backed toward the door, her hand on the student's shoulder. "Of course. Next week?"

Alec waved. "Just let me know when."

Selene put her arm around the girl's shoulders and led her away. It looked so sweet, so caring, that it left a lump in Alec's throat. She hoped the girl was okay, but she'd seen enough women with that look in their eyes, and that physical presentation, to have an idea of what was going on. She sighed and tried to focus on the moment.

Alec looked around, searching for the person who'd been watching them. But the feeling had gone, which made her uneasy. If it hadn't been Alec someone had been watching, who was watching Selene? And what's more, why didn't Alec know about it?

Chapter Seven

S elene stood at Mika's kitchen counter dicing tomato for their salad. Mika was finishing a bit of work at the kitchen table, and the room was silent, with only the tap-tapping of Mika's fingers flying across the keyboard. Though Selene liked music on whenever she was in her own kitchen, Mika preferred silence when she was working on anything. Selene was considering how to broach the subject of Alec. She was also feeling guilty about keeping Frey's offer a secret. This was supposed to be a real relationship, unlike the few surface dalliances she'd had before, and she knew things like that weren't kept quiet.

"There. All done, and now I'm all yours." Mika closed her laptop and set it aside. "Sorry about that. I know you prefer to have all my attention on you when you're here. This case just has me engrossed." She came up and slid her arms around Selene's waist. "But it's not nearly as engrossing as you. So, tell me about your day." She nibbled Selene's neck.

"It was a difficult day, in one sense. One of my students was attacked on campus, and I had to help her call the police and fill out the report and such. I sat with her while she called her parents as well. I felt so helpless, even doing that stuff. The poor girl."

"Terrible." Mika kept placing small kisses along Selene's exposed skin.

She pulled away slightly, finding the wetness of the kisses irritating. "But, aside from that, I have a new friend." She waited, unsure what Mika's reaction would be.

"Oh? That's nice. Another teacher?" She continued to press her body against Selene's, suggesting her attention was elsewhere.

"Kind of. She's got an interview. We had coffee today."

Mika's wet lips traced a line along the top of her sweater. "Nice. How long till dinner?"

Selene made a pretense of going to the fridge to escape Mika's caresses, which she was finding exasperating rather than arousing. "About five minutes, I think. Set the table?"

Mika looked slightly annoyed before covering it with a smile. "Sure."

She watched as Mika set the table quickly, taking the time to light the taper candles in the center. She'd liked Mika's hands, when they met. They seemed so sure, so strong. And they were. *They still are.* She placed dinner on the table and filled their wine glasses. Tonight, something about the red wine seemed more sensual and it made her grin slightly.

Mika clearly took the grin as a sign and moved around the table to push against her once again. "We could skip dinner." She lightly bit Selene's lower lip.

"I've got something to talk to you about, actually. Hold that thought?" Selene tried to smile flirtatiously, but knew she'd failed when Mika huffed around to her side of the table and sat down stiffly.

"Sure. No problem." She began dishing up their food, slopping it onto their plates.

Selene held her temper. She knew Mika disliked being told no, or to wait, and her sarcasm was her fallback response. "Thank you." She waited until Mika had finished serving them and had begun eating before she started talking. "I've had an interesting offer."

"Oh?" Mika said, continuing to stare at her food.

"Frey Falconi came by my office."

Mika stopped with her fork halfway to her mouth. "What?"

Selene smiled slightly. "I know, right? He came to ask me to work with him. On some big project he's doing for TV. He wants me to help get people to understand sociological evolution and the destructive nature of believing blindly." Mika looked so astonished for a moment, Selene almost found it funny. Almost. "Well?"

Mika took the bite of her food and chewed slowly, as though she were formulating her words carefully. "Did he say why he chose you?"

Something about the question rubbed her wrong. "Why do you think? Because he's read my journal articles and papers on humanism, and he thinks we'd do well working together."

"Wow, that's amazing, babe. You must be ecstatic. When do you start?"

"I haven't decided to do it yet."

Mika looked at her incredulously. "What do you mean? That could take your career in entirely new directions. You could do totally new research. Work with one of the most amazing men in your field. Why wouldn't you do it?"

"I'd have to move, first of all. Which I don't want to do. I'd have to be on TV, in the public eye, and you know how much I hate that. My interest is philosophy, not religion. And what if I end up not liking him? Or he doesn't like me?"

Mika shook her head and kept eating. "You'd be making a mistake. Moving isn't a big deal. It's not like it's forever, and it isn't as if you can't ever come back. They have people who can make you look good for TV and the public, so you wouldn't have to worry about that. And you don't have to like him, you just have to work with him. Don't be stupid."

Selene pushed her plate away. "You wouldn't care if I moved away?"

Mika sighed and took a sip of her wine, not meeting Selene's eyes. "I think it might be good if we took a bit of a break anyway."

Selene's stomach lurched. "You're breaking up with me?"

"No. No, I'm not. And I don't think we should see other people. I just think we could use some time apart. Time for the heart to grow fonder." She shrugged, still looking at the table. "We've become stuck in a rut, and that's not good for either of us. You can get out of it by taking the job with Falconi, and that, in turn, will help us rekindle our interest in each other." She finally looked at Selene's face. "It's a win all the way around."

Selene sat there, silent and stunned, for a long moment. Slowly, she stood and took her plate to the kitchen. She put it on the counter without scraping it clean and left it next to the other dishes. Mika hated a dirty kitchen. She gathered her purse and coat without saying a word. When she got to the door, she finally stopped, and without turning around, said, "You can have your break, regardless if I take the job with Falconi or not. Call me when you're sure you'd like me to come back around. If I'm available, maybe I'll come."

She left, allowing the door to close softly behind her. There was no attempt to stop her. She let her tears mix with the rare California rain as she headed for the train station.

Finally home, Selene lay in her deep claw foot tub, immersed in a steamy bubble bath. A cup of chamomile tea settled her stomach, but did little to calm her mind.

She broke up with me. Although Mika had said otherwise, you didn't tell someone you needed a break from them unless that's what you were doing. It was another person in a long line of people who didn't want her around anymore. *My mother didn't want me. None of my foster families even liked me enough to keep me around. And now, yet another girlfriend is tired of me.* A soft sob escaped her and she pushed herself deeper in the water. *What is it about me that drives people away?* Her shoulders shook as she held back the deeper sobs that wanted to break free. She wouldn't give in, though she desperately wanted to. Past experience told her just what it cost to give in to emotional devastation. It was astounding how many foster parents felt tears were a direct insult, a kind of judgment on their parenting, and found ways to quickly discourage any kind of crying. All her life, she wanted to be loved, without hesitation, without strings or barriers, but she'd always been just a bit too strange, a little too odd, and it had made those who were meant to care for her uncomfortable. And now, the thought that she'd failed, again…she felt a rip inside, in what she'd call her soul, if she were that way inclined.

With a sudden need to let out the rage building inside her, she threw her mug across the room and watched with satisfaction as it shattered against the pale blue tile. She curled into a ball in the water and wished it could embrace her. She longed for a hug, for human contact, in a way she hadn't since she was a child. Her house felt too big, too empty. She jumped from the tub and wrapped herself in one of her fluffy, oversized towels. She threw open her closet and started to rummage.

Tight black jeans, a sheer black blouse over a lacy black bra, and knee high black boots were what she finally left the house in. A mound of discarded clothes littered the floor and bed, all deemed too conservative or frumpy. Tonight she needed to feel sexy. Alive. She wanted to feel noticed. She grabbed her car keys and backed her CR-V out of the drive, but hit the brakes when she thought she saw something run behind the car. With her heart pounding, she got out and looked behind the car. Nothing. Up and down the street, nothing but a pair of squirrels chasing one another around a tree, and the howl of a coyote in the distance. Rubbing the goose bumps that rippled over her arms, she quickly got back in the car. *It's just this stupid feeling of being so alone.* She headed out, leaving her little mountain home behind in an effort to fling herself at the potential kindness of strangers.

❖

Alec watched as Selene left home. For a moment, she'd known Selene felt her, even though she had her guard up. When she'd gotten out of her car to check, Alec had felt a moment of panic that Selene would somehow manage to see her standing there in the trees, watching her. She was in her true form, and for Selene to see her that way now, before she'd had a chance to really explain things to her, would have been disastrous. Although Selene had looked almost directly at her, she'd not seen her. A blessing, and yet disappointing too.

Now, Alec debated what to do. Did she follow Selene to wherever she was going? Or did she have a look inside the house, to make sure there wasn't anything going on she wasn't aware of? She kept going back to the feeling of being watched, and it made her feel increasingly uneasy. Granted, it could have been a colleague or student, but it hadn't felt that way. It had almost felt like it was someone from the Company, but she knew she was the only one allowed near Selene, thanks to the oracle. And when Selene had left Mika's, Alec had sensed her pain and sorrow, and had been desperate to go to her, give her comfort of some kind. But she couldn't do that without giving herself away, and that wasn't acceptable.

Hell, it would've done more than give me away. I can't get involved like that. But damn, did she want to. She took a last look at Selene's house before she launched herself into the air, spreading her wings to catch the mountain thermals. Tonight, she'd watch out for Selene. There would be another time to look at the house.

Selene opened the door to the little lesbian bar in the middle of the desert. The one in the valley would have been closer, but this one pretty much guaranteed she wouldn't run into anyone she knew, and since it was a Wednesday night, it wouldn't be too crowded. It was dark, with horrible carpet that lit up under the black lights overhead. A pool table in a back room had a group of women gathered around it, laughing more than playing. A few bodies swayed on the dance floor, and a scattering of others sat at the small tables surrounding the dance floor and tucked into corners. The bar between the rooms looked well stocked, and a short-haired bartender watching a movie on a propped up iPad glanced up at her with a smile.

"Hey there. What can I get you?"

Selene considered the question. She always had wine when she was out with Mika, who believed it was classier than other alcohol. "Black and tan, please."

"Nice. Want a Mississippi Mud, or a fresh one?"

"Fresh, please."

She turned to make the Guinness and Bass mixture, and Selene admired the bartender's body. Short and stocky, she still seemed to have a nice layer of muscle under the Staff T-shirt she wore. She moved gracefully, as though she'd been behind that bar during her formative years. When she turned back with the overflowing glass, Selene gave her a genuine smile.

"Thanks. It's been a long time since I've had one of these."

The bartender took her money and handed over the change. "In that case, go slow. These can have a wicked kick if you're not used to them."

Selene took a sip and smiled as the bitter-smooth taste flooded her mouth. "I will. And hopefully, I'll dance some of it off." She took her drink over to an empty table near the dance floor. She felt conspicuous, but there was another feeling too, one she didn't recognize. She focused on it, analyzed it, worked it through her shoulder blades and lower back. Freedom. It was freedom running through her. A lack of expectation and obedience to social norms. Tonight, she could be herself. Just the way she wanted to be, regardless of anyone else's desires. She closed her eyes and reveled in the feeling for a moment. A tap on her shoulder had her looking up at an extremely tall woman with a pierced lip.

"Care to dance?" she asked.

Selene nodded, not trusting her voice not to break with nerves and excitement. She hoped she looked calmer than she felt. They began to move to the beat, a quick, thumping bass Selene felt from the bottoms of her feet to her scalp. She closed her eyes and let herself go. In a moment, she felt the stranger's body move closer, felt her thighs against her own. Startled, she started to pull away, but then relaxed into it instead. She opened her eyes and looked into the stranger's, and saw exactly what she'd wanted to see tonight. Desire. Lust. Eagerness.

She pressed back against the stranger and they moved together, hips swaying quickly as they moved forward and retreated. The stranger spun her around so her butt was pressed against her crotch. Strong hands held her hips tightly as they moved and Selene's body warmed like caramel in the sun. The song ended and she pulled away, breathless, warm, and buzzing. "Thank you," she said.

"My pleasure. Another later?" the woman asked with a lopsided grin.

"Sure." Selene retreated to her table and took a long drink of her beer. Energy coursed through her. She could almost see herself opening her blouse, offering herself up...she nearly laughed out loud and covered it by taking a drink. She felt wild, wanton.

Another person asked her to dance, and after that, another. A fresh beer appeared on her table, and another. Time slipped past and she was shocked when last call was shouted from the bar. The stranger she'd danced with first came back to her table.

"Every time I came over to ask for a dance, someone else beat me to it." She shrugged almost apologetically.

Selene giggled, and in that moment realized how drunk she was. She laughed outright. "No problem. I think you had other people to keep you occupied." She gestured at the group of women gathered around the pool table, who were putting on their coats and getting ready to leave.

"Yeah, well, none of them were you." She held out a hand and pulled Selene from her seat. "It seems to me you're in no shape to drive. So maybe I could take you home with me?"

The look in her eyes left no question as to what she had in mind. Selene's body responded in full. She felt her nipples harden and her panties grow wet. She could imagine the stranger's hands on her, in her. She pulled away slightly and looked at her. The mirror-ball light caught the side of her face, and suddenly, there was something not right. Something dark and unpleasant.

Selene slid her hand from the woman's grasp and tried to smile. She wavered on her feet more than necessary. "Another time, I would have liked that. But I think I'm too drunk to be good company. I don't think I can even keep my eyes open. I'll call a cab." She picked up her bag and coat and headed to the bar, backing away. She didn't like the look in the woman's eyes. "A rain check?"

The woman shrugged, but her smile didn't reach her eyes. "Sure, no problem. See you around."

Selene breathed a bit easier when she got to the bar. The bartender looked at her with a wise expression.

"Good call. How can I help?" she said.

"Thanks. Can you call me a cab? I'm not going to be able to drive home, so I'll have to get a hotel room. Can I leave my car here overnight?"

The bartender was already on the phone. When she hung up, she said, "Yeah, of course. I can't remember the last time we had a break-in. It should be fine. Your cab will be here in about ten minutes. You can wait in here with me, if you want?"

The group that had been at the pool table were gone, with just a few remaining people left in the bar. "No, that's okay, thanks. I think some fresh air will do me good."

"No problem. Come back in if you have any problems."

Selene waved and headed into the welcome cold air of early morning. It was the true dark before the dawn, pitch-black and freezing cold. She pulled her jacket tighter around her. A few cars were still in the lot, and as one pulled away, she reconsidered going inside. Just as she turned to do so, three figures came out of the shadows. She gasped and stumbled back.

"Hey there. Sorry, no need to be scared. We just thought we'd keep you company." The stranger she'd turned down stood in front of two others, people she'd also danced with.

"Oh, thanks. I think I'm okay, though. Actually, I was just going to head back inside. Too cold out here, you know?" Fear fluttered in her stomach, turning her legs to Jell-O.

"We can help with the cold, can't we?" the stranger said with a nasty smile to her friends, who laughed.

"I don't want any trouble. Please."

They advanced toward her, and she was forced to move farther into the parking lot, away from the bar's entrance. She moved into the shadows and realized they were backing her into a side alleyway.

"It's no trouble at all, princess. I promise."

The woman reached out and grabbed at her, her face twisted in an evil leer. Selene jumped back, and the stranger only managed to grab her shirt, which tore open. Selene pulled it shut, closing her jacket over it, and considered her options. She could see the street at the other end of the alley, with plenty of cars still passing by. If she could make it that far, she'd be safe. She ran.

There was a brief, muffled scream behind her, and then silence. No footsteps to suggest she was being chased. She turned, still backing toward the main street.

The alley was empty.

Chapter Eight

Alec rested her head on the table. She could hear the other staff on the floor going about their daily duties, getting ready for lunch, but she didn't have the energy to make small talk with anyone. Or conversation of a deeper nature, either. Too many questions pummeled her brain, too many emotions flooded her body.

She needed answers.

Zed came in, quickly followed by Ama. He slid into a chair and motioned for Ama to join him on his right.

Damn. He looks...old. Zed had always been old. No one really knew just how old he was, or when he'd come into existence. Records didn't go that far back. But no one remembered him being anything but old. But today, he actually looked elderly, as though he was wearing his age like a heavy cloak. She glanced at Ama, who returned her look of concern.

"You okay, Z?"

He nodded. "Weaker by the day, it seems. But I'll be fine. What's on your mind?"

She hesitated. Given his weakened state, should she trouble him? She thought of the previous night. "Zed, I need to understand some things. Can you answer some questions for me?" Regardless of the number of years behind them, Zed was her boss, and disrespect wasn't her thing.

"Go ahead, Alec. If I can answer, I will."

"That sounds ominously oracle-like."

He shrugged and gave her a tired grin. "Old habits, you know. Go on."

"Okay. When you chose me for this assignment, I accepted it, just figuring other folks were busy or whatever. But the truth is, I don't get it. Why me? And why me alone? Why aren't there other people helping me out? I mean, there are people way more powerful. Older, wiser, all that shit." She tilted her head apologetically. Zed disliked swearing. "It doesn't make any sense."

He nodded thoughtfully. "Anything else?"

"Isn't that enough?"

He looked at Ama. "Can you get the purple file off my desk, please?"

She nodded and left silently. Ama was rarely respectful, and even more rarely quiet. Something bad was going on for sure.

"Alec, I'll tell you what I can; you deserve that much. While we're waiting for the file, though, tell me how things are going with Selene."

She sighed and rubbed her neck. "There was an incident last night. She's got some personal stuff going on, and she took a risk last night that nearly got her in trouble. But I was following her, so I took care of it." The thought of what could have happened to Selene made her feel ill. She'd dealt with all of the women in her normal fashion, and they wouldn't be bothering other women again. "I think it probably scared her enough to keep her inside for a while."

"Then this is a good time to get close. Use her fear and vulnerability to further your connection with her. We can't take much longer to get things going."

Before Alec could continue, Ama came back with the requested file. She handed it to Zed, who pushed it across to Alec.

"This is all the information I've got, one of the original versions of the oracle. I've tried asking the Fates some questions myself, and I've got nothing more than what's already in there. I've even tried asking other departments if they have similar information, or a parallel situation, and not one of them does."

She opened the file and began to read the written version of the oracle, passed down by the Fates, as oracles always were. Once upon a time, they'd sat in caves or on hilltops and given out oracles orally. Now, it was done via computer, like everything else. She skimmed the pages quickly, then looked up incredulously when she was done. "Seriously?"

He looked morose. "Seriously. That's it. That's why."

Alec leaned back in her chair. Her wings itched to stretch open. "It doesn't say anything about me doing it alone."

"No, it doesn't. But if you don't, how do you propose to get close to her? Do you think showing up with a crew, or an entourage, in your case, is going to work for you? Maybe once you've got her here, and she accepts her role in this, then you can draw together a team for marketing purposes. Maybe even for recruitment. But until that point…" He slumped in his chair. "Until then, Alec, it's you."

He got up and left, and she thought he shuffled slightly. Ama watched him go before turning to Alec. "Can I help?"

"Ama, you're not from our department, so maybe you have a different perspective. Have you read the file? What's your take on it?"

"We have similar beings to your Fates in our department, obviously. We always have. But like Z said, when it comes to this, we've got a big blank spot. I've checked with the P.A.s and data workers in other departments, just in case the higher-ups didn't want to tell Z the truth. We're the only ones with the information, and we're the only ones with you." She reached across the table and took Alec's hand in her own. "If I can help, tell me. I'll do anything I can, you know that. You might have to do the contact and research work on your own, but you've got plenty of us behind you to support you through it. You're not alone, Alec."

"We've got five floors of people stronger, older, and wiser than me. And we're basing the fact that it has to be me because of this?" Alec waved a piece of paper from the file. "I thought we'd moved beyond this a hell of a long time ago."

"We did. We had. And then people started fading. I mean, fuck, Alec. Did you know there's a section on the second floor that no longer exists? It's gone. Just…gone. They were fading, yeah, but we didn't think they'd just go like that. But something must have shifted out there, because suddenly, we've got a bunch of empty desks and half-full coffee cups."

"Not half-empty?" Alec asked with a small grin, trying to lighten Ama's mood.

She squeezed Alec's hand before letting go and standing up to leave. "I'll believe it's half-full until you tell me otherwise. I believe in you, Alec. We need you to believe too."

She left and Alec put her head back down on the table. Belief seemed like a lake in the middle of a desert. Possible, but unlikely. She thought about what Zed had said. It was time to move forward.

She pulled out her cell and dialed Selene.

"Hello?"

Alec heard the tremor in Selene's voice. To a normal person, it wouldn't have been present. But Alec could hear nuance and emotion better than most beings, and Selene sounded sad.

"Hey there. It's Alec."

The relief in Selene's voice was almost palpable. "Hi. What a nice surprise."

"Good to know. It's a beautiful day, and I was wondering if you wanted to hit Venice Beach with me today, for a stroll and maybe some late afternoon pizza?"

"It'll be practically empty this time of year. And it's kind of cold."

"Venice is never really empty, and you can dress warm."

Selene laughed. "Okay, fair enough. What time?"

"Why don't I pick you up around four?"

"You can come here, but we'll take my car. Finding parking for your behemoth will be a nightmare."

"Hey now, be nice. She's a big girl, but she's light on her feet." Alec was glad to hear some of the fear leave Selene's voice. "I'll see you in an hour."

Alec hung up and headed for the kitchen. She could hear Edesia singing in Italian, and it eased her worries, if only for a moment. She stopped in the kitchen doorway and watched as the Roman beauty moved around the room as though it were an extension of her own body. Mouth-watering aromas filled the air, from the fresh herbs hanging from the ceiling to whatever delectable dish was in one of the many ovens. The Italian department ran the company's cantina, and the menus were always superb. When Edesia turned and saw Alec, she stopped singing and opened her arms.

"Alec, my lover of the ages. What brings you to my humble domain?"

Alec returned her hug. Edesia gave amazing hugs. Full body things that made you feel truly cared for. She didn't want to let go, but time was important.

"I was wondering if you could whip me up a picnic for the beach. Something low stress but nice."

"Of course I can, silly woman. Which beach, and for how many?"

"Venice, for two."

Edesia pressed her hand over Alec's heart. "Is this part of your mission?"

"Does everyone know?" Somehow, it rubbed Alec wrong that it was common knowledge. If she failed, everyone would know who it was that led them to their demise.

"No. Not everyone. Although everyone knows what kind of crisis we're in. People are fading from every department, all the time. The ones who don't have friends among us go even faster."

"I'm going to do everything I can, Edie. I promise."

Edesia gave her another bone-crushing hug. "I know you will. And we're all behind you." She gave Alec a playful shove away. "Now, go. Come back in thirty minutes and I'll have your basket ready."

She turned away, but not before Alec saw the tears in her eyes. It took a lot to make a goddess like Edesia cry, and Alec's heart ached. If she didn't succeed, tears would be the least of their worries.

On her way home to change, she considered her next move. Seduction seemed seedy. Clearly, something had gone wrong with Selene and Mika, and she wouldn't pretend to be sorry about that. As far as Alec was concerned, Mika was part of the problem they were facing, and she was glad to have Selene away from that influence.

Selene had looked amazing at the club the night before. Dressed in black, she'd looked sexy, sweet, and dangerous all at once. No one else knew just how scared and insecure she was under those figure perfect clothes. But that fear and naivety could have gotten her in serious trouble, had Alec not decided to follow her after all. Granted, she might have gone somewhat overboard with the attackers, who wouldn't be sleeping well for a very long time to come. But she'd be damned if she'd allow them to prey on women anymore. That it was Selene they'd attacked made it all the worse.

Once home, she stripped and unfurled her wings, letting them free, allowing herself to breathe deeply. She'd be completely covered today, as usual. The chill weather at the beach would give her good reason to keep on her sweatshirt. She didn't want any questions about her tattoos, not yet. The time for that would come. She pulled out her black jeans, a deep purple turtleneck, and her black boots. She pulled her wings back in, then dressed efficiently. She wanted to look nice, but not like she was trying too hard. If Selene found her attractive, so much the better. *Maybe.* Grabbing her black leather jacket on her way out, she glanced in the mirror. *Let's put on a show.*

"I'd forgotten how nice it can be at the beach in the winter," Selene said as they strolled down the boardwalk, stopping to look at the occasional painting or craft. There were far fewer street vendors and performers than usual, but as Alec had said, there were still enough to keep things interesting. The roller skating man and his electric guitar nodded at them and smiled as he skated past, not interested in money today, just in making folks happy.

"I love it at the beach in winter. All over the world, it's the same. People hunker down, hibernate. But being outside in winter can be magical."

Selene laughed. "I'm not sure I've ever thought of Venice as magical."

Alec grinned but motioned around them seriously. "What's more magical than people free to express themselves in any way they want, without fear of reprisal? People existing alongside one another, supporting one another, being creative and vocal?" They stopped to admire some African carvings. The man selling them gave them a polite nod, then turned back toward the weak winter sun.

They walked on, and Selene broke the easy silence. "I'd honestly never thought of it that way. I mean, I assumed Venice was unique, a nutty place found only in California. I know it's one of the older cities in California, and has a long history of being a slum. That often leads to a counter culture, which is probably why The Doors and Jane's Addiction formed here."

Alec raised an eyebrow. "I didn't picture you being a fan of either of those."

Selene laughed. "You don't have to be a fan in order to know things. Although, that said, there are songs by both I really like."

She blushed slightly and Alec laughed. "Okay, counter culture girl, where do you want to eat?" She swung the old-fashioned picnic basket. "This thing is getting heavy." It wasn't. She could carry fifty of them all day long and not notice. But she wanted somewhere more intimate, a place they could talk. "I hope it's okay I went with something other than pizza."

"As much as I love pizza, I can't wait to see what you brought. Can we sit out on the sand? Or would that be too messy?"

Selene looked hopeful, like a child asking for something but expecting the answer to be no.

"I love sitting on the sand to eat. There's nothing like filling your stomach with amazing food and seeing the surreal expanse of ocean in front of you. Let's do it." The excitement in Selene's expression made Alec wish she could take it back, and say it all over again, if only to see that expression once more.

Selene hurried over to the stairs leading down to the sand and took off her Birkenstocks. She rolled up the hems of her jeans and jumped down. "Oh, it's cold!"

Alec laughed and followed suit, placing her boots on top of the picnic basket. "I'll follow you. Anywhere you want to go." She winced inwardly, the import of the words far more true than Selene could realize.

"That sounds promising." Selene bit her lip and blushed again before she turned and set off toward the water. When she'd found a spot with no one near them for at least thirty feet in any direction, she knelt gracefully. "Here okay?"

Alec set the basket between them, needing a bit of distance. The more time she spent with Selene, the more she liked her. And while that would help them work together, eventually, she didn't want to have any deeper feelings that could complicate matters. *Like things aren't already complicated enough.* She took out the plates and silverware, then the tubs of antipasti, lasagna, and salads. She nestled them in the sand and handed Selene a serving spoon. "Go for it."

Selene looked at the food, then back at Alec. "Wow. I thought you just had sandwiches and chips in there. You didn't cook this, did you?"

Alec swallowed, her mouth suddenly dry. "No, not this particular dish, although I do like to cook when I have the chance." She concentrated on putting food on plates as she figured out how to lie without lying. "A friend of mine is a great cook, and she does this kind of thing for people all the time."

Selene moaned with a mouthful of food. "Oh my God. This is amazing. Please tell me your friend has somewhere I can get this again?"

Alec took a bite of lasagna and thanked Edie mentally for the delicious fare. "Not really, no. Maybe one day I'll take you to her place. It's…private."

Selene looked dubious. "Okay, I'll go with that, for now."

They ate silently, watching the waves crash onto the dark, reflective shore. When they'd finished and packed the food away, Selene leaned back on her elbows and stretched her legs in front of her. She dug her toes in the sand. "Who knew it would be so fortuitous to have coffee spilled on you by a stranger." She glanced at Alec, then back to the water. "Honestly, things have been really confusing lately, and last night was a perfect end to it. Being able to go out and be normal like this is so unexpected. And so…nice."

"I'm sorry you had such a bad week. Want to talk about it?"

Selene sighed. "I've got so much going on. My life was so quiet, so organized. And all of a sudden it seems like everything is up in the air. I hate it when that happens."

"You like things calm? Stable?"

"Exactly." She dug her toes deeper into the cold sand. "My life wasn't easy, growing up. It wasn't stable, and that's what I want now. I think it is, anyway."

Alec thought about Selene's mother, about the things she knew, and felt guilty at the subterfuge. "That makes sense. Difficult parents?"

"No parents, not really. I grew up in foster care. I never knew either of my parents. I don't know what happened to either of them. I went through a number of foster homes before I finally ended up with the Johnsons. A lot of foster homes, actually. One of them only lasted three months, before they decided I was a distraction their biological son didn't need. I think the mother was more worried about her husband than her son, though. Creepy bastard. I never fit in with the families I stayed with, and some of them…well, thankfully, I was able leave before things got really bad, usually. By the time I was fourteen, I'd been in twelve foster homes. I stayed with the Johnsons for four years, until I was eighteen. We're not close, but I consider them my family. I see them on holidays and we talk a few times a year."

"Do they live nearby?" Alec asked. She'd been to their home doing her research, but she still had to ask. Lying was making the lasagna sour in her stomach.

"No, they live in Denver. Most of my life was there. I just knew I needed to get away, somewhere warmer and not landlocked." Selene gave her a quick, sad smile. "Enough about me. What about you? What's your story?"

Alec's skin crawled and she glanced around, looking for the person she could feel watching them, but she couldn't see anyone lurking. *Unless it's someone I can't see…someone who doesn't want to be seen.* She looked up when Selene coughed lightly. "Sorry, I'm easily distracted these days." She shrugged and tried her most charming smile. "My story isn't nearly as interesting as yours. Two disinterested parents, two sisters. No drama to speak of between us. Pretty average, really."

"And does your family live nearby?"

"My sisters do, and we're pretty close. We do a lot of things together. My parents…they run a major company, so they're often traveling." She shrugged, hoping to derail the line of questions she couldn't truthfully answer. Yet.

"It must be nice, having a close family. I always thought I'd like to have siblings, but then, there were often other kids in the foster homes I grew up in, and I never really clicked with any of them. I was always so…different."

An answering dejection filled Alec in response to the sadness in Selene's eyes. When Selene found out the truth, would she want to help? Or would her resentment cause her to walk away? The thought of losing their one hope, as well as what small connection she already had with Selene, made her stomach turn even more. "Okay, enough serious stuff. Let's talk about fun things. What's your favorite board game?"

Selene laughed, the worry lines in her forehead easing quickly. "I haven't played one in years. Uno, maybe?"

"Uno isn't a board game, it's a card game. Try again." Alec grinned and wiggled her eyebrows.

"I didn't know there were rules to the 'what's your favorite game'! Okay, Sorry."

"You don't have to be sorry. I wasn't being serious."

Selene laughed and shook her head. "I mean Sorry the board game. That's my favorite."

"Ah, got it. Mine is Rummikub."

Selene frowned and tilted her head in the way Alec was coming to know meant she was giving something serious thought.

"I don't know that one."

"It uses domino type pieces. It's a strategy thing. Maybe I'll show you one day."

Selene looked down at Alec's hand in the sand, picked up a handful of sand in her own, and drizzled the cool grains over Alec's knuckles. Somehow, it was more erotic than anything else she could think of having experienced. And she had a fair amount of experience. She shivered and pointed at the horizon. "Watch."

Selene followed the direction of Alec's finger and sighed. The sun looked like it was sinking into the ocean, bit by bit, and then faster as the middle of it was obscured by waves, until finally, the edge sat like a crescent over the pulsing water.

Alec leaned closer to Selene and whispered, "Now. Right now is my favorite part. When the tip…" She waited as the very edge of the sun dipped below the horizon. "The tip leaves in a last little flashing gasp, like it's struggling to stay with us." *Just like the world I'm trying to save.*

Selene placed her hand gently over Alec's. "That's beautiful. And so sad."

Alec shook off the feeling of melancholy sweeping over her. She concentrated briefly, but the feeling of being watched had disappeared. Whatever it was, she'd figure it out later. For now, she could focus on Selene. "We were supposed to be having fun. Now. What's your favorite color?"

Selene flopped backward onto her bed. It felt like her smile was permanent, and her cheeks hurt. They'd spent the next hour laughing over each other's favorite things, and unlike Mika's teasing, which was often sharp, Alec's was gentle and sweet. More than once she'd seemed almost shy, embarrassed to be sharing things about herself.

Selene stretched, her body feeling light, infused with a kind of happy she couldn't remember feeling in a long time. *If ever.*

The phone rang and she jumped to answer it, part of her hoping it would be Alec. *Not that she'd call when she just dropped me off. But still.*

She answered and was momentarily taken aback when it wasn't Alec, but a deep man's tone instead.

"Selene. Good to hear your lovely self. How are you, philosopher extraordinaire?"

She blinked, trying to place the voice, her euphoria over her time with Alec still clouding her mind. "I'm sorry, who is this?"

There was a moment's pause before the man answered. "It's Frey. I'm disappointed I'm not more memorable."

Selene flushed, instantly on guard. "Mr. Falconi, my apologies. We have only met the once, though, in my defense. How are you?"

"I'll let it go this time, but I hope you'll learn it well enough to hear it across a crowded room soon. Have you given my offer any more thought?"

Selene thought fast. "I have, of course. However, I'm discussing it with a friend of mine at the end of the week. Someone who has often advised me in business matters. It's obviously not a decision I want to make in a vacuum." Again, there was a pause, and she wondered what he was thinking. She'd never needed business advice in her life, and there sure as hell wasn't anyone around to advise her, but she needed to buy some time to think things through.

"Of course not. I wouldn't expect a woman of your intellect to do anything else. Are there any questions I can answer?"

"Honestly, Mr. Falconi—"

"Frey, please."

"Honestly, Frey, I'm not sure the public life is for me, and what you're talking about isn't just writing a textbook. I've seen what you do, and I know I couldn't do that. So I'm being very cautious. You're asking me to change my entire life."

"You're right. I am. I have an idea. I'm throwing a little soiree tomorrow night. Why don't you come along and meet some of my colleagues and friends? Maybe that will give you some insight into what we do and what we're working for. And, perhaps, set your mind at ease enough to join me."

"A soiree?" Fear swept up her spine. "I'm not really the type."

"Nonsense. All you have to do is talk to people, which you do all the time. And feel free to bring a date. Ciao for now."

Before she could protest further, he was gone. *Oh God. What am I going to wear?*

She opened her closet, and the first thing she focused on were the gorgeous heels she'd never been brave enough to wear. *No time like the present.* She riffled through her more dressy clothes and flung herself back onto the bed, in an entirely different mood from the one she'd been in the last time she'd done it. Her clothes screamed "crazy professor," not "soiree." What she wouldn't give for a girlfriend to call in a panic, someone to take her shopping and give her advice. She briefly considered calling Mika, but dismissed the thought. Mika had made her position known, and there was no way she would give her the satisfaction of saying Selene needed her. Just when she decided to call him back and decline, her phone rang again.

"Hello, Frey, I really don't think—"

"Hey there."

Selene stopped midsentence and tried to calm the butterflies brought on by Alec's voice. "Hi. Sorry, I thought it was someone else calling back."

"Should I let you go?"

Selene couldn't think of anything worse. "No, please don't. Did you forget to tell me one of your favorite things?" She laughed, the unexpected desire to flirt making her feel giddy.

"I did, actually, and I couldn't let it go. I wanted to tell you about one of my newest favorite things."

"Go on?" She heard Alec take a deep breath and hesitate for a millisecond.

"One of my newest favorite things is picnics on the beach with genius professors. I just wanted to let you know."

Selene's stomach flipped over and she slid down the side of her bed and onto the floor. "That's...wow. That sounds like a great favorite thing."

Alec laughed softly. "Indeed it is."

Inspired by Alec's statement, Selene said, "Are you free tomorrow night? I've been invited to this party, or soiree, or get-together, or something. And I really, really don't want to go alone."

"I'm a huge fan of all three of those options. I'd love to. But a soiree isn't just a party, so I need to know what to wear."

Selene groaned. "I'm trying to figure that out myself. I have a feeling it's going to be a well-heeled crowd, and I've got zilch in my closet for anything fancier than a faculty mixer."

Alec laughed. "Well, how about I pick you up after your last class tomorrow and we run to the mall? Maybe I can help you try some things on. I mean, you know, suggest some things. Not actually help you dress or whatever. You know what I mean."

Selene could practically see Alec's blush, and that same giddy feeling rushed over her again. "Really? You'd do that? You don't seem the shopping type."

"Ah, see, that's where you've got me wrong. I like shopping, when I'm in the mood. And thanks to my parents, I've had to attend lots of swanky parties. Does that plan work for you? We could have a quick bite to eat before we go to your grand ball, if we have the time."

"That would be fantastic. Thank you so much."

"No problem. I'll pick you up at three thirty. Be ready for an adventure in textiles."

Selene said good night and headed for the shower. Suddenly, Frey's invitation had become far more enticing.

CHAPTER NINE

Alec pulled up in a loading zone in front of the E&T building at three twenty-five. If she didn't want anyone to see the Hummer, it was easily concealed, much like her home. But that didn't work when she was picking up someone who needed to see her. While she waited, she scanned the area around the building, not just with her eyes, but with her senses. There was no darkness, no eerie feeling of being watched. Just a beautiful winter day in California.

Selene stepped outside and shielded her eyes from the weak California sun. Alec's breath caught slightly. Even in clothes at least a size too big for her, she was truly stunning. Her flawless, pale skin practically glowed, and when she saw the Hummer and smiled, Alec felt like someone had pushed sunlight directly into her soul.

Selene pulled open the door. "Are you sure you want to do this?"

"Hi yourself. And yes, I'm sure. Are you?"

"Geez, I'm sorry. Hi. I'm actually looking forward to it, which is saying something. I don't usually like buying clothes."

Alec pulled out and headed for the super mall fifteen minutes up the freeway. "And why is that?"

Selene sighed and Alec felt her energy plummet.

"Because nothing is ever quite right. I don't like tight clothes because I feel too conspicuous. But baggy clothes never seem appropriate for social gatherings. They're barely appropriate for work, but no one really cares what the philosophy professors wear, so I get away with it. I don't like colors, and I feel frumpy and formless in just about anything, no matter what it is." Selene put a gentle hand on her forearm. "This was a stupid idea. I shouldn't have accepted the invitation to the party at all. What say we forget about it and go get pizza?"

"Comfort food. You must really be panicking." Alec shot her what she hoped was a comforting smile. "We're totally going shopping, because you sounded up for it last night. Maybe even a little excited about it?"

Selene moved her hand away from Alec's arm, and she missed its warmth.

"That was yesterday. Now, in the light of day, I know I'm a moron. Pizza?"

Alec glanced at her. "Tell me honestly. Do you want to go to this party?"

"Honestly? I don't know." She sighed again and rubbed her shoulder absently. "The host has made me a career offer I'm considering, something potentially life changing. So in that sense, yes, it would be good to attend." She shrugged. "But then, he's a kind of public figure, and the other people there might be too, so I probably won't like them or have anything at all to say to them. At best, I'm socially awkward. At worst, I'm like a vampiric hyena in a hen house."

Alec laughed. "Well, that's descriptive. Which side, logically, makes more sense to you, and which will you regret least?"

Selene sighed. "I think I should go."

Alec slapped the steering wheel. "Then we're going shopping!"

❖

"Seriously? No. You're kidding, right?"

Alec pushed the black dress back at Selene. "Yes. I'm completely serious. And we don't have a lot of time, so you need to trust me."

"It's sheer. And tight. Did you not listen to a thing I said?" Selene hung the offending material on a rack next to her and blew out a frustrated breath when Alec picked it back up and turned away to grab another.

"You asked for my help. I've had years of dressing women, and I know what I'm talking about."

"You don't even know my size. And I won't even ask about the dressing women thing."

Alec raised an eyebrow and grinned. "No, *you* don't know your size. I do. I have an eye for these things." She grabbed another dress and pushed the bunch into Selene's arms. "Now, head for the fitting room, and I'll be right there. I want to see each one—you only get one veto."

"Rules? Now there are rules to shopping for my own clothes?" Selene grumbled as she went to the fitting room. As she undressed, she slowly began to smile, and that smile turned into a soft giggle. She clamped a hand over her mouth. She couldn't remember anyone ever making this kind of fuss over her, and although it was slightly scary, it was also exhilarating. She pulled on the first black dress. Backless, it had thick black pieces that crisscrossed over her breasts and then folded into a rain of material down the front. Although it hugged her curves, it also somehow managed to minimize them. She thought she might be in love.

Shyly, she poked her head out. Alec was sitting patiently in a chair right outside.

"I don't know if I can do this." An army of butterflies began a war with the nerves in her stomach.

"Come on. You know I don't bite."

The image that flashed through Selene's mind was far from innocent, and she flushed. "Okay. No laughing."

She stepped out. In that second, she wished she could take a photograph of Alec's expression. She looked...dumbstruck. Selene executed a little turn, letting the folds of the dress flare out. "Well?" she finally asked, when Alec continued to be silent.

"Yes. Yes, you should get that. Get that right now."

Selene laughed, feeling like a schoolgirl. "Really? You like it?"

Alec's gaze traveled the length of her body, and she felt it like a caress.

"No. Like isn't the right word." She cleared her throat and looked away for a moment. "But you should try on the other two, just to be sure that's the right one."

Selene grinned and moved back into the cubicle. She put a tiny bit of extra sway in her hips, hoping Alec was watching. When she latched the door she heard what sounded like a soft swear from outside, and once again, she felt like she was floating. The next dress, a deep crimson number with an almost embarrassingly low neckline was also backless, and this one had a slit up the side almost to her thigh. She turned this way and that, and liked the way it made her feel sexy, almost wanton.

She opened the door and laughed out loud when Alec pretended to collapse.

"You're going to give me a coronary. Good gods, woman. That's…you should get that one."

"I thought you said I should get the other one?" Selene turned so Alec could see the plunging back.

"Get them both. Wear one before dinner and one after. Damn, woman."

Selene giggled and put a hand over her mouth, mortified. When Alec began laughing, so did she.

"One more. This is your fault, by the way. The consequences must be accepted as a part of your choices." Selene thought she saw a flash of something cross Alec's expression. Sadness? Fear? Whatever it was, it disappeared quickly enough to make her think she'd imagined it.

"Too true, lady professor. Last one?"

The next dress was navy, with a high neck and tight bodice. It was nice, but nothing like the other two, and she knew she wouldn't be comfortable enough in it to enjoy herself at the party. She shrugged out of it and got redressed.

Alec stuck out her bottom lip. "I didn't get to see the last one?"

Selene shook her head. "It wasn't right, so there was no point. But now I have to decide on which dress to wear."

"Like I said, I think you should get them both."

"That's awfully frivolous, isn't it?"

Alec frowned slightly. "You don't have any party dresses, right? And you said this party is important for your career, right?"

"Well, yes, but—"

"Then you might have to go to more than one of these swanky things, right? It's not like you won't get to wear them both." Alec held up her hands. "But I don't want to pressure you, not really. They just both look really amazing. And a woman like you should have things that make you feel good about yourself."

Selene hugged the dresses to her and went to the cashier without another word. No one, ever, had told her she was someone worth feeling good about. The words sank in, burrowed into her heart, and stuck. She felt weightless, breathless, and defenseless all at once. Impulsively, she turned and threw her arms around Alec, hugging her tightly.

"Thank you," she whispered.

Alec hugged her back before gently releasing her. "Anytime."

When Selene had finished paying, Alec suggested heading downstairs for an iced coffee before they got on the road. She carried Selene's packages, along with a small bag of her own.

"I didn't see you buy anything. Did you get something for tonight too?"

Alec blushed, and Selene found it both charming and adorable.

"Kind of. It's a surprise. I'll show you later."

They both turned at the sound of someone calling Alec's name, and Selene felt Alec stiffen when the woman came strolling toward them.

Selene felt like a grubby, substandard grandmother figure.

The woman was a good three inches taller than Selene, with a body that seemed to have been shaped by an hourglass. Long, flowing black hair swung in time with her hips, and her fire-red heels seemed to have sex with the floor as she walked.

She gave Alec a full body hug and flicked a glance at Selene. "Imagine seeing you in a mall. I didn't think you stepped foot in these places anymore."

Alec tried to disengage herself from the woman, somewhat mollifying Selene's sudden rush of possessive jealousy. "Melina, this is Selene. Selene, Melina."

Melina's hand was dry and scratchy, her nails sharp and pointed. Something about her made Selene shudder. "Nice to meet you."

"It always is, dear. Until it isn't."

Alec stepped back and took Selene's hand in her own. Selene was filled with warmth and calm, and the fact that Alec had chosen to take her hand, rather than the femme fatale's, made life bright again.

"I'm sorry, I don't understand."

Alec shook her head. "You don't need to. We're heading out, Melina. Sorry, no time to chat. Good to see you again though."

They left Melina standing there watching them with an ugly smile on her face. Selene followed Alec into the food court, where they ordered their coffees. Finally, Selene turned to Alec and simply gave her a questioning look.

Alec sighed and rubbed her temples. "I'm sorry about that. We've got…history."

The thought turned Selene's stomach slightly. "Yes, I gathered that. And is it still history?"

Alec looked surprised at the question, then bemused. "Ancient history, actually."

Selene relaxed and felt her shoulders relax. "I never asked you if you were dating anyone. I guess I just assumed you were single."

"Oh, and what gave you that idea?"

"You said you would have asked me on a date, if I'd been available. I suppose that suggests single to me."

Alec grinned, the worry lines around her eyes easing. "And I would have, too."

Selene stirred her coffee while they waited for Alec's. Without looking up, she said softly, "You can, you know. Ask me."

Alec softly touched Selene's hand. "Problems in paradise?"

"We've broken up. I think. We've separated for the moment, anyway. It's complicated."

A look of sadness flashed over Alec's features when she said, "Most things are." She seemed to shake off her mood and she took Selene's hand in her own. "Then, sweet lady, may I ask if tonight can be our first date?"

Butterflies turned into hummingbirds in her stomach, and her knees felt like cotton balls. "I'd like that."

Alec grabbed her coffee and tugged Selene toward the exit. "Then we'd better get you ready for the ball, Cinderella."

❖

Alec insisted on driving Selene home, as the party was closer to Selene's home in the mountains than it was the university, and taking the train meant it would take longer for her to get ready. She'd said she'd get a hotel for the night, not far from Selene's, so she wouldn't have to drive back to her place at the beach after. They'd quickly backtracked to Alec's place after the mall, so she could grab her clothes. Selene was impressed at the size and beauty of Alec's home by the canals, and was slightly disappointed when Alec didn't invite her in. With a quick, "I'll be back in a flash," she was gone, leaving Selene waiting in the soft winter sun, watching the water flow gently through the canal. It gave her time to wonder if she was doing the right thing. She was unquestionably attracted to Alec, and wanted to spend more time with her. But she had also just gotten out of her relationship with Mika, if she was, in fact, out of it at all. She wouldn't want to damage any kind of relationship she might have with Alec by diving into a rebound situation. She sighed, wondering if she should call the night off, when Alec opened the door and bounded back to the car.

Any rational thought she might have had blew away like dandelion puffs in the wind. Alec carried a suit bag and small duffel bag, and she looked so strong, so sure and sexy, Selene couldn't back out tonight even if she could think straight.

"Sorry, hope I wasn't too long." Alec got in and started the car. "I would have invited you in, but I haven't had anyone over in a long time, and the house is a mess. If you get addicted to my charm and are desperate for a second date, maybe I'll cook you dinner." She grinned and winked, and Selene's stomach did a somersault.

"Can you cook, really? I know you said you liked to when we were at the beach, but you might have been trying to impress me."

"After a fashion, I can. I have some specialty dishes I like to make, and there's something comforting in making your own food. My sister, Meg, she's the real cook of the family, though. She throws a lot of parties, and people angle for an invitation just so they can get to her food."

"You haven't said much about your family. Tell me about them?"

Alec smiled, but Selene could see she was uncomfortable.

"Like I said, not a lot to tell. And it's boring stuff, really."

"We've got a long drive ahead of us. Plenty of time to bore me."

Alec laughed. "Well, Meg likes to throw parties and cook. Tis, my other sister, is the bookworm of the family. She was a lawyer for a long time, but gave it up when the cases started to get to her."

"Who's oldest?"

Alec looked vaguely surprised, then started to laugh. "I didn't mention we were triplets, did I?"

Selene laughed. "No, you forgot to mention that. Wow, I've met plenty of twins, but never a triplet. Identical?"

"No. We have some similar traits, but we look very different."

"So, if Meg is the outgoing cook, and Tis is the bookworm, what does that make you?"

Alec flexed her bicep and grinned wickedly. "I'm the jock. I love to read too, but I'm all about the outdoors. I love experiencing new things, and I've rock climbed on pretty much every continent."

Selene tore her attention away from Alec's defined biceps, ignoring her sudden urge to lick the line of muscle and feel it flex under her tongue. "Every continent? Including the poles?"

"Yup."

Alec looked like she might shut down, as though the memory bothered her, and Selene decided to change the subject. "So, where did you go to school? I don't take you for a California native."

"You mean I don't fit in here? I'm distressed."

Selene lightly touched Alec's thigh. "No, goodness no, I'm not saying that. You're just so down-to-earth, so genuine. You don't find a lot of that in people living in Venice."

Alec raised an eyebrow and glanced at her. "That's a rather sweeping generalization, Professor."

Selene felt her face flush. "You're right, I'm sorry. I didn't used to be that way. I suppose my years with Mika have changed me a bit."

Alec shrugged. "There's no question there's a falseness about California, especially Southern. There's an element of needing to be more, different yet the same, but better, always better. But I've met some really amazing people here too. People who know what it means to live tough lives but still see the magic in life."

"Magic? What kind of magic would that be?"

Alec shrugged, looking shy. "The kind of magic we'll have to discuss later. Right now, I need you to guide me to your place." She pulled off the exit leading to Selene's little mountain town.

"How…that's not possible. We can't possibly already be here."

Alec laughed. "Magic, I tell you. My Hummer can get anywhere in an instant."

Selene was utterly out of sorts. They hadn't been talking that long, and her place was a good hour and a half from the university. She stared at Alec, baffled.

"Selene? I need to know which way to go."

"Left. But I don't understand."

"Do you need to?"

"Left here. Of course. Understanding leads to knowledge."

Alec deftly maneuvered the Hummer up the long mountain pass. "Always?"

"Usually. Or at least an understanding of what other questions need to be asked."

Alec motioned at the passing scenery of pine trees and desert scrub. "How long have you lived here?"

"Changing the subject? Okay. I've lived here for eight years. I can't imagine living anywhere else now. It's my sanctuary." She poked at Alec's shoulder. "We're going to come back to that once I figure out what questions to ask." She tried to cover a yawn. "How long have you lived at your place in Venice?"

"Tired already? We've got a long night ahead of us. I've lived there for about ten years now."

"And before that?" Selene didn't want to admit she wasn't sleeping well, that dreams of a certain woman were invading her most private thoughts.

Alec looked lost in thought for a long moment before she said, "Europe. I moved around a lot before I settled here."

"That sounds idyllic. You said you taught while you were there?"

Alec nodded. "It was idyllic, in many ways. But every place has its demons. And I spent time there *not* teaching as well. Just enjoying the landscape and history."

Selene gave a few directions once they entered the village, and Alec pulled up outside her cabin. "I'll pick you up at six thirty, okay? That should give us plenty of time to get there fashionably late."

"Apparently so, in your magic carpet Hummer. Did you want to come in and change here?" Selene swallowed hard as she considered the offer she'd made without thinking. Alec, naked in her house.

"Thanks, but I'll go check in at the little hotel down the street and get ready there. See you in a few."

Selene climbed out with her new packages in hand, and before she could shut the door, Alec said, "Oh, and, Selene? Thanks again for inviting me tonight."

Selene smiled as Alec pulled away. She juggled her packages, and her hands began to tremble slightly. *A date.* She had a date with a sexy, funny woman, for a party at Frey Falconi's house. The pressure began to weigh on her, but she tried to shake it off. *I can do this. People do this all the time, and I can too.*

CHAPTER TEN

A lec sat in Selene's living room, waiting.
Every few minutes, she heard a frustrated sigh come from the bathroom, and it made her chuckle softly. When time began to get short, and they were going to be my-time-is-more-important-than-yours-late instead of fashionably-late, she knocked tentatively on the door. "Selene? Everything okay? Anything I can help with?"

Selene cracked the door open, but not so Alec could see her. "I'm having some hair issues."

"You know, because of my sisters, I'm pretty good with hair. Want some help?"

The door slowly opened, and it took all of Alec's willpower not to laugh. Not at Selene, or the distressed look on her face, but at the frizzy mess she'd made of her hair.

Selene looked ready to cry. "I don't know what happened. Granted, I don't usually do anything with my hair. I just blow-dry it and go. But I thought I'd try a few curls tonight, because it's our first date, and an important party, and all that stuff. But every time I tried, it got worse, so I tried again, and well…" She motioned at the puff of hair almost obscuring her face.

"Okay, sit down. I've got this. Where are your hair products?"

Selene's shoulder's slumped. "I've only got a few. In that cupboard."

Alec rummaged for a moment and found a few things that could help. She poured small amounts into her hands and turned to Selene. "Trust me?"

She shrugged. "You can't exactly make it worse, can you?"

"That didn't answer the question, but I'll go with it." She ran her hands slowly through Selene's hair, and soon her hair was straight once again. She picked up the blow-dryer and slowly ran a brush through it as she blew it out. Within ten minutes, Selene's hair was glossy. "Want some waves at the front?"

Selene nodded slightly. "Whatever you think works. I'm all yours."

Alec's mouth went slightly dry at the thought, but she pushed it aside. She expertly used the brush and blow-dryer to give some wave to Selene's hair and then held the tools up with a flourish. "And...done." She set them down and grinned. "Now, you'd better get dressed before we're even later."

"Alec...Oh my God. I don't think it's ever looked this good." Selene was staring at the mirror, her eyes wide. "Thank you so much."

Alec smiled as she shut the door behind her. "Get ready, woman!"

Fifteen minutes later, Selene entered the living room, and Alec decided she would've waited another decade if necessary. The black dress hugged every curve, and the material crossed over her full breasts, but left exposed her smooth, pale chest and a small diamond cut flash of stomach below, before the material gathered together and fell in a waterfall effect down to her ankles. Classy black heels, a thin silver necklace with a tiny book charm on it, and small diamond earrings completed the outfit. Alec quickly gave silent thanks she wasn't a man, because if she had been, she wouldn't have been able to walk, let alone hide the effect Selene had on her. As it was, she was going to have wet underwear all night.

She stood and took Selene's hand. "You look stunning. Stunning isn't the right word, really, but I'm at a loss to think of others. I can't believe I get to show up with you."

Selene blushed. "Thank you. You look pretty impressive too."

Alec had grabbed her outfit quickly, not wanting to risk Selene coming into her place yet. There were too many artifacts from her previous life, too many things she might have to explain. Like furniture placement, which necessarily left large open spaces for her wings. So she'd grabbed an outfit she'd worn to Meg's last big party, which was a suit with an onyx black button-down shirt and patent leather shoes. Her only color was the deep purple tie and matching cufflinks. The outfit had gotten her plenty of welcome female attention at the party, and she was glad to see the appreciation in Selene's eyes.

"Then we'll be a hell of a good-looking couple. You ready to go?"

Selene grabbed a small handbag. "I think so. To be honest, I'm pretty nervous."

Alec held her hand and helped her into the Hummer. "Why is that?"

Selene waited until Alec was back in the car and pulling onto the street before she answered. "I'm so awkward at these kinds of things. I never know what to say or how to act."

"Why act at all? Just be yourself."

"You know what I mean. If I were just myself, I wouldn't laugh at stupid jokes or smile at people I don't like. And you can't get away with that kind of thing at parties. Or in general, really."

Alec frowned. "No, I don't suppose you can, if you're talking about your career. But if it's more important to be true to yourself than about what people think of you, then maybe you shouldn't be around people you can't be yourself with anyway." She looked over at Selene and felt her pulse skip. With the streetlights highlighting her silky hair, her smooth skin, and her full lips, she looked like something from a fairy tale. A sexy fairy tale, she thought, looking at the expanse of skin showing.

"That's part of the problem. I'm going tonight, but I'm not sure I should be."

"Why? Is it a party full of zombies? Or drunk hippies?"

"Both of those would be more fun and probably more interesting. The person throwing the party, Frey Falconi, wants me to come work with him on a major project. But I'm not sure about it, and this invitation is meant to provide me with impetus to say yes."

At Frey's name, Alec shivered slightly, an ominous feeling coming over her. She'd heard of him, but hadn't paid much attention, figuring he was just another bag of wind blowing meaningless words at people. "What makes you uncertain about it?"

Selene laughed. "You ask me so many questions, but I can't seem to ask you any."

"You can ask me anything. But I told you, I'm boring." Alec hoped Selene wouldn't ask her anything that forced her to outright lie.

"I think you need to turn right on the street ahead," Selene said as she scanned the directions in her hand.

"I think you're right. Look at the line of cars."

Selene looked up, and Alec thought she saw her visibly pale. "I don't think I can do this."

Alec pulled into the line of cars waiting to be taken away by the valet and turned to take Selene's hand in her own. "I'll be right beside you, okay? And if I think you're getting stuck, I'll jump in. Like I said, my parents made me go to all kinds of these types of things. I can make small talk with the best of them. And if you need my help, just nudge me."

"Nudge you? How?"

Selene's smile lit up the Hummer, and Alec melted just a bit. "Step on my toes or pinch my arm or something like that. I'll get it, I promise."

Selene seemed to relax. "Okay. If you promise."

The valet tapped on the window. "May I?"

Alec held up her finger to ask him to wait. She reached into the glove box and handed Selene a small bag. "I got you a little something for tonight."

Selene touched the bag almost as though she was afraid it would disappear. "What is it? Why?"

"Open it and see, and because I wanted to."

Selene took the small box out of the bag and opened it to find a slim silver bracelet with a round charm. She held it up to look at the flat circle and smiled. "The tree of knowledge."

Alec tilted her head and shrugged slightly. She couldn't remember the last time she'd given a gift to someone outside her family or co-workers. "It seemed appropriate. Do you like it?"

Selene held out her arm. "I love it. Will you put it on me, please?"

Alec slid the bangle over Selene's thin hand and tightened the sliding clasp. It looked perfect on her, just as Alec had known it would when she saw it.

The valet tapped on the window again, looking more impatient. Alec looked at Selene. "I'm ready if you are?"

Selene took a deep breath, and Alec tried to keep her eyes above Selene's chest.

"I'm ready."

They entered the enormous white mansion, replete with stone lions standing guard at the entrance. Stone animals and statues always made Alec think of Medusa, and although she'd long been gone, Alec still missed her occasionally. She'd had a wicked sense of humor, often pulling pranks on people, like turning their food into stone right as they were about to take a bite. History hadn't been kind to her, and Alec wished she had the capability to change that. *But history will be what it is. All we can do is try to live for today and plan for the future.*

Selene shivered and Alec took her hand. The massive living room was overflowing with people, the conversation a cacophony of false laughter and fake interest. Even from the landing above the room, Alec could feel the tension and desperation in the room, but she couldn't get a handle on the source. She smiled at Selene, hoping she couldn't see Alec's unease. "Why don't we start with a drink? Looks like the bar is over there." She lifted their linked hands to motion in the direction she meant, and Selene nodded gratefully.

Alec deftly led the way through the crowd, with one or two people stopping them to say hello to Selene, but only briefly when Selene failed to respond with the expected false enthusiasm. At the bar, she asked Selene what she'd like, and noticed the slightly panicked look at the variety of cocktails and wines. There wouldn't be any Guinness at a place like this. Alec leaned over as though to nuzzle her ear and asked softly, "Alcohol, or no?"

"No, please," she murmured back.

"Can I get a red wine, and a Shirley Temple with orange juice, in a wine glass, please?" Alec grinned at the bartender and winked, and the woman practically fell over herself pulling together the request.

Alec handed Selene her glass. "If anyone asks, it's just something the bartender whipped up for you." She tapped her glass to Selene's. "To a night of adventure."

Selene's eyes sparkled. "To adventure in general."

Alec took a healthy sip of her wine and let her hand linger on Selene's naked lower back. The dress left the small dimples in her back exposed, and Alec imagined running her tongue over each one.

"Selene! You made it. I was beginning to think you'd declined my invitation after all."

Alec turned toward the booming voice, and the hair on the back of her neck stood on end. Dark, swirling energy surrounded the man who shook Selene's hand for a moment too long, and she recognized it as the same energy that had been stuck to Selene once before. Her impulse was to step in front of Selene and protect her, although she kept her place. Somehow, the energy seemed to surround him, rather than come from him. *Strange. Whose energy does that?*

Selene managed to extricate her hand and gave him a polite smile. "Frey Falconi, I'd like you to meet my friend and fellow professor, Alec Graves."

He glanced at Alec and gave her a smile that looked genuine. "Nice to meet you. Selene, I've got several people I'd very much like you to meet. Come with me?"

Selene stiffened next to her and Alec said, "You really should, Selene. And if you don't mind, I'll tag along and meet some new people too, so I don't continue to use you as my only social outlet." She felt Selene's body relax a little, and knew she'd made the right call.

Falconi shrugged and grinned. "Of course, the more the merrier, as they say."

He led the way, and stopped here and there to introduce Selene to various people. Producers, both TV and film, writers, and other philosophers went by in a whirlwind. Selene was polite to all of them, though Alec could tell she hadn't really taken much of it in. Falconi seemed to think she should be suitably impressed, however, and when he wasn't getting the overawed reaction he was clearly expecting, he seemed deflated.

"If you don't mind terribly, I'm afraid I should attend to some of my other guests. Please, Selene, mingle and talk to people about the vision we're running toward. Anyone here could answer at least some questions, and I'd really like to put your mind at ease about the project."

He gave Alec a cursory nod before he moved off into the crowd.

Selene gave a heavy sigh and leaned against Alec, who put an arm around her. She tried not to notice that Selene fit perfectly against her.

"Can we go, do you think?"

Alec laughed. "I could. I have a feeling he'll notice if you're gone. But do you care?" The man's intense energy was wearing on her, so it must be tiring for Selene.

"I don't know. If it's true that this could change my career, then maybe I really should talk to some of these people and see if it's worth taking the risk. Certainly, there are people here who are way above me in the field, and under different circumstances, I'd love to simply talk to them. But if it's not worth the risk, and I'm happy where I am, then I can leave and never take one of his phone calls again. I can contact the other people on my own terms."

Alec frowned. She didn't like that the man with the horrible dark energy was trying to pull Selene into his frenetic little world. "Just what is this project, anyway?"

Selene did her best not to cry. Alec had been silent since they'd left Falconi's. In fact, she'd been silent since she'd told her about the project Falconi wanted her assistance on. And, looking at it objectively, she could somewhat understand why. Falconi wanted people to stop believing in religion and to start thinking rationally. Alec taught theology and felt people should believe in what made them happy. Naturally, Alec would be against that kind of plan. What she hadn't considered was that Alec would actually be offended and not want to spend any more time with her. The thought made her achingly sad, and she had to blink back tears.

"Alec—"

"Look, Selene. I'm sorry. I'm not feeling very well. Can I call you in the morning?"

Alec looked straight ahead, and Selene felt bereft. "Sure. Of course. Thank you for coming with me tonight."

Alec got out and opened Selene's door for her. After helping her down, she sighed. "I'm sorry. I was a bit thrown. I just need to think." She kissed Selene's knuckles, her lips feather light over the sensitive skin. "But I'll call first thing tomorrow. I promise."

CHAPTER ELEVEN

After a long night spent in the trees outside Selene's house, just to make certain she was safe, Alec headed home to freshen up, and then hit the boardwalk for a diversion from her swirling thoughts. She hadn't called Selene yet, because although she wanted to, she needed to sort some things out first. That Selene was contemplating working directly against religion, and on a massive scale, seemed far too coincidental. And that she was doing it with someone whose energy had a signature she couldn't read made her distinctly uncomfortable. The last thing she wanted to do was drive her in that direction, so she decided to get some perspective before she made her next move. She bought a deep fried croissant-donut covered in chocolate, or a cronut, from the street vendor on the Promenade. She thanked him, and without looking at her, he said in a heavy Irish accent, "No problem, duckie. Enjoy it. There's less time than you think."

She nearly choked on her artery-clogging fried dough. "Still dishing out the philosophy to the masses, Fin? You sound like a nutter."

He looked at her sharply and then broke into a grin. "Alec! Blazes, woman, it's been a long time. You live and work nearby, and yet I see you once a century. What's that about?"

She licked chocolate from her fingers, glad she couldn't actually get diabetes. "If I saw you more than that, I'd be the size of Bacchus."

He laughed and handed another patron their donut and change. "Nothing wrong with that. At least he's enjoying the hell out of his existence." He frowned briefly. "Or is he?"

Alec nodded. "For now, he's still throwing his famous parties every month. Debauchery and douchery."

Fin gave her a mildly disapproving look. "So jaded. What brings you to my little sweet stand?"

"I need some advice, and I need it from someone outside the organization. Could we meet up over a drink later?"

"You know I'll never turn down a drink, lovey. King's Head at two? I'll be sold out by then."

She gave him a hug, glad to feel his solidity. "See you there."

Alec left him to his line of customers and wandered aimlessly down the Promenade toward the beach. It was crowded with the usual combination of desperately optimistic street performers, tourists, the homeless, and locals ignoring them all. If she closed her eyes, it could almost be her original home, where the marketplace was always abuzz with almost the exact same groupings of people. *Minus the occasional royalty.* She smiled slightly, trying to picture any of the modern day owners of airlines or fashion designers wandering along Santa Monica Pier. At least in her time, the royalty had occasionally mixed with the rabble, if only to see just how far above it they really were. *My time. What does that even mean anymore?*

Arcade game music was background to the roller coaster, and as she left it behind to go to the farthest point on the pier, she sighed with relief at the quiet. There was so little of that these days. She could remember when there was true silence. No bells, no whistles. Especially at night, when they'd lived out in the open, perching in trees or cliff tops. Bird cries and animal howls, perhaps. But they were nothing compared to the constant, ever present buzz in this century. At night, when all should have been silent, there was still the zapping of power lines, the ringing of phones, partygoers, and general nightlife. She stood on the end of the pier and watched the waves roll in and crash against the posts. They continued, crash after rolling crash, pounding against all in their path, only to roll back out again, sweeping whatever they covered into the ocean.

She felt the tide in her soul, as though she were being swept to sea, caught in a current there was no swimming against. She rested her chin on the cold metal railing, her arms dangling over the water.

A face appeared below her and shot up out of the water, grinning maniacally.

She jumped back. "For fuck's sake. Seriously. Do you have to do that?" she snapped at the water nymph. A quick glance around her told her they were covered by their otherworldly cloaking.

"Zed wants you back at the office."

The creature's voice was preternaturally high, like that of a bat. Alec winced. "Now?"

"Now. He said to tell you it's orders. Want a ride?"

"I'll pass, thanks. Tell him I'm on my way." Alec rolled her eyes and waved the mischievous little creature away. While it wouldn't kill her, being under water without gills wasn't pleasant for anyone, and the nymph knew that well. It gave her a pouty look before diving back into the water.

She closed her eyes and spread her wings, basking in the feeling of stretching them wide open in the sea air. The ocean seemed to race beneath her as she flew over the waves, unable to resist diving toward them and then up again, into the salty winter air. *I'd forgotten what freedom it is to fly.* The thought sobered her, and she headed back inland to the office.

Once there, she folded her wings but didn't tuck them away. It felt too good to have them out. She knocked on Zed's door and poked her head in. "You wanted me?"

He waved her in, and she thought she saw his hand flicker slightly, but when she looked again, it seemed normal. A tremor of fear rushed through her. He looked so tired.

"Sit."

She sat.

"How is it going?"

She sighed. "Well, we're getting along. I'm learning about her, and she seems to trust me." She hated to lay another thing on his shoulders, but he needed to know. "Zed, what do you know about Frey Falconi?"

He looked lost in thought for a moment. "The philosopher? He's a bit of a Socrates of his day, isn't he? Lots of questions and no answers, with the hordes of pseudo-intellectuals flocking to his sock-and-sandal feet?"

She laughed. "Kind of, yeah. But he's got money. And people are listening, Zed. They're planning on putting him on TV, so he can tell the masses that believing in a deity is wrong. But he'll say it in ways that even the good ol' boys will understand. He might not get the hardcore believers, but he'll get the ones on the fence. And there are a hell of a lot more of those than there used to be."

Zed paled, and she nearly reached out to him, but quickly thought better of it. He might be old, and he might be fragile, but he was also proud.

"Could he be the reason the rate of nonbelievers has gone up?" He pointed to the holographic map he had of the building. "Sectors seven and twelve have had mass fades. Nearly fifty percent of their workforce is gone."

"It could be, but I doubt it. He doesn't seem to be working in other languages yet, which has restricted him to English-speaking countries. But once he goes on TV, or if his plan to go viral works, then we're going to see some drastic changes."

Zed got up and closed his door. "Remember the old days?"

Alec had a feeling she knew what was coming. She inclined her head for him to continue.

"If someone behaved irresponsibly, or if we just didn't like someone, we took care of them. We made sure things went the way they were supposed to."

"I don't think turning him into a tree or a cow is going to work this time. He's too well known to just disappear." She shifted her wings away from the uncomfortable chair. "Different times, different measures, old man."

He pointed a finger at her and a bolt of lightning shot from it, sizzling the air next to her head. She laughed.

"Don't call me an old man. I'm ageless. As are you. What are we going to do about him?"

"I think Selene may be the key to dealing with him too. He seems to have made her a major part of his plan, although I admit I'm not sure why. His energy was off, like he'd been hanging out with a bad crowd. I'll need to convince her, somehow, that Falconi isn't the way to go. If we get her where we need her, maybe we can turn the tide in our direction."

Zed looked thoughtful for a long moment. "I want to know who he is. If he's using the same wild card we are, I think there's more to this than we can see. I'll see if one of the other sectors has a spy they can spare. In the meantime, focus on Selene. I'll keep you in the loop if I find anything out. You do the same."

She got up, aware she'd been dismissed.

"Oh, and, Alec?"

She stopped. "Yeah, Zed?"

"Tell Fin I said hello, and to come have a drink with me sometime. I miss our old poker nights."

She shook her head. It shouldn't surprise her Zed knew. He was omniscient when it came to his own sector, so it was obvious he'd know where she was and who she was talking to, especially if it was one of the company. "Will do."

❖

She entered the King's Head just before two. She despised being late, as it was an indication she thought her time was more valuable than someone else's. While there had been times in the past that was true, particularly during an especially narcissistic phase in the sixteen hundreds, it was rarely true now. She spotted Fin at a table in the corner and waved to him, motioning to the bar to see if he wanted a drink. He held up his glass and grinned.

She ordered a Guinness for him and a Diet Coke for herself. She'd learned long ago not to try to keep up with a Celt when it came to alcohol. And right now, she felt like she needed her wits about her more than ever before. The little Irish Pub was nearly empty this early in the afternoon, which was perfect. The feeling of being watched the last few days had made her edgy.

"One for you, none for me." Alec set their drinks on the table and returned his one-armed hug.

"You're a good one, lass."

They clinked glasses and sipped in silence for a moment.

"So? Tell me what's going on."

She ran a hand through her hair. "Where do I start? You know about the fadings?"

He nodded. "The grapevine is as fruitful as ever. I've heard it's getting bad."

"Bad doesn't cover it. Worse by the day." She wiped the condensation on her glass with her thumb, watching a tiny bit of steam rise from her hand. "The thing is, Fin, I'm the one tasked with stopping it. Because an oracle said so. And you know what that means."

He laughed and took a drink of beer. "It means you don't know your ass from your head right now, and it won't matter in the long run because you'll do what you're supposed to do, no matter what you do." He shrugged. "So, why worry about it? Do your best, because whatever you're doing is the right thing. The only thing you can do."

"That's the thing, Fin. What if I shouldn't be doing anything? What if we ignore the Fates and just see what happens?"

"And leave people to fade?"

He didn't look judgmental, just interested. She sighed. "Maybe some want to, now that things are so different. Maybe I shouldn't be making that choice for them."

He held up a hand. "Wait a minute. Hold on to your white horses and put down your shield. You're not making a choice for anyone. We can all choose whether or not to stay." He shrugged. "Well, maybe not all. Not the big boys. But the rest of us? We can trade in our cloud shoes for rubber soles anytime, sugar. Look at me. I wanted out of the game, and now I bake and sell, and no one tells me what to do, and the only thing people want from me are thick pieces of bread slathered in sugar. I come and go when I please, and I still have the benefit of traveling back to Ireland whenever I want. That's a choice almost everyone there has, kid."

Alec grinned at his endearment. She was older by a good thousand years. "I hadn't thought of it that way. But what about those who don't want to fade? Who blink out because they aren't given a choice?"

He scoffed. "Please. Like that happens. We all get a little less substantial when it comes down to it, so we know it's coming. They had a chance, and they didn't take it." He took her hands in his. "Don't let Zed tell you otherwise. Yeah, do what you can. We all have to do what we can." He let go of her hands and picked up his drink. "Until we can't. And then we choose."

"What if I let people down, Fin? What if I can't do it?"

"Don't do it alone, Alec. Reach out. Hell, I'll gladly place some ears in walls for you. Do this your way."

She rolled her glass between her hands. *What is my way?* She started to consider the people at the company and all they could offer. Fin was right. She might be the one to make things happen, but maybe she didn't have to be the only one.

"One more question. Have you heard of Frey Falconi?"

He frowned slightly. "Who hasn't? But I can't get a feel for him. He seems to really believe in what he's spouting, and truth be told, he's got some valid points. But there's something about him that doesn't sit right."

"Any chance you could get some ears in that direction too? Find out who he associates with? I could really use some more info."

He nodded. "Zed doesn't have what you need these days, huh? The higher-ups don't get their hands dirty. Not the way they used to."

He said it with such wistfulness it made Alec laugh. "Different times indeed, old friend." She finished her drink and stood. "I've got a task to get back to. Thanks for your input, Fin. I needed it."

He got up and gave her a tight hug. "Don't forget your friends are different from those who give you shit to do, Alec. Sometimes they're the same, but in your situation…well, be discerning, lass. And if you need anything, shout. You know where to find me. And if I hear anything, I'll send it your way."

Alec hugged him fiercely. She'd forgotten what it was to have a conversation outside the company, with someone who knew the ins and outs of the operation. She felt lighter, and more determined than she had in a long while. She'd do this, but it was time to take control, whether anyone else approved or not. It was time to call Selene and move things forward.

CHAPTER TWELVE

Selene lay on her stomach on the couch, reading from Rousseau's *Confessions*. Guilt niggled at her slightly, since she should have been grading papers. But it had been so long since she'd simply relaxed on a weekend and taken the time to read, she couldn't resist. She read the many confessions of a man baring his not-inconsiderable misdeeds to the world and felt strangely moved by it. There were plenty of times she'd had to choose between doing the right thing because it was right, and doing the wrong thing because it had a better outcome, or was more interesting. Life in foster care often meant making those sorts of choices. Although she'd almost always chosen the high road, she'd lost plenty of nights of sleep over making the choice. She often wondered if other people had the same dilemma.

The phone rang, and she nearly fell off the couch leaning for it, and it made her giggle. "Hello?" she said somewhat breathlessly.

"Sorry, sounds like you're not alone. I'll call later."

"Mika, wait. I'm alone. I just did something silly. I'm surprised to hear your voice."

Mika hesitated. "Yes. Well. I find myself missing your company, and I thought perhaps we could have dinner."

"Oh? What is it about me you miss?"

"Come on, Selene. Don't be narcissistic. It's unbecoming."

Selene had to fight the urge to hang up. "It's not narcissism, Mika. It's a genuine question, as I don't feel compelled to have dinner with the woman who broke up with me."

"I told you, I wasn't breaking up with you. We just needed some time—"

"No, *you* needed time. I was fine, but that didn't matter." Selene took a steadying breath. "You should know, I'm seeing someone." *I think I am, anyway.* Alec hadn't called that morning like she'd said she would, but Selene had decided she wouldn't freak out about it until the following day.

The silence stretched so long she almost thought Mika had hung up.

"Oh. Who?"

"Another professor."

"Of?"

Selene grimaced, knowing what was coming. "Theology."

Mika's laughter sounded both forced and sarcastic, if laughter could sound sarcastic. "Religion? Seriously, Selene. Why on earth would you date someone like that?"

"She's not religious, exactly. And you know I'm open to belief."

"Open to the *idea* of belief is different from believing, and you're no believer."

"But that doesn't mean I can't be okay with someone else believing."

Mika gave a sigh Selene knew meant she was trying to be patient.

"Selene, baby, you're meant to be with someone like me. Someone rational, a thinker." She stopped for a moment. "And besides, we do have phenomenal sex."

Selene shook her head and glanced at *Confessions*. Should she simply admit to Mika that the sex was far from phenomenal? That it was outright dull, and the thought of having to go through that process with Mika again nearly made her throw up a little in her mouth? Part of her wanted to do it, to put Mika in her place and take control. But the lighter side of her responded, not bothering to consult with the darker side. "Be that as it may, you made it clear even that bored you slightly."

"True, I did. But we've had our little break, and now it's time to continue forward. Together."

Selene felt a headache threaten. "No, it's not. I don't know that it ever will be again. And if I take Falconi's offer, I'll be gone anyway, so there's really no point." With the words out of her mouth, Selene felt like she could go jump in the pool naked, or run down the street in the rain, or sing from a rooftop. That distancing herself from Mika made her feel so much better told her what she needed to know. "I'm sorry, Mika. When you broke it off, I was crushed. But it turns out you were right."

"Fine. When you realize I'm the best option you've got, and certainly a more likely one than a religion professor, give me a call. I'll try to make time for you."

She hung up, and Selene was happy to allow her the final word. She'd always walked on eggshells around Mika, feeling like she was inferior. While it might be true, she decided she much preferred the way she felt around Alec. Not superior, or less than, but equal. A unique feeling indeed.

She folded back onto the couch and picked up her book, but the thought of Alec inspired other, more base thoughts. She put the book down and headed to the bedroom. Maybe some time with her vibrator would ease the tension she felt thinking about Alec. *Or make it worse.* Either way, she wanted some fantasy time.

The thumb-length silver bullet vibrator sat in her bedside drawer. It was simple, no bells and whistles. A bit of physical stimulation and a lot of mental visualization usually got her off quickly. She got comfortable, closed her eyes, and imagined Alec. Her hands massaging Selene's breasts, her mouth closed around an aching nipple, her fingers sliding slowly inside her—

The phone rang.

She was tempted to ignore it, but the incessant ring made her sigh and reach for it.

"Hello?"

"Selene? Hi, it's Alec."

Selene's stomach flipped, and she felt the blood rush to her face. The object of her fantasy on the phone at the moment she'd been making use of her image was somehow embarrassing, though Alec would never know. "Hi. I was hoping you'd call."

"I wanted to apologize for last night. I was just thrown, and I didn't handle it well. Can I make it up to you?"

"What did you have in mind?" *Please say sex.*

"I'd like to take you to dinner at one of my favorite places. And then maybe dancing? Do you dance?"

Selene pressed her hand to her stomach to quell the rush of nerves. The thought of dancing with Alec was more enticing than a philosopher's book about confessions. "I do like to dance, yes. Should I meet you there?"

"If you want to. But parking isn't easy, so it might be best if we take one car. I don't mind driving, if you don't mind being stuck in a car with me."

Selene could hear the teasing in Alec's voice, and it made her warm inside. "As long as you're not going to drop me off like a sack of trash again." She laughed to show she was kidding, but it needed to be said.

"Geez. I'm really sorry. I promise tonight will be different."

"Seriously, though. It's not like I live near you. Why don't I take the train and meet you at the campus?"

Alex hesitated. "Well, how about I give you a choice? Dinner and dancing in West Hollywood, or dinner and dancing in the high desert?"

Selene thought about it. The last time she'd gone to the bar in the high desert hadn't been terribly successful, and the thought of seeing those women again made her twitch. "West Hollywood, definitely. If we're out late, I'll need to get a hotel room, because I'll miss the train back."

"I know a great one in the area. Why don't I book it now, and we'll make that the plan?"

A hotel doesn't mean no sex. That's a plus. "That sounds great. Eight?"

"See you there."

Before she hung up, Selene said, "Alec? I'm really glad you called. Thank you for not being angry with me."

"I've got no reason to be angry with you. And I'm looking forward to apologizing."

Selene could practically see Alec's mischievous grin. They hung up, and Selene threw the vibrator back in the drawer. With any luck, she wouldn't be needing it any time soon.

❖

Alec waited nervously on the train platform. Things were getting out of control. She'd meant to become Selene's friend, maybe. A serious acquaintance, anyway. She needed to be close enough to tell her the truth, to get her to believe. But here she was, taking her on a date. *Another date.* She knew full well Selene was seeing something more than what Alec had to offer. Although Selene was beautiful, intelligent, witty, and sweet, Alec couldn't go there, not really. She'd been down the path with humans before, and it never led to anything good. And how would Selene feel when she found out the truth? Would she think she'd been betrayed, or lied to? *Hasn't she?*

The train pulled up and Alec sighed. It would have to happen soon. Tomorrow, maybe. They could have breakfast together and she could take her to the office. *So, Selene, this is where your logic has no place. Excellent.*

Selene got off the train, and Alec decidedly ignored the way her stomach looped and her pulse raced. She looked gorgeous in her skinny jeans and loose sweater, paired with a silky gray scarf and knee-high boots.

"Hey there."

Alec felt like she could swallow her tongue. She cleared her throat and concentrated on making word noises. "Hey yourself. You look great."

Selene smiled. "Likewise. Do you ever wear anything other than black? It suits you; I'm just curious."

Alec tried to remember the last time she'd worn colors. The French Renaissance, maybe? When she and her sisters had decided to be more in style, taking the time to have a real life rather than just doing their job twenty-four hours a day. They'd even taken a decade-long vacation, although the workload when they'd gotten back had been horrendous.

"Not really, no. I guess I'm a creature of habit." She took Selene's hand and nearly sighed out loud at the warmth and softness of it. "Ready to go?"

"I can't wait. I haven't been dancing in so long I've probably forgotten how. I'll look like a clown having a drunken fit."

"Not likely. And if you need some help, I'll be right beside you." She opened the door to the Hummer, and noticed Selene's head tilted as though she were thinking. "Something wrong?"

Selene glanced at her and looked back at the car. "It's the strangest thing. Sometimes, when I'm looking at the Hummer, it's like I can't quite see it properly. It gets...fuzzy, or something." She looked at Alec. "In fact, the same thing happens when I look at you. If I look directly at you, or in your vicinity, it's fine. But if I try to look at you out of the corner of my eye..." She shrugged, looking perplexed. "You go fuzzy, or something, too." She shook her head. "I must need my eyes checked. Maybe something's wrong with my peripheral vision. Although, it doesn't seem to affect anything else."

Alec gave her a hand up into the Hummer, her heart racing. She didn't fully understand it, but there was a reason Selene had been chosen. This confirmed she was at least on the right playing field. What it meant beyond that, Alec couldn't fathom. "There's a special paint job on the Hummer, and like you said, I'm always in black. Maybe you can't see either of us because we blend in with the shadows." She grinned to show she was teasing and hoped Selene couldn't tell the truth behind her words. But if her expression was any indication, she hadn't fallen for it.

"I thought we could go to the French Market for dinner, and then maybe to The Hollow for dancing. Does that work for you?" *Please let me change the subject. I'm not ready.*

Selene searched Alec's eyes for a moment, before her shoulders dropped slightly and she relaxed into the seat. "I love the French Market. Their onion soup is to die for." She moved her hair off her shoulder. "But maybe I'll avoid onions tonight. Just in case."

Alec winced. *Don't do anything stupid. Don't say anything stupid. Don't be stupid.* "In case?" *Well, that was stupid.*

Selene looked at her. "In case I can convince you to kiss me before the night is over."

"Ah. Then stinky foods should definitely be out."

They drove in silence for a few minutes before Selene said, "Did you ever find out about the job, by the way?"

Alec had nearly forgotten the reason she'd given Selene for being on campus. "I did, actually. They chose the other guy, but said they'd like to consider me for a position in the fall."

"I'm sorry to hear that. I would have liked to see you in action."

"Yeah, well, maybe you'll still get the chance. Who can tell, right?" Alec gripped the steering wheel tightly. Why did everything feel like it had a double edge tonight? She shifted uncomfortably, an itch in her right wing making her desperate to reach back and take care of it. But with Selene's ability, albeit slight, to see beyond the veil of magic, she didn't want to take the risk.

"Are you okay?"

"I am, just an itch. Got it, thanks." *Or I've got fleas.*

They pulled up at the restaurant, and as the parking lot was full, they managed to find a space down the street. They got out and Selene laughed. "I used to go into this shop a lot when I first moved here." She motioned at the witchcraft store, with its dark wooden door and smell of incense wafting out.

"Really? It seems way out of your jurisdiction, Professor."

Selene took Alec's hand. "I was searching for something to hold on to, something non-judgmental, and this was right at the time. Can we go inside? I just want to remember."

Before Alec could think of a suitable excuse, Selene pulled open the door and dragged her inside. It was dark, the air heavy. Selene wandered around the small shop, a tiny smile playing on her lips.

"Well now. If I had to guess which random person from my past would walk through the door tonight, it sure as hell wouldn't have been you."

Alec glanced at Selene, who was at the far end of the store. "Hey, Iza. How's things?"

Iza glared at her. "How's things? After all this time, that's what you've got?"

Alec raised a hand to quiet her. "I'm kind of working right now. Maybe we could have this conversation another time?"

Selene touched Alec's shoulder. "Everything okay?"

Iza gave a harsh laugh. "Sure, it's fine. You go and enjoy your little friend. Because she'll be long gone in the morning. She's not one for hanging around, are you?" Iza's arms were crossed over her chest as she stared at Alec.

"This isn't the time, Iza." She turned to Selene. "Ready for dinner?"

Selene nodded slowly, looking back and forth between them. "Sure."

Alec took her hand and led her outside, glad Iza hadn't continued her tirade at their backs. It was going to be hard enough to explain as it was.

They walked in silence for a moment. Alec said, "I'm sorry about that. Iza can be...volatile."

"Is that why you didn't stick around, as she says?"

"In a way." Alec tried to think of a way to explain things without having to explain everything. "She was always volatile, and I never knew what to expect. And she had a fascination with death I couldn't handle." *It's true. Kind of.* Iza had wanted Alec because of her obsession with vengeance after she'd lost a favored human in World War I. The sex had been insanely hot, but not worth the raging outbursts.

They were nearly to the restaurant before Selene said, "The woman at the mall, and now this one. Are there many?"

Alec smiled at the hostess and waved Selene in front of her as they were shown to their table. It gave her seconds to think of an appropriate response. But she couldn't think of one. They sat down and Selene ignored her menu, clearly waiting for Alec's answer.

"Yes, in a way, I guess." She took a deep breath. "Honestly, Selene, I'm not really the relationship type. I've been in a few, but I always manage to mess it up. I work long hours. I don't always call. I forget anniversaries. I travel incessantly. I find that if I don't leave, the other person does, eventually. So I stay unattached, for the most part, and just live my life the best way I know how."

Selene began folding her napkin into some kind of origami figure. "Okay. I didn't realize that, but okay. So, this thing between us…"

"Can be fun. And interesting. And maybe even excellent. But it won't be forever."

They ordered their drinks and sat in awkward silence. Alec searched Selene's face for a sign of emotion, but there was none. It was an impassive mask, which was far more worrying than if she'd broken down or gotten angry. "I really like you, Selene. I enjoy spending time with you, and I'm enjoying getting to know you. Can that be enough?" *Please don't let me have blown this chance. Zed will kill me.*

Finally, Selene looked up from her swan napkin. "I'm not looking for forever, not right now. So fun and relaxed is a good way to be, for both of us." She squeezed Alec's hand. "Thank you for being honest with me."

She opened her menu, effectively ending that line of conversation. Alec knew she should feel relieved, and yet, her heart ached for what couldn't be, and for the pain she knew she caused Selene, regardless of what she said. *And what about what I've yet to do?*

Chapter Thirteen

Thumping bass slid over Selene's skin like an energetic lover. Bodies of every shape and size moved on the dance floor, and all kinds of beautiful people sat relaxing under heat lamps on the patio. Inside at the back, groups lounged in oversized plush red booths covered in throw cushions. A few had the curtains pulled for privacy, although their silhouettes were still distinctly clear.

Selene closed her eyes and let the vibe fill her. Dinner conversation had been nice, but more stilted than any they'd had yet. Though she'd told Alec it was no big deal to keep things casual, it was an out-and-out lie. She didn't do casual sex. She didn't do casual anything, really. And it had seemed like they had such a great connection. She was hurt, but trying hard not to take it personally. After all, they were out on a date, and if Alec didn't really like her, she wouldn't have made all the fuss she had already. So why did she feel so empty?

Alec's hand settled on her lower back and said in her ear, "Drink?"

Selene nodded and Alec headed for the bar. She liked the way Alec's black jeans hugged her slim hips, the way the black leather jacket sat exactly right on her broad shoulders. Selene looked at the women on either side of her, and Alec went fuzzy. She frowned and looked away. She wasn't going to worry about anything more tonight. She wanted to dance, lose herself in the music, and let go. Tomorrow, she could return to the life where she felt like a penny in a pool.

Alec returned with their drinks and handed Selene hers before taking her free hand and leading her to a surprisingly empty table near the dance floor. She shrugged off her leather jacket and hung it on the back of a chair before motioning at the dance floor and raising an eyebrow. Selene took a swig of her drink, savoring the rum on her tongue for a moment, before taking Alec's hand and pulling her onto the dance floor.

They started dancing, and it took all of Selene's willpower not to press her body against Alec's. She looked good in her leather jacket, but she looked unbelievably hot in her ribbed black tank top, which showed off the flat planes of her stomach and the solid bulges of her biceps. Selene closed her eyes and concentrated on the beat rather than how much she wanted to trace the lifelike snake tattoo on Alec's arm with her tongue.

They stayed on the dance floor for three songs, their bodies moving closer together, until by the last song Alec had her leg pressed firmly between Selene's and they were moving as one. Selene tried to keep her eyes closed and concentrate on the music, but the connection with Alec's body was like being touched with a blowtorch. She was on fire and could think of nothing more than the feel of Alec's hand on her waist, her hard legs, and the marble-smooth skin of her shoulder under Selene's hand. She felt a need like she'd never felt before consuming her, and she didn't see any reason not to give in to it.

The song ended, and they made their way back to the table. The music was too loud for conversation, which suited Selene just fine. This way there were no words to get in their way. They could let their bodies speak through the music, which seemed far more honest. She watched the people on the dance floor, particularly the couples. Few people realized just how loud their body language spoke, and as she watched, she drew conclusions. The couple who left virtually not a thread's space between them were probably newly together, while the couple who danced apart but only had eyes for each other seemed solid, more mature. Then there was the couple dancing together, but not together. Both watched other people, barely glancing at each other except for the occasional polite smile. Either they weren't together, or they weren't going to be together for long. She took a sip of her drink and wondered what people saw when she and Alec were dancing together. A leggy brunette in hot pants threw Alec a smile, and Selene wanted to leap on her like a tigress and claw her eyes out. Instead, she took Alec's hand and pulled her back onto the dance floor. They might not have a lot of time together, so she'd be damn sure to make the most of it now.

The songs stayed hot and fast, and they hardly stopped for a drink before going back out again. Selene's nipples ached from being so turned on, and she knew her panties were soaked through. Alec's hard body pressed against hers was driving her insane. The lights blinked twice, and she looked at the bar in surprise. The last call indication brought a few people to the bar, but for the most part, the crowd had thinned out substantially. They went to their table and downed the last of their drinks.

"Wow, I can't believe it's that late."

A slow song came on, and Alec held out her hand. Selene took it and let Alec lead her back onto the dance floor.

"Did I mention you look beautiful tonight?" Alec said as she wrapped her arms around Selene's waist, pulling her close.

"You might have said something to that effect, but feel free to say it again." Selene tried to quell the butterflies trying to migrate from her stomach to her mouth.

"You look stunning." Alec brushed a lock of hair away from Selene's face. "Exquisite. I'm so proud to be here with you tonight."

Selene closed her eyes as Alec's lips met hers. Soft, cool, tender. She opened her mouth and let Alec's tongue in, and was grateful for Alec's arms around her as she felt her knees go weak. The kiss was slow, deep, and wanting. She pulled away and saw her desire mirrored in Alec's eyes.

"Shall we go?" she said.

Selene nodded, unable to say anything. *Thank God the hotel is nearby.*

Alec grabbed Selene's coat from the chair and held it out for her before she slipped on her own. She took Selene's hand and led her from the bar.

The night was quiet compared to the constant noise inside, and when the sidewalk tilted slightly, Selene giggled.

"I think I had more to drink than I usually do."

Alec laughed. "I haven't had that much to drink in a long time. I'm not drunk, but I've got a nice buzz going." She slipped her arm around Selene's waist as they walked to the Hummer.

"Ouch!" Selene jerked forward, holding her shoulder.

"What is it?"

"Something just hit—Ow!"

A small rock bounced off Selene's shoulder and hit the sidewalk in front of them. Alec spun around, pulling Selene behind her. Three men stood behind them. One held a handful of rocks, one held a bat, and one held a pipe. The rest of the street was deserted.

"Hey there. We saw you come out of the bar and thought maybe we could have a talk." The one with the bat motioned with it, his face set in a malevolent grin.

"I have a feeling we don't have much to say to one another. Why don't you find someone else to talk to?" Alec crossed her arms and stared him down.

"Well, see, we would, except that you two look like you need to hear what we have to say." They moved closer, and Alec pushed Selene away from her slightly, farther back.

"Believe me, buddy, you don't want to have any kind of conversation with me. Ever. If I have to talk to you, it'll definitely wreck your night."

They all snickered. "I like your spirit. Too bad I need to beat it out of you. See, this whole lesbian thing really gets under my skin." He looked over Alec's shoulder at Selene. "That one there, she shouldn't be with the likes of you. She needs to be with a real man, one who can show her what's good in life." He raised the bat. "And when we're done with you, we'll show her exactly what she's been missing."

He was fast, so fast. Selene barely had time to scream before he lunged at Alec, swinging the bat. She looked behind them and across the street. No one. She looked back at the fight and was stunned.

Alec held the bat in one hand, looking almost bored as he tried to yank it from her grip. The other man jumped forward with the pipe, and Alec grabbed that with her other hand. No matter how many times they tugged or pushed, she held steady. The third man, seeing her occupied with his friends, took advantage. He darted around them and grabbed Selene. He pulled her against him, and she could smell his fetid breath as he yelled at Alec.

"Hey, bitch. I got your dyke girlfriend. What you gonna do now?"

"You don't want to do this. Really. Go away, guys."

Selene cried out slightly when the man twisted her arm behind her back. He'd dropped his rocks and pulled a knife instead, something far more terrifying. Suddenly, the two men tussling with Alec went flying backward. She flung their weapons at their feet and turned so she could see Selene and her attacker, while not turning her back on the other two.

"Close your eyes, babe. Please."

The knife dug into the soft skin under Selene's chin. She whimpered.

And then hell broke loose.

Alec…changed. She grew taller, impossibly tall. And…*wings*. Thick, jet-black wings spread from her back. Her eyes turned the color of slate, the whites gone. She held up her arms, and from beneath her jacket sleeves slithered two massive diamondback snakes. Instead of dropping to the ground, they leapt, and one struck the man with the bat, while the other flew toward Selene and her attacker. She screamed, but the snake bypassed her and hit her attacker in the throat. He shoved Selene away from him and fell to the sidewalk, screaming and trying to pull it off him. The man with the pipe was scrambling backward, watching his friends with terrified eyes. He held his hands up in defense when Alec turned toward him.

"Please, don't. I'm sorry. I didn't know you were this kind of freak. I just thought you were a dyke."

Selene watched as Alec held up her hands, and a black mist formed between them. She turned them toward the man and the mist slithered over his body, twisting and turning around him until it entered his screaming mouth. He choked and gasped.

The other two men were writhing, nearly unconscious, and the snakes slithered back to Alec's feet, up her legs and back under the cuffs of her jacket. She lowered her arms slowly and turned to face Selene.

She stumbled back. "Alec…what…I don't…"

Alec sighed, and returned to normal size. Her wings folded and disappeared from sight. Her eyes returned to their normal color. She stepped over the man who had been holding Selene and reached for her. She winced when Selene pulled away.

"I can explain. I promise, just give me a chance—"

"A chance? Give you a chance? Are you serious? What…I don't even…What are you? Have I gone insane? Did someone spike my drink? Oh God, I've been drugged, haven't I?"

Alec motioned toward the Hummer. "You haven't been drugged, as much as I'd like to blame it on that. Can I take you to your hotel, please? And maybe we can talk this out?"

"Talk it out. Just like that. You want to talk about the fact that you've got wings. And your tattoos just came alive and did… something…to those men. And what the fuck was that between your hands?" She looked at the men on the ground, all looking like they were stuck in some kind of horrific nightmare. *I know how they feel.* "I need a minute, Alec. I'll take a taxi to my hotel. You can call me in the morning. I think. I don't know."

Alec sighed and looked utterly forlorn. "I'm so sorry. I didn't want you to find out this way. But when I saw him hurting you—"

"You what? Decided to become a…a…an evil fairy?"

Alec looked surprised, and then she grinned slightly. "I don't think I've been called that before. I like it."

She turned and flagged down a passing taxi. She opened the door, and Selene kept her distance, wary of the snakes she knew were under her sleeves. *Tattoos. They're tattoos. Tattoos who come alive and do things to people. Sure. Right. Okay.*

"I'll come by your hotel in the morning, okay? Please give me a chance. I'll explain everything."

"How do you explain...no. Nevermind. Not now." She gave the driver her hotel name. "I'll wait for you in the morning. If you're not there by ten, I'm getting on a train home."

"I'll be there, I promise."

The taxi pulled away, and Selene turned to look out the back window. Alec stood on the sidewalk, looking like her usual gorgeous self. Except for the three men twisting in some kind of agony at her feet, everything looked normal.

Normal. The woman I wanted to go to bed with tonight is apparently over six feet tall and has wings. Sure. Normal. She closed her eyes but saw the situation play out again and reopened them. *Please, let me be having a breakdown.*

Chapter Fourteen

Alec stood outside Selene's hotel room, a bag of bagels and cream cheese in one hand, a holder with two lattes in the other. She'd been standing there for nearly fifteen minutes. Fear and indecisiveness weren't part of her nature. For centuries, she'd tracked down the worst of humanity, become something even nightmares couldn't conceive of, and handed out judgments. Now, in front of a woman's door, faced with her anger, she was a marshmallow of apology and contriteness.

The door opened, and Selene looked at her warily. "It's creeping me out, you standing there like that." She looked at the bag in Alec's hand. "And I'm starving."

Alec let out a deep breath. "Sorry. I couldn't figure out how to knock with both hands full."

"What, your wings aren't that versatile?"

Humor. That's unexpected. "No thumbs on them. Yet. I'm waiting to evolve."

Selene stepped out of the doorway and motioned Alec inside. "Don't change on me, okay? Just stay...you."

Alec winced internally but smiled. "I can manage that, as long as no one pulls a knife on you."

Selene moved to the little kitchenette with the bag and took an appreciative sniff. "There are a lot of bagels in here. Were you intending on kidnapping me and letting me have these as my only meals?"

"That's right. No plain bread and water for you. Bagels are chewier. They last longer."

They stayed quiet as Selene dug into the cream cheese with determination. She brought one over on a paper towel and handed it to Alec, though it was clear she did so carefully, making certain they didn't touch. *Not so great, then.* She took a long, slow sip of her latte.

Alec took a bite and waited. When Selene didn't say anything, she couldn't stand the tension any longer. "Questions?"

Selene looked at her incredulously. "You think?" She shook her head. "I don't even know where to start." She looked Alec over, her gaze lingering on her jacket cuffs. "I suppose the logical question, if there is such a thing right now, is what are you? Did I really see what I thought I saw last night? Because that's not possible. Right?"

She looked so desperate for Alec to agree, to be told her world was the way it should be, Alec was tempted to make up some ridiculous story. Maybe involving an acid tab in their drinks or something. *It's too late. And we're running out of time. Step up.* "The thing with life, with the world, is that there are a whole lot of things that seem impossible, but aren't. They just aren't likely."

"Not likely? No. Not likely is a grandmother lifting a bus off her grandchild. Not likely is the ability of a peacock to fly or salmon to swim upstream. Those things are unlikely, but possible. You…" She closed her eyes as she chewed. "Tell me what you are. Start there. Then we'll deal with unlikely."

Alec's stomach churned, and she put her food down, only half eaten. "Okay, fair enough. I'm a fury."

Selene opened her eyes. "Sorry? What?"

"A fury. One of three, actually. Myself and my sisters."

"Oh. Well. That explains everything." Selene got up and began to pace, motioning with cream cheese covered fingertips as she talked. "Please, continue. Explain to me how you're a mythological being? Tell me how you're something that doesn't *exist*?"

Alec raised her hands. "Selene, please try to keep an open mind. I know you're stressing, and I know this is some weird shit. But please try to really hear me."

Selene stopped pacing and stared at her. With a sigh, she flopped into the overstuffed chair. "I'm listening."

"Thank you." Alec pinched the bridge of her nose. *Where the fuck do I start with something like this?* In all her existence, she'd never had to explain what she was. "I'm a fury. I was born in the time of ancient Greece. BC, just before the Bronze Age. My sisters and I were the ones who dealt out justice, in a time when things were pretty black-and-white. We still do it now, even though things aren't quite as simple as they used to be."

Selene looked contemplative, and Alec loved the way her brow furrowed and she bit her lip. She forced herself to focus.

"How is that possible, Alec? You're telling me that mythological beings, from more than three thousand years ago, exist." Her eyes got wide. "You're telling me you're five thousand years old." She laughed, a hoarse, choking sound. "If I hadn't seen…if you hadn't done…I'd say you should be locked away. I'm still not sure one of us shouldn't be."

Alec reached for Selene, but lowered her hand when Selene flinched away from her. "I can't imagine how hard this is, especially for someone so devoted to philosophy and logic. But I can assure you, I'm very real."

Selene covered her face with her hands and looked at Alec through her fingers. "Next you'll be telling me unicorns and fairies are real. Leprechauns? Are they real? How about demons and succubi? Santa? The Easter Bunny?"

Alec sighed. "The unicorns died off before I was born. All the rest…yes. They're real, to some extent."

"I think I'm going to be sick." Selene rushed for the bathroom, and Alec grimaced at the sound of her vomiting. She went in quietly and held her hair back, then placed a cold cloth against the back of her neck. She closed her eyes when Selene slumped against her legs and rested her head against Alec's thigh. A flicker of hope licked at her subconscious. Maybe, just maybe, it would be okay after all.

"I don't understand," she whispered.

"I know." She helped Selene stand and offered her a cup of water. "Why don't we take a walk and talk a bit more? That way we've got some fresh air, and if you have to vomit again, you can do it in the sea?"

"Excellent. I've always been a fan of public spewing." She ran her hands through her hair. "Give me a few minutes to pull myself together."

Alec nodded and squeezed her hand. "I'll wait outside."

She turned to go but stopped when Selene tentatively touched her forearm.

"Wait. Before you go…I need to see. I need to see what I saw last night, right here in the light of day. So I believe and I don't just think you got me so drunk I hallucinated you as something else."

Alec searched Selene's eyes but found only determination. "Are you sure?"

"More than you can know. I believe in things I can see. If we're going to have this conversation, I need to believe you."

"Okay." She pulled gently on Selene's hand and moved her to the bed. "Sit down. And please don't scream."

"Do I look like a screamer?"

Alec gave her a wicked grin. "I'm hoping I'll still get to find that out."

Selene gave a surprised laugh and looked away for a second. "Do it. Please."

Alec stepped back and raised her arms. She let the magic fall away and breathed a sigh of relief as she spread her wings. Mostly spread them, anyway. The room wasn't quite large enough for her to spread them fully. She let her eyes change and her teeth sharpen. She looked down at Selene.

"This is me. This is what I am, Selene." She'd never really noticed how her voice hissed slightly. That must scare the crap out of people too. *Nice.* "I'm not a monster. I'm a myth, I'm a form of law no one ever thinks about anymore, and by the time someone knows I exist, I've already begun shredding their mind. But I'm not ashamed of what I am."

Alec waited and watched as Selene took in what she was seeing. She was startled when Selene stood up and lifted her hand.

"Can I touch them?"

"My wings?"

Selene nodded. When Alec flicked her wing and brought it closer to Selene's hand, she jumped slightly before stroking them. Alec shivered at her soft caress, the feeling running straight through her.

"They didn't look soft. Last night. I thought they looked like... bat wings. But they're feathers."

Alec tilted her head. "They looked like bat wings because I wanted to scare the shit out of those guys. And those kinds of wings seem scarier today than wings with feathers."

"Today?"

"As opposed to a thousand years ago, when feathered wings had a reputation for being some kind of terrible curse. It was a phase."

"Of course it was," Selene murmured. She stepped back. "And your tattoos?"

Alec shook her head. "Let's take it a little at a time, okay? How about that walk?"

Selene nodded and moved away. "Okay. Five minutes."

❖

The drive to the beach was quiet. Alec could feel Selene processing, trying to work through the little she'd already been told. *Wait till she hears the rest.*

"That's why I couldn't see you properly. Isn't it?"

Alec nodded. "It's rare, but sometimes a human is sensitive enough to notice that something isn't quite right. You're one of those, apparently. I use a form of magic, a kind of shield, so no one sees my wings, or the things related to me. That goes for the Hummer and my house too. I can cloak everything completely, or just to a degree. Whatever I need to do." There would be time to tell Selene the rest. For the moment, a bit of information was better than all of it.

"Does the Hummer have wings too? Is that how we got to my place so quickly the other day?"

"Kind of. I mean, not wings, but it moves through time and space differently."

"Of course it does." Selene sighed, a heavy, deep sigh. "I imagine there's more?"

"Well...yeah. I mean, I'm only one kind of ancient. There are plenty to go around."

"I need coffee. Or something stronger."

"How about an iced coffee, and we'll take it down on the sand?" Alec turned onto the Promenade and parked in a back lot.

"Sure."

Selene looked slightly defeated, almost sad, and Alec wasn't sure what to do about it. She could still feel Selene's caress on her feathers. It had been a very long time since she'd allowed someone to touch her that way.

They got their coffee and started walking. When they passed Fin, he gave Alec a nearly indiscernible nod and she returned it, before returning her attention to Selene. If Fin needed to talk to her, he'd let her know. Still, it was nice knowing he was around.

Selene shook her head. "I was one of these people. Who walk around not knowing there's something...else. Something completely unknowable, undefinable...well, not undefinable, because we know what you are. But, I mean..." She shrugged helplessly.

They walked to a spot on the sand. The beach was nearly deserted, the waves crashing softly, rhythmically, onto the shore. Alec sat and motioned for Selene to sit next to her. Selene hesitated only briefly before doing so.

"What if I pretend? What if pretend I never met you and didn't see what I've seen?"

"Could you?" The thought sent a shot of pain, and panic, through Alec.

Selene sighed. "No. Of course not. But I really, really wish I could."

Alec rolled her coffee cup between her hands. "I get that. And I'm sorry you had to find out that way, I really am."

"You were going to tell me anyway?"

Now or never. Do it, you coward. "Selene...it's not just me that exists. There are others. A lot of others."

"Alec, you've told me you're a five-thousand-year-old fury. Unless I am actually having a total mental breakdown, which I admit I'm really rooting for, then that's not an entirely surprising statement."

"The thing is, Selene, there's logic to this."

Selene's look of disbelief was so strong it made Alec laugh. After a moment, Selene started laughing too. "Okay. Hit me with the logic. I'm ready."

"Human beings are believers. They have been since they crawled out of the primordial ooze."

"You, of all people, are going to talk to me about evolution?"

"You promised to listen."

Selene shrugged and threw herself backward on the sand. "Yes, I did. Go ahead."

"The moment people, humans, started believing in things, and believing in them wholeheartedly, they started creating things. People are made of stardust and energy. The world itself is built of it and perpetuates it. When groups of people start thinking of something simultaneously, their energy, the energy raised by their collective thoughts, creates the thing they think about. The longer they think about it, the stronger it becomes, infused by the energy, the actual matter, of life."

"Thoughts manifest reality? If that were true, we'd all be lottery winners."

"No. Group thoughts, mass-group thoughts, manifest beings, not outcomes. A singular thinker can begin the nucleus of the process, but it doesn't go any further than that unless a substantial amount of others add their energy to that process."

Selene closed her eyes, and Alec sat quietly, allowing her to contemplate the idea. After a few minutes, she shot up from the sand and looked at Alec, her eyes wide. "You're telling me God is real?"

Alec nodded. "He is. She is too. Enough people believe to have made both aspects real, although she isn't quite as high up the food chain as he is, because of his number of followers."

"I think I'm going to be sick again." Selene moved quickly to the water's edge. She let the waves crash over her boots, not seeming to notice. Alec stayed still, unsure what the next move was. Would this kind of thing break Selene's mind? Alec thought she was strong enough, but she realized the enormity of what she was asking Selene to believe. She'd lived with the idea for so long, it seemed natural to her. But now…

Selene came back, her feet squelching in her boots. She crossed her arms and stayed standing, staring down at Alec. "Go on."

"Are you sure? I can take you home, let you breathe for a while. It's a hell of a lot to take in."

"No. I want more. I want to understand. I think I can follow, to some degree, your idea about energy, although there are a billion loopholes in it. But if there's more, I want to hear it."

"Okay." Alec pointed over her shoulder with her thumb. "See that big building, with the mural of clouds on the side?"

Selene looked where Alec was motioning to. "There's no…No. That building was *not* there before. Am I having a seizure of some kind?" She fell to her knees, staring.

Alec looked over her shoulder at the building. "You can see it now because I've told you it's there, and allowed you to see beyond the veil, so to speak."

"How very kind of you," Selene said, not taking her eyes off the building. "What about it?"

"That's called Afterlife, Inc. It's where God works. All the gods, actually. Every god with a large enough group of followers, in every religion, works in that building."

"They work. From a building in Santa Monica."

Alec ran her hands through her hair. When Selene put it that way, it did sound ludicrous. "Yeah, maybe it sounds a bit weird. We used to work from places all over the planet, the way you think we would. But then people started moving. Really moving. It used to be only nomads, bards, or crazy people left their countries and moved around. But then, humans created transportation, and suddenly, believers are all over the globe." She tilted her head toward the building. "So they decided to start a kind of cooperative, where they could work together and support one another."

"Of course they did. Why not?" Selene looked at Alec. "I've spent my entire life disproving religious belief and teaching logic. Now…" She stared at the building. "I feel like I've been swept out to sea, and I'm going to drown."

Alec took her hand, relieved when she didn't pull it away. "You're not alone. I'm here, and I'll help. Trust me."

"Trust you. Trust." Selene looked angry. "Trust you. I was so into you. I wanted you, bad. You made me feel…happy. Sexy. Wanted. I haven't felt that way in so long." Tears flooded her eyes and began to course down her cheeks. "And now you tell me all this. You show me this other world, and now I don't know you, now I don't know me. I don't even trust the ground beneath me."

Alec took her hand away. Patience had never been her strong suit, and she felt it slipping. Convincing someone that she existed, that her friends existed, and had their own place in the world was a little harder than she'd anticipated. Why couldn't showing Selene that she was an ancient being be enough? Her irritation rose. "Should I have left you in ignorance, Selene? You don't strike me as the type who would want to spend her life believing in something that isn't true. In a world that doesn't exist the way she thinks it does."

"The way I think it does? You mean the way every frigging human on the planet thinks it does?"

"There are plenty of believers—"

"And where has that belief gotten them? Can you just walk in there and make an appointment with God? Can I go ask him about the meaning of life, about why bad things happen to good people, why there are wars?" She got up and started pacing, kicking wet sand in her wake. "Can I ask him about plagues, and poverty, and genocide?"

Alec was out of her depth and flinched in the face of Selene's anger. Her irritation died out, replaced with a sense of weary capitulation. "He doesn't really take appointments anymore. A few of his angels do, and Mary, she does—"

"For fuck's sake. This is…insane. It's insanity. I'm locked in a mental hospital somewhere, aren't I? On some good fucking meds."

Alec let her pace and rant, waiting her out. When her tirade slowed, Alec said, "Maybe I should take you home."

Selene turned and pointed at her. "Oh no. Nope. You don't get off that lightly. You'll drop me off and I'll never see you again, and then I'll think I've had some intense, crazy-ass hallucinatory experience." She grabbed the front of Alec's jacket and tugged on it. "No. You're taking me there." She pointed with her other hand. "You take me and show me where God works."

Alec covered Selene's hand with her own. "Are you sure?"

Selene threw up her hands. "Sure? What the hell does that have to do with anything? No, I'm not sure. But I want to go in there and see what you're talking about."

Alec stood and brushed the sand from her jeans. "If you think you're ready, I'll take you." She held Selene's upper arms gently, stopping her pacing and forcing her to look at her. "Remember this: don't leave my side. Stick with me, and I'll introduce you—"

"To God. You'll introduce me to God." She crossed her arms over her chest and glared at Alec.

"No. I told you, he doesn't see people anymore. Not he himself, anyway. But there are a lot of other great…people…I can introduce you to."

Selene stepped back and hugged herself. "Lead on, your Fury-ness."

Alec sighed and started walking. She thought about texting Zed to let him know they were coming, but he had eyes everywhere, so in theory, he knew. One of his nasty little sea nymphs had probably been eavesdropping the whole time. She heard Selene grumbling behind her.

Maybe it's us who need saving from her.

Chapter Fifteen

Selene looked up at the building in front of her. *Surely it's a bizarre dream.* Some surreal, drug or coma induced dream. She'd fallen and hit her head, and her brain was messing with her while she was out cold. Strangely, she wasn't sure she wanted to wake up from it just yet. The concept was fascinating, and she did want to know more. *If it's a dream. If it's not...* She shuddered at the idea she might have no true knowledge of her world anymore. That everything she trusted in, had learned and taught, was somehow false.

Alec cleared her throat softly and Selene started, realizing she'd been standing there lost in thought. She looked at Alec, and her stomach did that irritating flip thing. *How can I still feel that way when she's...what? Human-ish? Batwoman?* Still, standing there in her faded jeans, her soft black sweater, and her hands stuffed into her pockets, she looked adorable, and Selene desperately wanted to tell her it was all okay. But it wasn't. Not yet. Not in the least.

"Sorry, lost in thought. I just can't believe I never saw the building. That people don't. I don't understand."

Alec nodded. "I know. I really do. It's going to take some time. Maybe meeting some of the others will help."

"Maybe. Or maybe it will convince me I've gone batshit crazy."

"Yeah. Or that." Alec opened the door and motioned for Selene to go in.

Selene took a deep breath and crossed the threshold, reminded of Dante's line about abandoning hope.

The receptionist at the desk smiled at them, though she looked slightly puzzled. "Hey, Alec. Who's your friend?"

"Hey, Cerb. This is my friend Selene. Selene, Cerb."

Selene held out her hand, and only just managed not to pull it back when the hand that shook hers was far more claw-like than it should be for the tiny blond woman.

"Oh. Well. Really?" Cerb stared at Selene, wide-eyed.

Alec took Selene's hand. "Yeah, so we're heading up to Zed's office. Will you let him know, please?" She pulled Selene toward the elevator and then turned back. "And no one else, please. No gossiping."

The woman pouted. "But—"

"No. Seriously. Don't."

She nodded and picked up the phone, still looking petulant. "Fine. Just Zed."

The elevator doors closed on them and Selene saw the quick furtive glance she threw at them before picking up the phone again. Alec sighed next to her.

"Cerb?"

Alec winced slightly. "Cerberus."

Selene laughed and knew it sounded slightly hysterical. "The guardian to the underworld? The three-headed dog? She only had one head. And she wasn't a dog."

"She wears her modern look well, don't you think? But her true form, like mine, can come out when it needs to. In fact, she's often in real form when I come in."

Selene closed her eyes. *Coma. Drugs. Something.*

The doors opened and Alec tugged gently on her hand. "Zed will be waiting."

Selene followed silently, glancing around as they went. It looked like any other open-plan office. Cubicles dotted the room on either side of the soft carpeted path leading to a row of glass meeting rooms and offices. People worked quietly, tapping away on computers or talking softly on the phone. "Are any of them normal?"

Alec let go of Selene's hand and faced her. "Look. You need to watch your language, okay? I mean, it's one thing when it's directed at me, but it's downright rude to insinuate that the other people working here are abnormal, just because you don't get it yet."

Selene stared blankly at Alec. "You're upset that I'm saying hounds to the gates of hell and furies aren't 'normal'?"

Alec crossed her arms. "Yeah, that's exactly what I'm saying. Consider your ideas about perception and reality. Think about what you teach, and apply it here, to some degree." She uncrossed her arms and held out her hands, almost pleadingly. "Please, Selene. I brought you here because I thought you would be open-minded. Please don't prove me wrong."

Selene regretted her words. The situation might be absurd in every sense of the word, but they still had feelings. *Probably.* "I'm sorry. You're right, that was rude. I'll rephrase and ask if any of these beings are human?"

Alec grinned and Selene caught her breath. It transformed Alec's face, and she seemed to light up from the inside. She was truly gorgeous.

"No. You're the first human to step inside this building." She motioned with her head. "Come on. We don't want to keep him waiting."

Selene followed Alec into a large glass office with floor to ceiling windows overlooking the ocean. The winter sun created a golden path across the water that seemed to lead straight into the room, an almost magical effect. She turned when a man came around the desk, and once again considered the idea she'd fallen down a rabbit hole.

He was at least seven feet tall, with snow-white hair and a matching beard. His face was angular, strong. In fact, she'd seen it thousands of times, in books, on statues and painted on vases. She reached for a chair and felt Alec help her into it, although she couldn't take her eyes off the man. Finally, she said, "Zed. The letter Z in Europe. Short for Zeus. Is that right?"

He threw back his head and laughed, a booming sound she felt in her stomach.

"Indeed. That's me." He picked up a pair of glasses from his desk and motioned at her with them. "Although I find my eyes aren't what they used to be, what with all the typed print they use now. Stone tablets were easier."

He grasped her hand in his, and she wondered if she'd ever see it again, his hands dwarfed hers so completely.

"It's such a pleasure to meet you, Selene. Really, I can't tell you how much."

From the corner of her eye, Selene saw Alec shake her head slightly. He frowned but recovered quickly. "Any friend of Alec's is a friend of ours."

She glared at them both. "Spill it. I don't care if you're some ancient god. I don't care if you're some kind of flying woman demon thing. What the hell is going on?"

Zeus looked at Alec. "I'll let you handle this, and if you need me, I'll be in the cafeteria. It's Hindu day, and I do love their date parcels with the drizzled honey." He gave them a nervous smile and left.

Alec sighed.

"Alec? What the hell?"

"Why don't you ask some specific questions and we'll go from there? Or I could give you a general rundown?"

"A rundown is a good idea. I'll ask questions as you go. Or later. Or both." Selene poured herself a glass of water from the heavy pitcher on the table, but hesitated with it nearly at her lips. "This isn't going to make me ten feet tall or grow fangs or anything, right?"

"I think you're getting your tales mixed up, but no. It's just water." She waited until Selene had taken a long drink and motioned for her to continue. "Okay. We're on the Greek floor. All ancient Greek deities and beings work from this level. We're ancient, and although there aren't a lot of people who still pray directly to us, there are enough relics, museums, books, and general historical information about us, to keep people believing. We're also the oldest, and by virtue of that, we have the most say in board meetings and things like that."

"And if people don't believe in you? What then?" Alec physically flinched and Selene narrowed her eyes. "Alec—"

"Wait. Let me continue, and we'll come back to that. So, like I said, this is the Greek floor. The Roman floor is in a similar situation, although theirs isn't quite as big, because they took a lot of their pantheon from other cultures, and diluted their gods, so to speak. So our work tends to overlap a lot."

"You said they work. Work doing what?"

Alec motioned toward the cubicles. "Answering prayers. Responding to people who want responses, cataloguing large-scale issues going on in the places that house the majority of their followers, and attempting to give people what they want, in a way that doesn't negate the other people praying to them. In the old days, that meant actual home visits. But now it can be done almost entirely virtually in most cultures. There are still some outlier cultures, with lesser known gods, who still need physical visits. But for the most part—"

"They answer prayer by email."

"Well, yeah."

"And you? Where do you fit in?"

Alec shrugged. "I guess I'm lucky that way. There are plenty of mentions of me in history, so I've got the belief. But more than that, I have a purpose, and it's a purpose that never goes away, because the concept, the ideology behind it, is always there."

"What concept would that be?" Selene watched as normal looking people stood talking at a cubicle. If it weren't for the long, snake-like tail peeking out from under the woman's skirt, she would have thought they were in any other office building.

"The ideal of justice. And vengeance, and morality. Although they're vague concepts, and are often conceived differently in different cultures, the core of it remains the same. There are things you can't do, shouldn't do, aren't allowed to do, in any society. And that's where my sisters and I, and a few others from various departments, come in. We don't need belief in who we are, as much as we need people to continue believing in right and wrong on the most basic levels."

Selene rubbed her temples, feeling a migraine coming on. "You're some kind of avenging angel? Is that what you're saying?"

Alec scoffed. "No way. Those guys are stuck way up their own asses."

"Sure. Of course." She took another drink of water, needing to do something that felt normal. "Earlier you said something about God not taking appointments, at least not himself. I'm thinking, just to be clear, about the Christian version. What did you mean by that?"

Alec stared out at the cubicles for a long moment, her brow furrowed. Selene quashed the desire to run her thumb over the frown mark and smooth the stress away. Suddenly, Alec smiled slightly.

"You know how, at Christmas, there are Santas in every mall? None of them is the real thing, they're all just stand-ins?"

"Excellent. Santa and the Easter Bunny are real too. Brilliant."

"Wait, let me finish before we move into that territory. So, there's the original God, the one in the Bible. He's like the real Santa, the main guy people think of as a whole." She held up her hands and ticked down on her fingers. "But then you've got the varieties of that God. You've got the one the Jehovah's Witnesses believe in, the ones the snake handlers pray to, the ones the Jews and the Muslims pray to. All of those manifestations, because of the people who pray to them, also work on God's floor, dealing with their particular followers."

"Offshoots of God. Can I meet any of them?"

Alec looked at her watch. "I think so. I can take you to that floor, anyway, and we can see who's around. But the thing is, right now it's lunchtime, and Zed is right, Hindu day isn't something to miss." She stood and held out her hand. "Want to see?"

Selene avoided taking Alec's hand and felt bad when Alec looked saddened, but she just wasn't ready. As much as she wanted to touch her, she needed some distance. "Do I want to see a cafeteria full of gods, goddesses and...others?" She shrugged. "Sure, why not?"

They walked through mostly deserted areas to the cafeteria, which was loud and crowded. When they walked in, it was like some kind of awful high school nightmare. Slowly, the room went silent as everyone stared at them. Selene saw horns, eyes in every color, a person with multiple arms she assumed was Kali, and even a satyr. Alec reached back, her hand open, and Selene took it willingly, deciding distance could wait.

Alec stopped at the line of food. "Something sweet? Or salty?"

"Alcoholic."

Alec grabbed a tray and put various small dishes on it. At the end of the row, she took two bottles from a fridge and placed them on the tray too. She went to pay, but the woman waved her past while staring at Selene.

Alec glanced over her shoulder. "Want to eat here, or upstairs?"

"Are you kidding? I suddenly know what an animal in a zoo feels like. Upstairs, please."

Alec led the way out, and Selene heard the chatter start up again, even louder than before. She heard her name, and human, before the doors swung shut.

She followed Alec silently back to Zed's office, where he was sitting at his desk eating. When they came in, Alec set their tray on the table and said, "Zed, why don't you come eat with us while I tell Selene more about the company."

He sighed and looked at them for a long moment before picking up his lunch and joining them. "You know how much I love my lunch."

"I know how gluttonous you are, yes, you ungrateful butthead."

Selene choked on her date pastry and Alec clapped her on the back. "Did you just call God a butthead?"

Zed laughed and Selene found herself laughing with him. "She did. She does that kind of thing all the time. No respect at all."

Selene watched as food spilled onto his beard and seemed to just disappear. "I suppose that's not surprising."

They all looked up when a woman stopped in the doorway. Zed motioned her in. "Come eat with us. Ama, Selene. Selene, Ama."

Selene struggled to remember the many gods' names, but Ama didn't ring a bell. The stunning woman sat down next to Alec and picked a bit of bread from her plate. The intimate gesture set Selene's teeth on edge.

"I heard you were here, and I had to see for myself. It's really wonderful to meet you, Selene."

Selene shook her hand, marveling slightly at how smooth and soft her skin was. "Nice to meet you too, although I admit to being utterly confused. Why does everyone seem so interested in me?"

"Oh, I can't even imagine." Ama plucked some food from Zed's plate and he batted her away with his fork.

"Get your own." He shoved in another mouthful of food. "Go ahead, Alec."

Alec opened her mouth as though to begin, and then shut it again, shaking her head. She seemed like she was just about to start again, when another woman, this one with fire-colored hair, burst in. She pulled Alec into a tight hug, then released her so suddenly Alec lost her balance. She turned to Selene.

"I heard you were here, and I just had to meet you. I can't believe you're actually in the building. I mean, how incredible is that, right? You just *have* to come to my party on Friday night; you just have to. Everyone will be there, and they're all dying to meet you. Say you'll come?" She grabbed Alec's bicep. "Tell her, Alec. Tell her to come."

Alec grinned and pulled her arm from the woman's grip. "Selene, this is my sister Meg. This is her rather abrupt way of saying nice to meet you."

Selene stood and shook Meg's hand. "So, you're a fury too?"

Meg laughed and looked at Alec. "How adorable is that?" She looked back at Selene. "I sure am, sweetness. But we're all more than our job, aren't we? Come Friday and we'll talk all about it."

She stopped talking and an expectant silence filled the room. Selene hated not being able to think things through, so she could make a rational, informed decision. Too many things kept happening before she could formulate her questions. But if this was teaching her anything, it was that her way of looking at things had to change. "Sure. I'd love to."

No time like the present.

Chapter Sixteen

On their way back to her place, Selene fell sound asleep, only waking when she felt Alec's fingertips on her cheeks. "Hey, sleepyhead. We're here."

Selene yawned and stretched. Her body cracked and popped, and she ached for her bed. Surely this had been the longest, and strangest, twenty-four hours of her life. She gathered her things before turning to Alec.

"I don't really know what to say. Thank you doesn't seem quite right. Nor does, I had a lovely time." She smiled to show she was teasing, although there was unquestionably truth to her words. She hadn't received a hundredth of the answers she wanted, but she was so overwhelmed she couldn't really remember what the questions were.

"Selene, I can't imagine how you're feeling. I can't fathom what you're thinking. All I can ask is that you consider what we've shown you, what you've seen. And we can talk about it, as much as you want, whenever you want."

Selene shook her head. "Right now, I want a hot bath and bed. Tomorrow, I'll think about everything. I need to understand, and more than that, I need to understand where my position is now that things have changed."

"I can appreciate that." Alec took her hand and brushed her lips over Selene's knuckles. "Just don't shut me out, okay? Talk about stuff with me first?"

"I can promise that. There are far too many questions, things I don't understand…"

Alec looked crestfallen and pulled her hand away slowly.

Selene realized it wasn't the answer Alec was looking for. "I'm sorry. I don't know about us. It's not like I can say you're not my type, or that I've been with women like you and it hasn't worked out, can I? But you're…I just need time."

Alec nodded and looked away. "I get it. I do. I'll pick you up at the station at five on Friday, if you still want to go. If you don't, just let me know."

Selene nodded and climbed down from the Hummer. She trudged to her door and looked over her shoulder as Alec pulled away. Once inside, she put her keys in their usual spot, set her bag down by the bedroom door, and then pulled a beer from the fridge. She pressed it to her forehead, thankful for the cold against the budding migraine, and slid onto her couch. With her knees against her chest, she sipped the beer and thought. She replayed every element of the date. The way she'd felt so sexy, the way Alec had looked in her all black clothing, the way they'd danced…God, the way they'd danced. She could practically still feel Alec moving against her. But then…reality itself had turned inside out.

She closed her eyes and pictured the moment Alec had changed into…*into herself. What she really is.* She could picture the enormous wings, the terrifying visage of her face, which had morphed into something…not human. *Well, yeah. Obviously.* If she hadn't seen Alec change right in front of her eyes, she'd never have believed anything about religious icons working out of a business at the beach. She'd have bemoaned Alec's mental health and walked away, unwilling to get involved with someone who had such massive hallucinatory type visions.

But I saw it. I saw a fury. She wondered how many, if any, people saw a fury and lived to tell someone about it. She jumped off her couch and grabbed her copy of *Orestes.* The furies in that were merciless, driving him on to do a number of things until he had atoned for the death of his mother. As she read them, she pictured Alec and her sister Meg, and it was as though they came to life. She became so engrossed in her reading, she nearly missed hearing the phone ring.

"Selene, my girl. How are you? Anything I want to hear yet?"

She froze. What had felt like a gargantuan decision before, now felt like a train barreling down on her. "Hi, Frey. Not quite. I can't seem to put some relevant questions to rest."

"Fair enough. Why don't I take you to dinner tomorrow, and we can talk philosophy? No work stuff, just the kind of mind-bending, out-of-body experience kind of talk we can only have with people who get it. What do you think?"

She hesitated only briefly. She needed another logical mind, another solid, human, person to bounce ideas off. Clearly, she couldn't tell him about Afterlife, but she could certainly get his take on possibilities.

"I'd really like that, actually. How about the Green Mango?"

"That's perfect. I love Thai food. Six thirty?"

"I'm looking forward to it."

They hung up and Selene went back to her beer and stories about the ancients.

❖

By the time she was ready to leave for dinner with Frey the next evening, she'd exhausted her personal library of books that had any reference to ancient religions. She spent most of the day trolling the Internet, reading journal articles about the furies, or the Erinyes, as they'd been called later. One thing she did know, was that Alec was older than Zed. *No wonder she could call him a butthead.*

She started up her CR-V and realized how much she missed driving. Between taking the train to work and being picked up by Alec, it seemed like forever since she'd been behind the wheel. She headed down the back pass of the mountain, taking the shortcut into Rancho. Old pine trees quickly gave way to desert scrub and giant yucca plants. She loved the way California could change landscapes in a breath. She looked in her rearview at the receding trees and saw a black van coming up behind her. There were a few tight turns ahead, and she considered pulling over to let the driver pass, but then decided he could pass her anyway, as the road was as deserted as it usually was.

It came up fast but braked and kept a car length between them. She couldn't make out the faces inside, and suddenly, she was ultra-aware of how alone and vulnerable she was. The lone farmhouse on the road was often empty, the apple growers there only coming when it was time to press cider. She bit her lip and wondered if she should call Alec. *Why Alec? Frey is closer.* It wasn't Frey she wanted at her side if things were going to get freaky again, though.

She made the first tight turn, and the van stayed well behind her, as it did for the rest of the turns, until she made it onto the 15 Freeway. Once on, it dropped farther back, but stayed in her lane. She grabbed her phone from her bag and hit Alec's number. *Voice mail. Imagine a fury having voice mail. What the hell.*

"Alec, it's me. I'm on my way to a meeting, but I'm almost certain I'm being followed. It's creeping me out. Call me when you can?"

She hung up and switched lanes. So did the van. She switched back. So did the van. *Shit, shit, shit.* She sped up, darting around cars and across lanes, until she couldn't see the van for a moment. As she took her exit, she looked at the freeway and the van as it sailed past.

She thought she might be sick.

The faces inside weren't human. They weren't anything she recognized, but they looked like something from a horror film. They were smiling at her as they drove past, their pointed yellow teeth stark against their off-red skin.

She drove to the restaurant in a shocked daze. Surely Alec wouldn't have her followed? And not by…those things. *Those things probably don't look all that different from her and her sisters when they're…them.* No, that wasn't true. Alec had looked just as gorgeous as usual. She'd just looked far more dangerous, and far less human. But she hadn't looked like them, evil and spooky.

She parked and rested her head on the steering wheel. *Well, Alice, we've gone down the rabbit hole now, haven't we?* She wondered for a moment if those characters were real, but decided book characters probably weren't, as people knew them for characters. *I'm sitting here wondering if Alice and the rabbit are real. Jesus Christ.* She let out a slightly hysterical giggle. *No, he's real.*

She pulled herself together with some deep breaths and headed inside. Maybe Frey could help ground her in some way. *When in doubt, always return to knowledge.* She looked at the cloudless sky. *Except now, I have entirely new knowledge. So what am I returning to?*

❖

Frey kissed her cheek on both sides when she was shown to his table, an affectation she'd never liked from someone who wasn't European.

"I'm so glad you could join me tonight, Selene."

"Thank you for the offer. Actually, I'm looking forward to picking your brain about a few things." She scanned the menu, even though she knew she'd be getting the pad Thai, as she always did.

"Intriguing. I can't wait. Wine?"

She looked at the server. "Jasmine tea, please."

"Are you sure? If you wanted a drink or two I could always drive you home."

He said it innocently enough, and she didn't feel anything beneath the statement, and yet it felt off, somehow. "No, that's okay, thanks. I've got a lot on my mind, and I like having a clear head when I think."

He laughed. "But think of all the minds that have been opened, new thoughts and concepts brought about, by the use of mind-altering substances."

"True. However, I'm not one of those geniuses. Hence, the tea."

He leaned back and smiled at her. "Fair enough. So, tell me the issue you wanted to pick my brain about, as you say."

Well, see, there's this fury, and these gods...No, perhaps not. "You've worked tirelessly to teach people logic and critical thinking. To get people to stop believing blindly." He nodded and sipped his wine. "I've done the same, mostly. Except I've always felt that people have the right to believe, even if I personally think it's misguided."

"But belief in an afterlife of any kind creates false hope, and it allows people to pass the blame onto other people, or governments, or situations. It means they stop caring about other people, about humanity as a whole, because they think God will take care of them." He frowned and leaned forward. "It allows groups to commit terrible atrocities against people, all in the name of whoever they worship. And no one stands against the perpetrators because they too believe it's sanctioned by some deity, that it's punishment of some sort and they just have to endure."

Selene pondered his words as they ordered their meal. She thought about Alec and the others she'd met. Was Frey right? Were the people...creatures...at Afterlife simply catering to the need in humans to forsake true responsibility? Were they the ones doling out punishments like those in the Old Testament? She thought about Alec's point of view. "Doesn't it also allow for hope? For those people in dire circumstances, such as ill health or in war-torn areas? Does it give them something to hold on to, in a world that often turns its back?" She toyed with her fork, moving it from side to side on her placemat. "What if what we're teaching takes away people's hope? Maybe some people need the idea of an afterlife because life in the present is often unbearable?"

"So we feed into their delusions?" His hands started motioning like they had in her office when they'd met. "If we get people to understand that they're ultimately responsible for their own lives, that being proactive and helping one another is better than praying to someone to do it for them, then surely they'd be better off. Surely the whole planet will be better off."

Their food came, and they ate quietly for a little while. What would Alec say? Much of what Frey said made sense. It always had, when she'd been teaching similar principles. But now, having met them, knowing they were real...did it change anything? The questions about belief, about responsibility and the afterlife remained. "Some people are only good because they believe in an afterlife. In consequences for their actions here. Take that away, and aren't we asking for a society of faithless, narcissistic beings who don't care about right and wrong?" She speared a piece of chicken covered in peanuts. "And by saying people should take responsibility for their own lives, even if it's something like illness we're talking about, aren't we placing the blame on them, suggesting they aren't working hard enough, that there's no reason for their suffering other than pure bad luck?"

He shook his head vehemently, his hands moving so quickly a noodle flung from his fork onto another table, where the woman looked both baffled and irritated. "No. We're asking them to believe in science. In evolution, in illness as a function of the body, and viruses and bacteria. We're asking them to use reason and do some research themselves. To ask questions." He chewed quickly, watching her the whole time. "Ultimately, the illness will take its toll, whether they pray about it or whether they use logic. But in the end, at least they'll understand what happened. They won't feel forsaken by some guy playing in the clouds."

"But in the end, how comforting is it to think your loved one is just a pile of pink mush in the ground? And how do you mean to get to the true believers? The ones who are devout enough to kill for their belief systems? If there's one thing I've learned, it's that you can't change the mind of someone who truly believes, whether that's in politics or religion."

He held up his hand to stop her. "As for the pink mush question, it's the circle of life, the nature of being. It can be magical to think we're all part of the same amazing ecosystem and all the beauty it brings with it. As for the true believer question, that's slightly more difficult. You're right. We're not going to get the holy rollers to give up their little baby Jesus. But if we can reach the people who aren't completely gone, the ones open to rational thought, we might be able to change their minds. And if we can make some inroads into what are deeply religious areas traditionally, then those people will start chatting with their neighbors. It will spread through word of mouth. There's no question it will take time, and we won't see a total change in our lifetimes. But the change we could see, here and now, would be amazing in itself. All we have to do is keep talking. We do it simply, we do it clearly, and we make sure there's no ivory tower involved. We use social networking, TV, podcasts, and whatever other medium might work. We talk, and people will listen." He motioned the waiter over and asked for another glass of wine and a refill of her teapot. "Selene, what has you asking these questions, if you don't mind my asking? I've read your papers, I know you think along the same lines I do. That's why I chose you. Has something new come up?"

There's this wicked sexy fury, and these gods, working in Santa Monica... "Nothing particular. As I said, I'm giving your offer serious thought." She sipped her tea, trying to figure out how to say what she wanted to say, although she wasn't sure what exactly it was she wanted to say at all. "Frey, what if we're wrong? What if the believers are right, there is a god, or gods, and we're telling them to stop believing like we're some kind of Antichrist..." She drifted off, realizing that if God were real, then Satan must be too.

"Selene? Do you really believe that? With what you know about theological history?"

She snapped back to the conversation. "I'm concerned that we're being too narrow-minded. Telling people our way is the right way, the better way. Does that make us any different from the religious people who go house to house, trying to convert people to their way of thinking? And if we're wrong, what have we condemned people to?" *I need to ask Alec about the afterlife. About the location and souls. And how they answer prayers. And—*

"Selene, I'm surprised. I wouldn't have taken you for a doubter."

He looked so dismayed, so disappointed and let down, she regretted her words. But they were true, and she wouldn't say otherwise. "I'm just trying to see it from every side before I make a decision on your offer. What you're asking is a big thing. You've already got a bajillion followers online. You've met with people I could only dream of meeting. Working with you would mean agreeing with you and working toward the kind of change you're talking about. I just need to be sure it's the right change, the right argument."

He toyed with his glass, staring at it thoughtfully for a long moment. Suddenly, he began to smile, and then he began to laugh outright. His laughter was contagious, and she found herself smiling along with him.

"I knew it. I knew you were the right choice. Yes. Absolutely yes. You should be looking at it from every angle. You *should* be dissecting it and playing devil's advocate all over the place." He settled back as though satisfied after a good meal. "Selene, I chose you because you're a thinker. Because you genuinely consider the various channels and options. And because you seem to really like people."

I like furies more. She didn't actually like people as a whole that much, but she didn't have the heart to tell him when he looked so excited.

He waved to indicate the whole room. "I like people too. I think they're worth saving, and I want to make humanity better. I want it to go to the next level of evolution, which is more than physical now. I truly, honestly believe the world will be a better place when religion is no longer an excuse or a crutch. When wars are waged honestly, we can face them honestly and create real dialogue, instead of under a guise of divine right, which is so absurd it leaves no room for discussion. When we see the connections between humans, the ways forward through our collective brains, through technology and science, then we can truly evolve. But damn, I respect you for looking at all sides of it." He frowned and then gave a rueful laugh. "I'm not used to anyone challenging me anymore. I'm glad you have."

She flushed under his compliments. "Thank you. You see why I haven't been able to give you an answer."

He nodded and shrugged sheepishly. "I got carried away. That's what I do. I get passionate and want everything to happen right now. Have you seen my video about entropy?"

She smiled. "The existential meaning of existence is ultimately that everything dies, so you must enjoy everything to the fullest, because everything is temporary. Entropy as an entrance to the sublime."

His face lit up. "Yes! Exactly. And because I think that way, when I dive into a project I want it all to happen right away, quickly, because you never know when you'll have another chance, when that bus will come hurtling at you from nowhere, or that particular batch of malignant cells will begin to replicate. None of us knows what time we have left, so we need to make every second count." He squeezed her hand before letting it go. "I want to change the world. I want to make it a better place, and I seem to be having an impact. I think together we can make that impact even stronger. But I'll stop pressuring you. I'll keep going with my project, and if you decide to join me, awesome. I'll take you on board whenever—if—you decide to work with me. Deal?"

Relief washed over her. She didn't like being pressured, and between Alec and Frey, she'd felt caught in a slowly closing vise grip. Now she could process, truly process, what Alec was showing her. And then she could make a decision about Frey's project, with even more information and knowledge than he had about the subject. His ability to step back and respect her need for time made her like him just that much more, and made the decision that much harder. *If it weren't for Alec coming into my life...but then I'd be living in ignorance. The same ignorance the rest of the world is living in. Why me?* The question suddenly seemed incredibly important, and she needed that answered perhaps before any others. *Why me?* She forced her attention back to Frey. "That would be really excellent. Thank you. I promise as soon as I've come to any conclusion, I'll let you know."

He raised his glass and she raised her teacup. "That's all I'll ask. To passion and philosophy."

And to worlds you can't imagine exist.

Chapter Seventeen

*W*hat do you wear to a party with creatures, people, who aren't supposed to exist? What do you wear to mingle with God?*

Selene flopped back onto her bed. She'd tried on everything, including the dress she'd bought with Alec, the one she hadn't worn yet. But nothing felt right. It didn't help that she had no idea what the dress code for the party was. Now, lying on a mountain of clothing, she considered just going in her underwear. Surely there wasn't much the people at this type of party hadn't seen. *Wow. What have they seen?* She couldn't fathom what it must be like to watch the world change the way it had. Empires had risen, fallen, risen again. Weapons had been created from stones and developed into nuclear bombs. They'd gone from candlelight to video conversations across the world. The concepts began to feel overwhelming. *To have lived through those things...*

Her "Bad to the Bone" ringtone went off, but it was muffled. She started digging through the pile of clothes, flinging skirts, blouses, and underwear behind her. She found the phone under an ugly floral top that set her teeth on edge. *Why on earth did I ever buy that?*

"Hello!" She fell back on to the pile, out of breath.

"Did I interrupt something, sexy?"

Selene grinned. "I wish. And no, you didn't. I can't figure out what to wear tonight."

"First things first. I'm sorry I didn't respond to your voice mail. I was actually getting some sleep for once. Tell me about your message? About the people following you?"

Selene thought back, but the memory was blurry, just out of reach. "It's strange, I can't quite remember it now. I know they were ugly, not human. And I was scared. Really, really scared. Were they from your…company?"

"Did you see anyone on your way home?"

"No, and I watched. Everything was fine." Suddenly, Selene didn't want to be lying naked in a pile of clothes. *Excellent. I'm going to be the girl in the horror movie in her underwear, running away from the bad guy in a forest.*

"I had a quick check, and I'm looking into it. I don't like it, and we're working out our next move." Alec chuckled. "Now, as to what you should wear, you could come dressed as a nun and still be the most beautiful woman there."

"Charming. I'm sure I'd fit right in." Selene got up and wrapped some clothes around her haphazardly. Her home was her haven, and yet she felt a definite desire to be elsewhere. "What do people usually wear to these things?"

"Selene, they're ancient gods. Some of them come in the stuff they used to wear in their heyday. Some wear jeans and flip-flops."

"That's no help whatsoever. What are you wearing?"

Alec hesitated and Selene could hear the embarrassment in her voice. "You know, I'm not much for fashion, or color. I'll probably be in black jeans and a black button-down. My go-to."

"Now that helps. I wouldn't want to show you up." Selene jumped up and dug until she found her favorite pair of jeans, the ones that hugged her butt just right and made her feel sexy.

"Glad to be of service. Don't worry, okay? It's just a party, with people. Mostly people, I mean. Anyway. I'll pick you up at the station soon. Text me if there's anything weird, and I'll be there."

"Will do. Thanks for calling back. See you soon."

She hung up and bit her lip. She was still upset with Alec for not telling her, for…*for what? For not saying, "Oh, by the way, I'm five thousand years old," when she told me she likes pineapple?*

When, exactly, is it a good time to tell someone you're a mythical creature? If she were honest with herself, the truth was that she felt stupid, and there was little she hated more than feeling stupid. She felt stupid for not knowing...*again, not knowing what? That a world exists no one knows about? They do, though. The believers. The ones who pray. They know, kind of. Plenty believe without question. And they're right. How can that be?*

She slipped on her jeans, loving the way they hugged her in the right places, but left the not-so-great places alone. She pulled out a black, sheer top that gathered between her breasts and fell waterfall style to just below her belt. She put a white lace camisole under it and paired it with calf-length heeled boots. *Sexy, but not slutty.* She very nearly changed her mind and put on a looser, baggier top. Something to hide in. But then she thought of Alec and her beautiful sister and steeled herself against the temptation. She didn't want to hide; she wanted to be noticed. Particularly by Alec.

So, what am I saying? That I want something with her? Even though she's...well, what she is? She couldn't bring herself to say, or even think, fury. It still felt too unreal, too illogical. But in not doing so, was she negating Alec's very existence? Was it just...rude?

She sighed and went to do her makeup. These weren't questions she had to figure out all at once. She had time, and in Alec she had a patient and willing teacher. A moment of elation stole over her. Who else had this kind of chance? The opportunity to meet and mingle with gods? She finished getting ready in record time and left the house in its utterly disheveled state, her excitement such that she couldn't wait any longer. She headed for the train, ready for the next step in her unexpected adventure.

Selene got off the train at the university stop, nearly forty-five minutes early. She figured she'd go grab a coffee somewhere, rather than ask Alec to come get her early. But when she made it to the top of the stairs, she was greeted by a fury holding a beautiful bouquet of African roses.

"But, how?"

Alec shrugged and grinned in that way Selene was quickly coming to adore. "Fury, remember? We know stuff."

Selene shook her head and sniffed the roses appreciatively. "Nope. Sorry, that doesn't fly with me. Explain, please?"

Alec rolled her eyes and smiled. "Can't just accept on faith, huh?"

"Is that even a real question?" Selene asked as she climbed into the Hummer.

"No. Not really." Alec went around to the driver's side and jumped in. "Okay, so, here's the truth. If I know someone pretty well, I can find them. Anywhere on the planet, at any time. I just have to focus on them, on their particular energy, and I'll know where they are. But I try not to do it often, because it feels like an invasion of their privacy." She looked at Selene with a half-grin. "I can't imagine that explanation is much better."

Selene frowned and thought about it for a long moment. "No. It's not."

"And that, my dear, is why it's called faith. You just have to believe me when I say that's what I can do, because I can do it, and it is what it is."

"I don't accept that. There must be a reason for the ability." She thought about Frey's idea about connections. "Maybe it's what you say about energy. That you're somehow connected to another person's particular energetic signature."

Alec looked skeptical but smiled. "If that's what you'd like to think, we'll go with it."

"I don't like that answer either. Engage with me."

"I will, I promise. But I think you need more questions to play with. You must have a ton of them, and I think you'll have a ton more after tonight." She reached over and took Selene's hand. "Tonight, let your imagination go wild. Enjoy the party like you would any party—"

"So, not at all?"

Alec laughed. "Okay, more than you would other parties. Ask questions, accept answers to mull over and pull apart later." She tilted her head and said seriously, "One thing, though. Remember that some of these folks, they have egos. Some of them have really, really big egos. I mean, they're gods, right? Not football players, or politicians, or doctors, who think they're gods. They're the real deal, and it's given some of them pretty big ideas about themselves."

"Are you telling me to toe the line?"

"No! Well, not exactly. I'm saying an angry god isn't always a nice party guest, especially when there's alcohol involved. They can get pretty irritating, and the last angry goddess did some major damage to Meg's roof. It's not like we can just call a contractor out, you know?"

"Can't you just wiggle your fingers and make a new one?"

"What, now you think we're genies or something?"

Alec looked affronted and Selene began to laugh. "This entire conversation is surreal." She held up her hands in surrender. "Okay, no offending the gods. I won't make any promises, but I'll do my best."

Alec nodded, looking mollified. "Deal."

They pulled up in front of Afterlife, Inc, and Selene looked at her quizzically. "I thought we were going to Meg's house?"

"We are. The building we went into the other day was just the main office building. This is actually a campus kind of setup, with lots of people living on it. Some of us, like me, choose to live elsewhere, but plenty of people feel safer and less exposed by living on campus."

"How does that work with regard to physical space? Where are these places located in Santa Monica?"

Alec frowned slightly. "They're not. In Santa Monica, I mean. It's a time-space-temporal thing. They're here, but not here."

"Of course."

They drove through the enormous black gate, which shut quickly behind them, and headed down a street to the left. "Darwin Street? Seriously?"

Alec shrugged. "We try to have a sense of humor. It's important when you live this long." She parked the Hummer outside a large, two-story house with a wraparound front deck. Aside from a convertible Mercedes and a Chevy truck, there were no other vehicles around.

"Are we early?"

Alec shook her head. "There's no real start or end time to these things. Meg cooks some amazing food and puts it out on tables for people to help themselves. People come and go throughout the night. Pretty relaxed things, most of the time." She grinned and flexed her back muscles slightly. "And not everyone drives."

Selene flushed at the thought of Alec's enormous, soft black wings, reminded of the dream she'd had that had involved Alec's wings wrapped around her...

"Selene?"

She snapped back to the moment. "Sorry, I drifted for a second there. What did you say?"

Alec grinned and flexed her back again, laughing when Selene looked away. "I said, are you ready?"

Selene looked at the house and saw people inside, milling around talking. Like Alec said, just another party. *Sure.* "As ready as I'll ever be. Just stay close, okay?"

Alec lifted Selene's hand to her lips and gently kissed her knuckles. "Without question."

The feel of Selene's hand in her own was like holding electricity. And given that she'd tried to hold it when it was invented in usable form, she knew the feeling. Alec tried to concentrate. She couldn't fathom what Selene must be feeling or thinking.

They stepped inside, and there was the usual hum of conversation, a few voices too loud, a few laughs too high-pitched. Alec glanced over her shoulder at Selene and nearly laughed at her wide-eyed stare. Alec followed the direction of her gaze and understood immediately. Durga stood talking to Ganesh, her eight arms octiculating, pressing whatever point she was making, several times nearly poking him in his elephant trunk.

Alec pulled Selene beside her and whispered in her ear. "Gives new meaning to 'talking with your hands,' doesn't it?"

"I don't know if I can do this."

Selene looked almost panicked, and Alec hated to see her so distressed. "Selene, it's not like you don't know a ton of stuff about the people here. You've studied most of them throughout your career. Use your knowledge. Yeah, of course it's a little different when you get to actually talk to someone rather than just read about them, but—"

Selene held up a hand. "If you had any idea how ludicrous that statement sounds right now, you'd stop speaking. There's a Hindu god and goddess, standing in a living room...is she drinking beer? And what on earth is he eating?"

Meg swept up beside them, her hands over her heart. "Oh my god, you came! I thought for sure you'd skip out. Alec always skips out. Well, not always, but most of the time. And she's never brought anyone before. This is a celebration for sure."

Meg put her arm around Selene and started walking her toward the kitchen, and Alec followed behind dutifully, careful not to step on Meg's trailing white gown.

"I hope I'm dressed okay? I wasn't sure what someone wears to something like this." Selene blushed and looked away.

Alec's stomach flipped, and she felt her wings twitch with the desire to pull Selene against her.

"Are you kidding? You look fantastic. I love that top. There's no dress code for these things, usually. Unless it's a costume party, obviously. Everyone comes in whatever they're comfy in, or sometimes what they come from work in. Whatever, as long as they're here. What would you like to drink? Soda? Wine, beer? Ambrosia?"

Selene blinked. "Ambrosia?"

"No. That was just a joke." Meg grinned and Selene began to laugh.

Alec was glad to see Selene's shoulders relax slightly. *Maybe this won't be so bad after all.*

"Guinness, if you have it?"

"We're gods, Selene my dear, we've got everything."

Meg took care of pouring Selene's drink, and Alec gently touched her shoulder. "You doing okay?"

She nodded. "So far. Thank you for asking." She took a sip of her drink and sighed happily. "That's perfect, Meg, thank you."

"My pleasure. Now, shall I introduce you to people, or do you want to stand here and chat for a while?"

Selene seemed to consider the question for a moment. "Can I ask you something personal? Well, I don't know if it's personal, but I think it might be."

"Shoot. I'm an open book."

"Do you have wings too? Like Alec's?"

Meg shot a glance at Alec. "She showed you her wings?"

Selene nodded, frowning slightly. "We were being attacked one night, and she…changed, in order to protect us. Me. To protect me. And then I got angry and made her show me them the next day."

Meg stared at Alec for a long moment, looking thoughtful. She turned back to Selene. "I do have wings, yes. But they're not really like Alec's. Hers are all broody and dark, like she is. Mine are bright, passionate. Like me." She looked around the increasingly crowded room. "I can't show you in here, but I could show you outside later, if you like?"

Selene looked like a kid being given a present. "I'd love that, thank you." She motioned at the guests around them. "There are so many people here who aren't hiding any aspect of themselves. Like the Hindu couple. Why are you both hiding your wings?"

Meg looked at Alec, clearly expecting her to answer.

"We're not hiding them, exactly. As you noticed, they take up a lot of room. And they drag on the floor when we relax, which means people stepping on them, or getting beer spilled on them, or dragging them through whatever muck has been left on the floor." Meg was nodding her agreement and Alec laughed. "Remember the first time you got gum in yours, Meg? I thought you were going to burn down the city."

Meg grimaced. "Gum is the most disgusting invention yet. Worse than Spam or that boxed mac and cheese stuff with the fluorescent powder. And it's made more disgusting by the fact that people just spit it wherever. Imagine getting something someone's been masticating for who knows how long stuck to your feathers?"

"No, I can't imagine that." Selene looked like she was giving the issue serious consideration.

"Come on, Selene. I'll introduce you to some of my friends."

Meg laughed. "Friends might be too strong a word. But go on and have fun, and I'll catch up with you later. Be sure to try my tiramisu. I got the recipe from Carmin Antonio himself, back in the sixties."

With a vague wave, she headed off to talk with other guests, leaving Selene and Alec on their own. Alec watched Selene carefully, wondering what was going through her mind, but too afraid to ask. She tried to imagine what it would be like, to not know any of the beings around her existed, and then to be surrounded by them. She couldn't, though. It was a denial of her world, and she couldn't imagine for a second that it didn't exist. *It won't, if I don't get Selene's help.* The thought was sobering. All the people around her would cease to exist if she didn't succeed.

"You're looking more serious than I feel." Selene lightly touched Alec's hand.

"I'm sorry, you're right. I'm not being a very good host." Two people walked in and Alec felt better. "I see someone we can talk to." She took Selene's hand and led her over. She gave Ama a big hug and kiss on the cheek before turning to Selene. "Selene, you remember Ama."

Ama's eyes grew wide and she looked back and forth between them. "Really? Wow, that's amazing. I can't believe she talked you into coming here tonight. I thought after coming to the office you'd be scared away."

Selene frowned slightly as she shook Ama's hand. "I'm not that easily frightened. It's confusing, and…and…bewildering, but there's no way I'd rather live in ignorance."

Ama glanced at Alec, who subtly shook her head, and Ama put on a bright smile. "It's just that Alec hasn't brought someone to a gathering in years. Like…fifty, maybe? Has it been that long?"

Alec laughed. "No, it hasn't been that long. Well, not since I was with someone, anyway. But yeah, I haven't come to a party with anyone in a while. It's not like it's a normal Friday night date scene, is it?"

Selene didn't seem to be paying attention, but rather scrutinizing Ama. "Given that Alec has told me that most of the people here aren't...people, in the traditional sense, I'm guessing you aren't either. But I can't place your name."

Ama's smile was slightly forced, and Alec winced. She whispered quietly into Selene's ear, "It's not really polite to ask a god who they are, or say you don't recognize them. It's like telling a celebrity you've never heard of them."

"Alec, that's being a bit unfair." Ama seemed to relax slightly, and she lightly touched Selene's arm. "It's true, we all have egos. You do, you know, when people worship you for centuries. It gives you an unhealthy sense of expectation and entitlement." She raised her arms slightly and tilted her head. "I am Amaterasu, the Shinto goddess of light." Light radiated from her entire body, and Selene squinted against it.

The light faded and Alec grinned. "You always did put on a hell of a display."

"You're...that's incredible. Truly."

Ama's chin raised slightly until she looked at Alec, who was rolling her eyes. She began to laugh. "You see? A bit of worship and we instantly become full of ourselves. If it weren't for Alec I would have been an awful person, but she keeps me grounded."

Alec felt herself flush. "That's my job. Goddess tamer."

Ama wiggled her eyebrows. "More than once, old friend." Another Japanese person walked in, and she made her apologies as she went to speak with him.

"Are you okay?" Alec asked, steering Selene toward a quiet corner. She hoped Selene didn't notice the many stares she was getting as people learned who she was. Alec needed time to explain. She wanted to take it slowly, show Selene the world and how important it was, before she dropped the other bombshell on her. As long as she kept anyone from saying anything stupid to Selene tonight, things would be fine. *Sure, right. Easy.*

"I think so. I keep thinking I'm dreaming, and I'll wake up any time with a wonderful story to write down. But I don't seem to be waking up, and you feel very real." She stroked Alec's arm, locking her gaze on Alec's. "Very real, 'goddess tamer,' Did you two—"

A booming laugh interrupted their conversation, and they turned to look. An enormous man with a goatee, followed by three satyrs and three beautiful women, drew everyone's attention. People greeted him as he passed, all looking genuinely pleased to see him. He spotted Alec and made his way over, his entourage separating to mingle.

"Alec, you old bat. It's been years. How the Hades are you?"

He scooped Alec up in a massive hug, one of the few beings who could do so.

"Bach, put me down. How many times do I have to tell you I'm not a bat?"

He winked at Selene. "Have you seen her wings? Tell me she's not an overgrown bat with a poor sense of proper femininity?" He motioned at the women who had come in with him, all of whom were incredibly tall, thin, busty, and half-naked. "That's the way a woman should look."

"Bach...as in, Bacchus, right?"

He opened his arms wide. "That's me! I don't think we've met. Are you a Noogie?"

"Noogie? I don't think so. Am I?" She turned to Alec.

"No, you're not a Noogie. Unless you've got a cult of followers I don't know about." At Selene's puzzled look she laughed. "A Noogie is a new god, one who's been created by a new cult of believers large enough to bring a new god into existence, but one who doesn't really fit one of the other, already existing gods. So they're not an offshoot, so to speak. They're totally new."

Bach looked between them before taking Selene's hand in his own massive one. "And you are?"

"Selene. I'm Alec's—"

"Date. She's my date. MY date. So don't go throwing your charm this way, big man. Stick with your nymphettes over there and leave us with our puny little selves, will you?" Bacchus was nearly as old as Alec, and she'd seen him seduce every type of human there'd been. Sex and gender didn't matter, as long as he was having a good time. The humans, though, rarely fared as well, unable to keep up with the god of gluttony and hedonism.

"My nymphs are beautiful, it's true. But there are times I'd give a barrel of ambrosia for a regular woman. A human one, flawed, with morning breath and pimples. You know what I mean, old bat?"

Selene put her hands on her hips and tilted her head. "Excuse me, I think we're more than that."

He leaned forward and whispered loudly, "Why don't you prove it to me?"

Alec was about to step between them, highly irritated, although she knew him well enough to know he was mostly joking. But the thought of anyone making a move on Selene made her want to flex her wings and let her snakes loose. Before she could intervene, however, one of Bach's satyrs clattered up next to him and whispered in his ear.

Alec nearly laughed out loud as Selene bent and tilted, trying to get a better look at the satyr's body. Bach stilled and his eyes narrowed as he looked at Selene.

He turned to Alec, his teasing manner gone. "You brought her here? Without telling us? Without allowing us to prepare and show her our best side? Is this how you work?" His presence seemed to fill the room, and it became dark and quiet. "How dare you spring this kind of thing on us, Fury?"

Alec moved in front of Selene and let her wings drop open to shield her. "Bach, everything is under control. There's nothing wrong, and she's here with me. Not alone. Back down, big guy. Let it be." She lightly punched his shoulder, to get him to focus on her instead of trying to see behind her. "I've never let you down before, have I?"

He seemed to shrink down to his regular-enormous size and his demeanor once again became jovial. "You've never let me down, that's true. Sorry about that. You know how much I dislike surprises of that nature."

She remembered the time he'd been imprisoned by another god for refusing to poison wine at a dinner party. "I know. But everything is cool. Just go join the party, and maybe we'll see you later, huh?"

He nodded, scanning the room. "I'll do that." He enveloped Alec in another hug. "Good luck with this one, old bat. It's a long damn road you've got ahead of you."

He walked away, and Alec slid her wings away again before turning to Selene. She wasn't prepared for the glaring, angry woman in front of her.

"What the hell is going on, Alec? Why do people seem afraid of me? Or…whatever emotion it is. Why do they seem to know me? Why was a god about to go ballistic because I'm here? Jesus, Alec, tell me the truth."

A man in a tank top, board shorts, and socks and sandals, turned around. "Pardon? I didn't catch that."

Selene blushed slightly. "I'm sorry. I was talking to Alec." She paused and then her eyes went wide. "Jesus. You're Jesus?"

He grinned. "I am. Selene, right? I've heard a lot about you."

She glared at Alec as she took Jesus's extended hand. "Yeah, that seems to be the case lately."

He shook his head. "Things play out the way they're supposed to, right? You have to trust."

In an effort to change the subject before Selene got into an argument about faith with the son of God, or, worse, learned about things Alec wasn't ready for her to know, she said, "Jesus has his own clothing line. He's really amazing at the marketing thing. No one else holds a candle to him."

He smiled happily at Alec's compliment. "Thanks, avenger. I do try." He lifted his arm and showed Selene the rubber bracelets on his wrist. "That whole WWJD, What Would Jesus Do, campaign? I started that. And Jesus sandals? Yup, those are mine too. Footwear and accessories is where it's at. That's how you stay in people's minds this day and age, right? By putting your name out there, keeping it visual. It totally works."

"But…but…why?" Selene asked. "Surely you don't need money. Or fame, since so many people believe in you already."

He tapped the side of his nose. "Ah, but see, you never know when people will stop believing, do you? More are straying into agnostic or atheist territory every day. Better to branch out now, fight entropy, than wait for the fade." He ran his hand over his shaggy haircut. "By marketing myself, I make sure people remember me."

Alec felt Selene lean against her slightly and was worried it was becoming too much for her. *Please let her be strong enough. Please don't let her have some kind of psychotic break.* She put her arm gently around Selene's waist and was glad when Selene leaned into her embrace. She tried not to think about how long it had been since a woman had leaned into her that way, and how good it felt to have it happening now. *Right woman, wrong time. The oracle said she's the one to save us. Not to jump her bones.*

"I suppose that makes sense, in a way."

He ducked his head like a kid about to do something naughty. "Watch this." He waved his hand subtly, near his thigh, and then put his hand over his mouth as they watched the people around them. Various people started spitting their drinks out, many searching the room just for him.

"What did you do?" Selene asked.

"I turned their wine to salt water. It kills me every time." He waved his hand again and this time people were able to drink again, though more than one threw him a dirty look. "I changed it back, but I never seem to get all the salt residue out. You might want to grab a fresh glass."

Selene raised her glass. "Beer, so no worries. But thanks."

The house grew dark, as though clouds covered the moon. Selene leaned into Alec once again as everyone turned to face the door. A massive black shadow filled the door, and the air in the room cooled noticeably.

"Who's that?" Selene whispered in Alec's ear.

"Death," Alec replied. "She's a good friend of mine."

❖

The figure stepped inside and the light returned. She smiled and nodded at people as she made her way across the room, but Selene thought she looked tense, unsure of herself. *Well, look at me. Analyzing Death's mental state.* She took another long gulp of beer. Everything was surreal, and yet felt strangely normal. She guessed it was an element of disassociation; her mind couldn't cope with the fact that her entire world was something other than what she thought, and so it accepted it as "normal." As Death stopped in front of them, she decided to just go with it. She could deal with any psychological cracks later. Instead, she took the time to study her. She was tall, like Alec. Imposingly so. She was handsome in a clean, classic way, with high cheekbones and short brown hair. Her T-shirt was loose over a thin but not scrawny frame, her khakis pressed and neat. If Selene had seen her on the street, she wouldn't have given her a second glance, except for her height. The thought that Death blended in and looked like everyone else was more disturbing than thinking of her with a cloak and scythe.

Alec gave her a big hug, and the relief on her face was clear. "Hey, avenger. How you been?"

"Good, really good. Dani, can I introduce you to Selene?"

She shook Selene's hand, and her smile was gentle and genuine. "Great to meet you. Any friend of Alec's, and all that. You must be finding all of this a bit disorienting, though?"

"Likewise. And yes, it's…Yes. Disorienting is a good word for it."

She glanced at Alec. "How about I get a drink and we go sit on the patio? I hate being stuck inside at these things."

Jesus laughed. "That's because people hate being stuck inside with you."

Dani winced, and her smile was forced. "Yeah, well, no news there." She headed toward the kitchen and Selene gave Jesus a questioning look.

"Death is a reminder, you know? Not only does she take our followers, sometimes by the truckload, but there's no telling if she might come for one of us. Well, not really, because we don't work that way. But she still represents finality, you know? Like, she's a bummer."

Alec shook her head. "She's no more responsible for the way life works than you are, or I am. Cut her some slack, would you?" She turned to Selene. "She has a hard time making friends because in a way, J is right. What she stands for disturbs even the gods."

"But you said she's a good friend of yours?" Selene said.

Dani rejoined them with a beer in hand. "She's been my closest friend for centuries." She motioned toward the patio doors. "Shall we?"

The four of them headed outside, and Selene felt like she was in the strangest conga line ever created. Death leading the way, followed by the son of God, an ancient fury, and…herself. Alec reached back, as though sensing Selene's need for contact, and she gratefully took her hand. Even amid this chaos, being with Alec felt like high ground in a flood. Once again, she pictured her wings, so massive, so soft, and the way Alec's eyes changed to an unknowable, impossible black the night she'd been protecting Selene. She shivered slightly.

Dani sat at an empty table near a heat lamp and patted the chair next to her. "Selene, you want to sit closest to the heat? Wouldn't want you catching cold."

The innocuous comment should have been sweet, but coming from Dani Death, it held a faintly ominous note. *No wonder she has trouble making friends. Everything she says feels like an omen.* She smiled at her with the sudden desire to make her feel less self-conscious. "Thank you, that would be nice."

They sat quietly for a few minutes, watching as guests roamed in and out. When they saw Alec, they often started to head their way. But when they saw who was at the table with her, they changed direction.

"Don't let it get to you, buddy. You know how they are." Alec squeezed Dani's shoulder.

"That's why I don't come to these things. I always end up feeling worse. But when I heard you and your guest were coming, I decided it was worth it."

"Then concentrate on that. I'm always worth it." Alec winked and gave her a saucy grin. They all laughed, and the tension was broken.

Dani turned to Selene. "So, questions. You must have a million. Can I help?"

Selene glanced at Alec, who nodded. "If there's anyone who can answer the basics, it's this lady. She's older than all of us put together."

"Well, that's not strictly true. My post is older. I've only been in the position for a bit longer than Alec. Jesus, here, is the baby of the group. There aren't many in the organization younger than him."

Jesus propped his feet on the edge of the table and sipped his Corona. "True enough. But there are plenty of my offshoots who are younger."

Selene wiped at the condensation on her glass thoughtfully. *Where to start?* "Death's persona is always portrayed as male. But you say it hasn't always been you?"

Dani shook her head. "No. The position has been in play since humans gained a level of consciousness about their world and became aware of the inevitability of death. I'll probably retire soon myself."

Selene processed that for a moment. "Okay, I suppose the first thing that occurs to me is why are all of you here? I mean, Alec said you're brought into existence by people's belief systems." She looked at Jesus. "So, that's why you worry about keeping people believing in you. But what happens when people stop believing in you?"

Dani looked at Alec, who tilted her head for her to answer. "For those who need belief to be here, losing believers means losing life force. The more life force they lose, the more insubstantial they become. We call it fading."

"But Alec and her sisters can't fade. And you?"

"No. That's why Alec and I have been friends for so long. She and her sisters understand the necessity of my post, and I understand what they do. We've worked together on many, many cases. Without death, the world couldn't exist properly. There's a natural cycle, and I'm a part of that. I don't need belief because I'm an undeniable fact." She took a sip of her beer, obviously considering her words. "And because the gods fade or, essentially, die when they lose their followers, they often blame me for taking those followers, even though there's no other option." She gave her a small, sad smile. "So you see why I'm not the most popular party guest."

Selene squeezed her hand, noting that it felt cold and bony. "I'm sorry. That must make for a lonely existence."

Her smile widened and she began to laugh. She squeezed Selene's hand in return. "Imagine, a human being one of the first people in centuries to acknowledge the loneliness of being Death." She looked at Alec. "Excellent."

Selene turned to Jesus. "I have to ask this, because it seems like the most logical, if clichéd question of all time. If you all really exist, and you're there working to answer prayers, why do bad things happen? Wars, poverty, plagues?"

Jesus sighed and tugged his socks up. "Okay. So here's the thing. Yeah, we answer prayers. But they're on a first come, first served basis, right? I mean, one prayer comes in asking for something, and we answer it. The next prayer comes in, asking for the opposite thing, and because we've already answered the first one, we can't answer the second. It's about who gets in first. At least, with the Christians it is. And the Jews. A few of the religions have a hierarchy, where if you're born in a certain caste system or whatever, you have to wait until you're reborn into another one to get your prayers answered." He shrugged and wiggled his sock covered toes. "It sounds harsh when you describe it that way, but it's true."

"Okay, so that covers prayer. Kind of. What about the other stuff? Bad things happening to good people?"

Alec leaned forward to answer, but Jesus cut her off. "That's where free will comes in. See, the gods are only as powerful as they're believed to be, and they're never more powerful than the people who created them, ironically. People have free will, and if they really believe they're doing the right thing, they're going to do it regardless of whether or not the gods approve or can help their cause. When big things happen, like wars, especially between religions or in one or more of our names," Jesus made air quotes at this, rolling his eyes, "most prayers go unanswered because there are too many opposing prayers coming in. People do the wicked, awful, horrifying things they do, and then we try to clean up the mess and provide some relief afterward. We don't honor the prayers of extremists, and the Afterlife constitution says we don't act on prayers against one another."

Selene pondered the answer for a long time, the sounds of the party in the house behind her growing more raucous. "So when times are okay, you're here for people. But when things get really bad, you don't do anything of use. Is that about it?"

Jesus sat up, his face red. "We give hope. We might not be able to help a lot in the face of humanity's messed up ways, but we can give those who have no hope in their lives a reason to keep going. And we do answer prayers, in a logical way. But when two football teams go out on the field, and they both pray for a win, you take the prayer that comes in first. That's fair. And it's answering a prayer. Being useful and shit."

That Jesus swore was something Selene filed away to consider later. For now, she needed to understand yet more of the world she'd been dropped into. She thought about her conversation with Frey, and wondered if he was right. Maybe hope, faith, and religion were only crutches, excuses for people to behave badly, or to behave well but only for a reward. But then, maybe without hope, without getting their prayers answered, people would give up on lives that were ultimately too hard to bear. The concept was too much to take on board all at once.

"Okay. And the afterlife?"

They all stayed quiet for so long Selene wondered if she'd spoken the question out loud.

Finally, Dani answered. "That's a tough one to explain. Each belief system has their own idea of the afterlife. Heaven, Hell, Nirvana. And if a group has enough believers, then those places exist in the way they've constructed them, but they tend to be loose, because no two people conceive of the exact geography the same way. So Heaven and Hell exist, as does Nirvana, and there are folks overseeing those spaces." She took a deep breath and shrugged slightly. "But those people who don't have a big enough group of believers, or whose idea of the afterlife is too fuzzy, well…"

Selene waited, but she seemed to have finished. "Well, what? What happens to them?"

"They meet me, or one of my staff—"

"Wait, your staff? Do you have your own offshoots? Death minions?"

She laughed and seemed to relax. "Yeah, kind of. There are seven billion people on the planet. Hundreds die every hour, all over the world. More, in war torn areas. I could do it myself once upon a time, but there's no way now. So I've got a staff, many of whom work for me from remote offices, all linked via the Internet. We Skype once a month to discuss issues and work out schedules, particularly if there are more wars than usual going on. It works well." She gestured at the group with her empty beer bottle. "I need another drink. Anyone else?"

All of them nodded and she left to get more.

Jesus said, "I just saw my mom come in, and I haven't stopped by her place in ages, I've been so busy. I'd better go say hi real quick. I'll be back in a second."

Alone for the first time since they'd arrived, Selene slumped in her chair, exhausted by the wealth of answers she'd received. Questions humanity had been asking for centuries were suddenly laid before her like nothing more than a paper napkin at a fast food restaurant, and she had no idea what to do with it all. How to process it. She flashed on Mika briefly and wondered what she would think if Selene told her about this whole situation. *She'd have me committed.* Alec cleared her throat softly and Selene looked up.

"You okay? Do you want to leave? Or talk to other people?"

The care, the genuine concern, in Alec's voice made Selene feel better. *I'm not alone.* "It's just a lot to take in. I can't really even analyze any of it yet. I guess I'll have to do that later, once I've got all the answers, right?"

Alec took her hand and she marveled at the way it grounded her and made her feel safe.

"There's no hurry. You can process all of this any way you want to, in whatever amount of time you need. And you're not alone. Remember that."

"Tell me what happens to the ones who don't believe? To atheists, like me."

Alec ran a hand through her hair. "Nothing. They don't go anywhere. Dani, or one of her crew, show up to claim them. They take the soul, the essence of any human, from the body. The believers go whatever direction they're supposed to according to their belief system. The non-believers…their essence turns to a kind of spirit dust, like something you'd take out of a fireplace, and they blow away."

Selene frowned, considering those options, and the possibility of being nothing more than crap sucked up by some cosmic vacuum. "I don't know how I feel about that. I mean, I would have been dust anyway, because that's what I think…thought, would happen. And is that so bad, compared to believing in and moving on to a place like Hell?" She wrapped her arms around herself, feeling a need to keep herself together.

"Hey, don't worry. We can talk all this stuff through. Life is about learning, right?"

Alec gave her a small grin, and Selene laughed softly. She leaned over and rested her head on Alec's shoulder, the feel of Alec's arm as it went around her shoulders a brace against the whirlwind of emotions and questions flooding Selene's mind and body. She murmured, "I need to go to the bathroom. Please don't tell me there isn't one because gods don't pee."

Alec laughed. "I won't bore you with the physicality. Yes, there's a bathroom. Come on. I'll take you." Alec stood and took Selene's hand to lead her through the crowded house.

Whispers and stares followed them, and Selene returned to her question that had now been avoided at least twice. They stopped in front of a bathroom in a quiet corridor, and she grabbed Alec's forearm. "When I come out, we're going to talk about why people are reacting to me the way they are. No more avoiding, okay?" She looked into Alec's beautiful eyes, determined to show her she was serious. "Please?"

Alec searched her face, for what she didn't know, before she nodded slowly. "Okay. I hear you. But let's not do it here, okay?

Maybe we can head down the coast, grab a drink somewhere by the water?"

Selene looked down the corridor at the mass of people laughing, drinking, and chatting. *People seems like a loose term.* "If we go, will you promise I'll have this opportunity again? I want to meet more…people. I want to know so much more."

Alec made an x over her heart. "I promise. But we can take it slowly, right? No need to dump it all on you in one night."

Impulsively, Selene pulled Alec into a hug. "Thank you." She pulled back slightly, unwilling to let go, and with their faces only inches apart, she licked her lips.

Alec groaned and closed the distance between them, holding Selene's face in her hands as she kissed her deeply, her tongue sliding into Selene's mouth, sending waves of heat crashing through Selene's body. Alec leaned Selene against the bathroom door, their bodies pressed together. Selene's hands slid into the soft, downy feathers of Alec's wings. She couldn't see them, but they were most certainly there.

The door popped open under the pressure of their weight and they nearly fell to the floor. Alec pulled away first, grinning. "Let's get out of here. I'll find Meg real quick and let her know we're heading out, and I'll come right back for you, okay?"

Selene nodded, breathless, unable to form words. She'd never, ever been so physically entranced by someone. All she could think about was getting their clothes off so she could feel Alec's perfect hands on her body. She wanted to feel Alec's mouth on her neck, her breasts…lower. *I want her everywhere.*

She closed the bathroom door behind her and leaned on the sink. If she weren't wearing makeup she'd splash cold water on her face, but seeing as she didn't want to look like a crying panda, she had to settle for patting some water on the back of her neck and on her wrists. She took several deep, calming breaths. She wanted answers, and getting into bed with Alec wasn't going to get her those. *At least, not yet.*

She peed, washed her hands, and stepped back into the corridor, feeling a bit more able to have a normal, nonsexual discussion. Alec wasn't there, but she didn't want to go wandering through the party on her own, so she decided to wait where she was. A light chuckle from behind her startled her, and she spun around. A dark-skinned man wearing a tall, half-red, half-white hat leaned against the wall behind her. His eyes glittered, though with mischief or malice she couldn't tell. Feeling defensive, she crossed her arms and looked over her shoulder for Alec.

"She's been caught up talking to her sister, the beautiful Megara. I'm sure she'll be right back."

His accent was Egyptian, and she tried to think of what few Egyptian gods she knew. "I'm sorry, I don't think we've met?"

He moved forward, too close for comfort, and held out his hand. "Esh, at your service. I wanted to meet the woman so many are talking about. The savior of the gods." He bowed, mockingly. "I'm sure your mother will be proud."

Selene's stomach turned, his words biting into her fragile emotions. "I think you must have me confused with someone else. When Alec gets back—"

"Ah, I'm sure she will clear things up, of course. But have no doubt, beautiful lady, you are who they say you are. Whether or not you believe it, or are capable of such a feat, well…that remains to be seen. I look forward to hearing your plan to keep us from fading into nothingness, or becoming fruit sellers on PCH, whichever the case may be."

He stepped even closer, and she could smell his nauseating, cloying cologne mixed with a smell that made her think of rotting vegetables. She tried not to gag and stepped back, but stopped when he grabbed her wrist in a cruel grip.

"You're supposed to save us, but you don't believe. An unbeliever, someone who disrespects us, and everything we stand for. A woman, a Halfling, a nothing." He abruptly let go of her wrist and stepped back. "You will fail. If it is our destiny to fade, so be it. I personally will not be held hostage to a human's intelligence." He turned and walked back into the dark of the corridor. Before he disappeared completely, he looked at her over his shoulder and gave her a malicious smile. "Say hello to your mother when you see her.

She's the same in every belief system, and she is truly magnificent. It's a shame you're such a pale comparison."

He disappeared, and Selene was left alone in the hallway. She slid down the wall and hugged her knees to her chest. She let the tears fall, not caring about her makeup anymore. Esh's energy had been malignant, and she felt dirty just from being near him.

Alec bounded into the hallway. "Selene, I'm so sorry. I got waylaid by about a hundred people—" She stopped and looked closely. "Selene?" She squatted in front of her and brushed the hair from her eyes. "What happened?"

Selene choked back a sob. "This man...he said things. About why I'm here with you, and something about my mother." She looked at Alec, desperate for her to say none of it was true, that it was just another ego-driven god with a grudge of some kind. "Alec, what the hell is going on? Is it...any of it...true?"

Alec rested her hands on Selene's shoulders and slid her hands down Selene's arms to her hands. She held them in her own and took a deep breath.

"Yes. It's all true."

Chapter Eighteen

A lec looked at Selene, who sat stonily silent beside her, still as one of Medusa's statues. She hadn't said a word since she'd gotten to her feet in the hallway and made her way out to the Hummer, silently pushing through the crowd as though she didn't see them. More than one sympathetic glance was thrown Alec's way as she left, which made her feel even worse. Many of them were likely resigned to their fates, unable to believe in Alec's ability to win Selene to their side. Now, with Selene radiating anger and confusion beside her, she wondered if they were right to doubt.

"Selene? Please say something?" Alec parked the Hummer at the far end of the Venice Strand. It wasn't the greatest area at night, but there wasn't anything she couldn't handle. *Until now.*

"I don't even know where to start," Selene said softly, her head resting against the passenger window, her eyes unfocused.

"Should I just start talking, then? And you can interrupt with questions?"

Selene nodded, and Alec took a deep breath. She hadn't wanted it to be this way, but the truth was, she'd been taking her time, reluctant to jump in. The choice had been taken from her, and that was probably a good thing.

"You asked what happens when people stop believing. The truth is, we fade. We get weaker and weaker, until we just…disappear. Sometimes you can watch people fading, people you've known for centuries, until one day you can practically see through them, and the next, they're gone. When people stop believing in us, we stop existing." She paused to see if Selene was listening. Selene flicked a glance at her before looking away, so Alec continued. "We have one option open to us, though. If we know we're fading, we can leave. We can renounce our godhood, and go live in the real world. We get real world jobs, real world apartments, and live among humans as though we're one of them."

"And are you? Does it make you human in some way?"

"Not exactly. We age, but far more slowly than humans do. We can still live for centuries. We're not immortal once we leave, because we *can* die. But unless some situation puts a stop to our life, we'll keep going. That means moving around a lot, of course, because that's the kind of thing people notice if you stay in one place for any length of time."

Selene stayed quiet for so long Alec didn't know if she should keep talking or just shut up. Then she turned and looked at Alec, and her eyes were cold.

"Why should it matter if you all fade? Or get jobs as accountants? If people stop praying to you and your horde, maybe they'll take responsibility for their actions. I've always believed the world would be a better place if only humanity took a stand and stopped waiting for some deity to take care of things. Why should knowing you make any difference at all?" She straightened and lifted her chin. "In fact, maybe knowing you all exist only because of belief means I should try harder to get people to stop believing, because it really is ruining the planet."

Alec winced, the words piercing her like a hot needle. It was the exact opposite of what she needed Selene to think. "Would you damn an entire group of people because of your personal beliefs?"

"Personal beliefs? Alec, what I believe is based on fact, on history and proof. From small scale to large scale confrontations, there's often a religious component, one that's been twisted by the people who believe. And as far as I can tell, your colleagues aren't about to do anything to stop that." She pushed open the door of the Hummer. "I need air."

Alec followed Selene as she stormed down to the water's edge. She didn't know what to say. She could see Selene's point, and it was hard to argue with.

The waves crashed at Selene's feet, and she spun to face Alec. "Why me? That...god? Esh, he said his name was—"

"Eshnu. He wore an absurd looking hat? He's an African god of mischief. He's constantly stirring the pot. I think I need to have a discussion with him."

"Whatever. He said something about me being important, about me being the one to keep you from fading. What the hell is that about? Is that why everyone stares at me? And why Bacchus found my presence so upsetting?" Selene pointed at her, nearly poking her in the chest. "And you'd better tell me the truth. All of it. Now."

Alec swallowed against the rising fear. She knew exactly how what she was about to say would sound. "An oracle. We've had an oracle in place for a few centuries, warning us about what was going to happen, and who could help us stop it."

"Convenient. And for some reason, you decided that was me?"

"We didn't decide, no. You were named, Selene. The Fates aren't wrong, ever. We don't always understand what the hell they're talking about when they pass an oracle down to us, but they're never, ever wrong. And apparently, an atheist philosopher is our ticket to continued existence." Listening to the explanation she was giving, resentment began to fill her. It did sound absurd. What kind of system did they have going that made their only hope someone who was least likely to help them? She threw a pebble at the ocean, unable to see where it landed. *Hopefully, on Zed's head.*

"Oh? And tell me again who wrote this oracle of yours? Who is it that decides who saves your asses?"

"They go by various names. You'll know them by the Fates, or maybe the Moirai Sisters."

"And do they work in your building?"

"Level five. But no one has access to it. We rarely even see them because they have their own elevator and they don't socialize with the rest of us. A conflict of interest, and all that."

Selene fell to her knees in the sand, her shoulders slumped. "And what does your oracle say I'm supposed to do?"

Alec thought back to the wording of the oracle. "It says the daughter born of the dark and the night's light will be the one to save our world. That without her, we'll soon become those for whom belief is no longer enough. We'll cease to be, if we can't get her to be the bridge. And the human world will descend into chaos and misery. The dark fury is the only one who can help the night's child become the bridge."

Selene looked at Alec incredulously. "Seriously? That doesn't seem the least bit self-serving to you?"

Alec shrugged and sat beside Selene. She pulled her legs to her chest and rested on her wings. "That's what it says."

They stayed silent for a long time, the crashing of the waves in front of them the only sound to break the night's silence. A path of moonlight lit the ocean, making either side of the light seem that much darker. Alec waited for the next obvious question.

"And what he said about my mother? You said the oracle says the daughter born of the dark and night's light. What does that mean?" She turned pleading eyes toward Alec. "I've been an orphan all my life, Alec. In one night, you tell me I'm supposed to save a world I didn't know exists, and that my real mother is out there somewhere." Tears slid down Selene's face, and she let them. "I don't understand."

Alec took Selene's hand in her own and was heartened when, instead of pulling away, Selene leaned into her. Alec shifted so she was sitting with her legs on either side of Selene. She pulled her back gently and wrapped her arms around her. The night air was cold, and when she felt the goose bumps covering Selene's arms, she cursed herself for forgetting her human nature. Slowly, she opened her wings and wrapped them around Selene. Alec felt her stiffen, then relax and begin to absently, slowly stroke her feathers.

"I can't imagine what you're feeling. But you're not alone. I'm right here with you." Alec rested her cheek against Selene's for a moment, gathering her thoughts. There was no reason to hold back now. "Your mom is Chandra, the moon goddess. She actually represents the moon itself, and so, like me, she doesn't need belief to exist. The problem is, she's not—"

"Not what?"

"She's an air goddess. Hard to pin down, not solid. Strong, beautiful. But...free."

"Is that why she gave me up? And why didn't my father take me?"

The pure sadness in Selene's voice was heartbreaking, and in it Alec could hear the child who had always felt rootless and less-than. "I don't know, to be honest. We knew Chandra had a child, but that's all we ever knew. She never talked about it, and no one was ever brave enough to ask who the father was, or where her child had disappeared to."

"No one cared what a goddess did with a child? And you're telling me I'm the child of a goddess? A representative of the moon, and someone or something else. Who the hell represents the dark?" Selene's laugh was nearly hysterical. "If I weren't wrapped in gigantic wings attached to a humanoid body right now, I'd think you were insane. But then, maybe I'm insane. Maybe I really am going crazy, and this is all one elaborate hallucination."

Alec trailed her hands up Selene's arms, letting her fingertips trace delicate lines along her skin. "Does this feel like a hallucination?"

Selene jerked to her knees and turned to face Alec. Placing her hands on Alec's cheeks, she whispered, "No, it doesn't." She leaned forward and kissed her softly.

"Selene, we probably shouldn't—"

"Please. Please don't say it. My entire life has become something out of a twisted fairy tale. For just this moment, keep me from thinking about it."

Selene's warm lips set Alec's blood on fire. She struggled to stay in her human form, but when Selene's tongue pushed into her mouth, she felt herself losing the battle. Her fangs extended and she shifted to keep them out of the way. She pulled Selene against her, wrapping her in both her arms and her wings as she fell back onto the sand with Selene's weight on top of her. She could feel the heat emanating from between Selene's legs, and her kisses were driving Alec mad. Selene's hands were everywhere, caressing her feathers, then her arms, sliding over her sides and up to her neck. She slid her hands under Selene's flimsy top and lightly raked her nails over her back, and when Selene moaned, she lost all sense of place.

She flipped Selene onto her back, still cradling her with her wings. She kissed her, deep and hard, and moaned when Selene's tongue slid over one of her fangs. She pinned Selene's hands to the sand above her head and kissed her way over Selene's collarbone to the swell of her breasts, which suddenly had far too much material over them. With a snarl, she ripped the material away with her teeth before resuming her exploration of Selene's perfect body. She released her hands and slowly dragged her fingertips over Selene's arms, over her shoulders and chest, to her breasts, which she palmed before leaning down to suck a hard, dusky pink nipple into her mouth. Selene's back arched and she pressed herself into Alec, who willingly sucked harder.

When Selene was thrashing with pleasure and begging quietly, Alec quickly undid her jeans and slipped her hand inside soft, silky panties to find the core of Selene's need. The moment her fingers pushed into Selene's welcoming wetness, she let her full change happen. If Selene wanted sex with a fury, then she'd get it.

Alec pushed deeper, faster, harder. She fucked Selene furiously, letting out all the frustration she'd felt as she'd grown to enjoy Selene's company, only to think she could never have her. And beneath Selene's need, she felt a desperation to be wanted. *I want you. I want you so fucking bad.*

"Alec...please...God, Alec. Don't stop. Please don't stop."

Alec had no intention of stopping. She wanted to make Selene come as many times as humanly possible, all while wrapped in her wings, comforted and sated by a creature she didn't know existed, but one who needed her more than she knew. More, even, than Alec wanted to admit.

Selene tightened around Alec's fingers, her body stiffened, and she bit down on Alec's shoulder to muffle her cries.

"No one can hear you," Alec whispered against her hair, loving the feel of Selene's orgasm crashing through her. As Selene rode through one orgasm and into another, Alec felt her own building in response. By Selene's third orgasm, Alec couldn't hold out any longer. She pulled her fingers from Selene and sat up, her wings open wide and her face to the sky as she let go.

When she opened her eyes, Selene was staring at her, but she couldn't make out with what emotion. When tears slid from Selene's eyes to fall in the sand beside her head, Alec pulled back, putting her human guise back in place. She lay beside Selene and brushed at the tears. Selene turned on her side to face Alec, seeming to search Alec's face for something.

"Selene? Are you okay? Was I too rough?"

Selene cupped Alec's face in her hand. "No. It was perfect. I've always wanted to have sex on a beach. Little did I know I'd be lying on a literal bed of feathers my first time."

She smiled slightly and Alec relaxed. "The tears?"

"Have you ever been told how beautiful you are in the moonlight?"

Alec froze, unsure what to say. There had been a moment in history when furies had been called Erinyes, and they'd sometimes been described as beautiful. But no one who had seen her true form had ever used the word beautiful. She felt tears threaten and cursed herself. *Furies don't cry, you idiot.* "No, I don't believe so. But trust me when I say no one could ever compare to you."

Selene snuggled into Alec's embrace. "I have so many questions, so many things I need to know. But right now all I can think about is falling asleep in your arms and dealing with all this when I can think again."

Alec pulled her tight, wrapping her wings around Selene like a blanket. "Then sleep, sweet one. And when you wake up, we'll face it all, together."

Within minutes, she felt Selene's breathing change and knew she'd fallen asleep. *She must be so emotionally exhausted.* She wished she could take some of the pressure from Selene's shoulders, but the truth was, there was far more to come, and nothing Alec could do to stop it, not if she wanted her existence to continue the way it currently did. Selene murmured and snuggled even closer, and Alec sighed.

Selene is right. Tomorrow. I can wait until tomorrow. For the moment, she could sink into the feeling of rightness, of not being alone anymore, that Selene's presence brought her. *For now.* She closed her eyes and allowed herself to drift to sleep.

Chapter Nineteen

Selene woke warmer than she'd ever been. She couldn't recall the last time she'd slept so well, without dreams fraught with confusion and stress. So often she felt as though she was being chased, or chasing someone, but nothing ever came of it. Now, she felt...safe. She shifted and went to stretch, but found herself encased to the point of barely being able to move. Her face was pillowed on Alec's chest, her hands buried in the feathers of her wings. She looked up at Alec's face and found her smiling down at her.

"Hey, sleepyhead. You must have been really exhausted."

"I'm so sorry. Have I kept you from anything? What time is it?"

"Nothing could have been more important than waking up with you this way. And my time is yours." She shifted slightly and laughed. "I'll admit, however, that the sand is making my wings itch."

Selene let go and went to sit up. When Alec's wings moved away to allow her to move, the morning air was cold and she immediately missed them. She looked down the beach and saw a few surfers coming back in from their morning rides. "Already coming back in. So it must be around nine?"

Alec looked at her quizzically. "You know what time the surfers go in and out?"

Selene tilted her head and stared at the ocean thoughtfully. "No. I've just always been really aware of the tides, when they're in and when they're out." She looked at Alec, the previous night rushing back at her. "I guess that makes more sense now, doesn't it?"

Alec stood and moved a few feet away to shake the sand from her wings. Selene watched, fascinated. The morning light glinted off the black feathers like flame on obsidian. Deep hues of blues and purples caught the light, making her wings more beautiful than anything Selene had ever seen. She tore her gaze from Alec's wings, only to be arrested by the sight of her beautifully muscled, taut body. She could see a six-pack under the tight T-shirt, and her biceps bulged, pulling the material tight. Selene swallowed, seriously trying not to drool.

Alec cleared her throat and grinned salaciously when Selene met her eyes. "Keep looking at me like that, and I'll take you somewhere to do more of what we did last night. For days."

Selene flushed and looked away, embarrassed by the way she'd jumped Alec last night, practically begging her to have sex. And what did it mean? Where did they go from here? Was it just a one-time thing? *Do five-thousand-year-old beings have relationships?* Panic started to turn her stomach.

"Hey." Alec knelt in front of her, her wings tucked away from sight. "Let's go get some coffee and figure out what you want to do next, okay?" She gently caressed Selene's cheek.

The panic receded and she nodded. "I'd like that." Selene stood, and her shirt fell in pieces around her. She crossed her arms over her chest, mortified.

Alec blushed. "Sorry about that. I have an idea, though." She wrapped her wing around Selene and cloaked them in her magic. When they arrived in the T-shirt seller's shop, the only one open this early in winter, she only dropped her cloak when Selene had pulled on an "I love Venice" sweatshirt. The proprietor screeched slightly when they suddenly appeared.

On the walk back to the Hummer, Alec took her hand, and Selene felt tears threaten. She'd always wanted to be with someone who was proud to be seen with her, someone who wanted to touch her whenever, wherever. While she wouldn't expect that level of anything from Alec, it was nice, just in that moment, to feel wanted.

They stopped at the 18th Street Coffee House, neither of them talking. Selene wasn't sure what was going through Alec's mind, but she knew she didn't want to talk yet and risk breaking the spell from the night before. Magic wasn't supposed to exist, and yet, magical was exactly what it felt like.

They sat at the outside patio, the morning sun promising a good day.

Alec took Selene's hand. "Want to start?"

Selene sighed. "I suppose. I just…where to begin?" She sipped her coffee for a few minutes, Alec allowing her the space to think. "Alec, does my mother work at Afterlife?"

"No. She's too free for that. She's not a big fan of walls."

"You know her? I mean, how well?" The possibility that Alec *knew* her mother made the panic flare up again.

"Yes. I know…knew…your mother well. Never romantically, if that's your concern." Alec squeezed Selene's hand. "We were incredibly close for a while, and have been off and on through the centuries. But when the industrial revolution hit, the buzzing and constant humming of machines and wires made her crazy, so she decided to make herself scarce. We're not always sure where she is."

Selene processed that. The idea that gods, omnipotent beings, might be bothered by innovations over the centuries, would never have occurred to her. The moon, a lump of rock without its own light, surely wouldn't be bothered by anything. But a representative of it…someone tied to the tides, gravity, storms…yes, she could see how someone like that might be bothered.

"Could you find her, do you think?"

Alec appeared to consider the question seriously. "It might take me a bit of time."

Suddenly, it felt like the most important thing in the world. To know her mother. To know why she'd given her up. To know who her father was…all the questions about fate, oracles, and religion paled in comparison to the promise of a possible family. "Can you start looking today?"

Alec nodded. "I can. Do you want to come to the office with me and hang around? Or do you want to go home and have some quiet time to think?"

Selene felt the sand in her jeans and knew her hair must be a frizzy mess. The sweatshirt wasn't exactly her style either, though it was surprisingly comfortable. "Home sounds good. But you can drop me at the train station, if that's okay? I like the quiet time on a train. And my car is still at the park and ride."

"No problem."

They went to the car and drove the few miles to the station in silence. Once there, Alec turned to Selene. "Thank you."

"For?"

"For not running. For last night. Selene, I won't say I haven't been with plenty of women. I mean, that would be ludicrous, given my age. But last night...that was special. I don't know if you felt it too, but...well. I just wanted you to know." She got out and opened Selene's door for her. She pulled her into a tight embrace. "I'll call you as soon as I know anything, okay? And if you want to talk, or want me to come to you, all you have to do is call, and I'll be there. I promise. And if anything feels off, or strange, just shout. If someone or something makes you think of those other creatures, call me right away."

Selene looked into Alec's eyes and saw something she thought only existed in fairy tales. True, genuine emotion. Promise. Care. A lump formed in her throat, and she kissed Alec's cheek softly.

"Thank you for wanting me. Call me later, even if you don't know anything?"

"You got it."

The train pulled up and Selene reluctantly let go of Alec and stepped on board. Alec scanned the train, frowning, but turned back and waved with a smile.

"All clear." She mouthed it, and the look in her eyes was one of concern and care.

Selene placed her hand to the window as the train pulled away, feeling strangely bereft at leaving her behind, even though it was temporary. *Is it, though?* She didn't know what the rules or guidelines were in this new world. What if one day, it all just... disappeared?

She closed her eyes and concentrated on Alec's promise. She'd said they'd do it together, whatever "it" was. Now Selene just had to decide if she was willing to take the leap.

Chapter Twenty

Glass shattered into hundreds of splintered pieces, like rainbow diamonds raining down in the sunlight.

"Who does he think he is? What the Hades does he think he's doing? Of all the stupid, childish, rash things to do, he has to go and nearly ruin everything?"

Zed and Ama stood against a side wall, well out of Alec's target range. She threw another glass, needing the release she felt when it exploded.

"Alec, Eshnu is the god of mischief. Frankly, it's amazing Loki, or even one of our own, didn't already try something like this. He can't help it any more than you can help having wings."

She spun to face Zed. "Bullshit. I call bullshit on that. You know why? He could have chosen to not speak. He could have decided not to go to the party. He could have gone somewhere, *anywhere* else. Instead, he waited for his chance, the fucking few minutes I left her alone—to pee, for fuck's sake—and then he made his move. It was calculated, and it was stupid. What if she'd been seriously pissed off? What if I hadn't been able to talk to her?" She hissed through her fangs. "I should rip out his tongue and feed it to him. Teach him not to say shit without considering the consequences."

"Alec, please stop giving me a new glass carpet and calm down."

She glared at him but set the glass she'd picked up back down and ran her hands through her hair. "Well, what now?"

Zed and Ama moved away from the wall. Ama went to Alec and enfolded her in a strong hug. "I know the stress you're under. But hold it together, okay?"

Alec felt some of the stress leave her shoulders. A benefit of having goddess friends was they often had soothing, healing touches. When they weren't angry, anyway. Then it was a different matter. "Thank you." She kissed Ama on the cheek, retracted her fangs, sheathed her wings, and sat down.

Zed sat across from her, Ama on his right. Alec noted the way Ama gently touched his hand. She was glad they'd found each other, even if it didn't last. Monogamy wasn't really an option when you lived forever, but you could certainly spend a good amount of time with someone before one or the other got bored and moved on.

"Alec, as much as I hate to say it, go back to the oracle. It says it's Selene, and it says it's you. That means no matter what happens, you'll be able to talk to her. This is her path."

"That's the thing about this oracle, though, Zed. Unlike ever before, there are two possible outcomes. We succeed, or we fail. Usually, there's an element of no matter what you do, you're fucked. But this time they're not sure. The *Fates* aren't sure, Zed. That means nothing is completely certain, except that Selene is caught up in this whole crazy mess."

Ama gave her a searching look. "Alec, last night, it looked like you were quite close. Closer than friends. Are you losing your objectivity?"

Alec started to give a sarcastic retort, but reined herself in and forced herself to consider the question. The truth was undeniable.

"Yes. I am. We slept together last night, and I'm feeling… things. Things I'm not analyzing right now. But you know what? It doesn't matter, does it? Because the oracle says it has to be the two of us. And if it goes down in flames, well, I'll deal with it then."

They sat in silence for a few minutes before Zed said, "Fine. I suppose you being emotionally invested can't hurt. Or maybe it can. You've been chosen, and we have to trust in that."

"Gee, thanks for the vote of confidence."

He waved away her words like gnats. "She wants to see her mother?"

"Yeah, and frankly, I don't blame her. Tell a mortal, who was raised in foster care, that she not only has a mother, but her mother is a goddess, and it seems pretty logical that she's going to want to meet her. The question is, do we know where Chandra is?"

Ama pulled up a page on her laptop. "The last address I have for her is Milwaukee, but I heard at a party a few weeks ago someone had run into her in the Alban Hills."

"Excellent. Milwaukee or Italy. Do we have anyone in those areas who can run quick checks?"

Ama started typing rapidly, her brow furrowed in concentration.

"What's your next step, Alec? After you take Selene to meet her mother, assuming Chandra is available and willing to talk. What are you going to do after that?"

"I don't know." And truthfully, she didn't. For the first time in her existence, she had no idea at all what the next step was. "It looks like I have to just go with it in order to see what's coming down the road. Like each step is necessary to understand the next one. I hate it, but that seems to be the way. Unless the oracle has changed, and it's given us some more information? Have the Fates sent down any more we can work with? Like what, exactly, Selene is supposed to do to help us? Or what I'm supposed to do in the scheme of things?"

Zed opened the ever-present folder and scanned it. "Nope. Same as it's always been."

Alec sighed. "You know, at some point Selene is going to ask to see it. The real thing. She believes far more in what she can see than in something she's simply asked to believe."

He shrugged. "I don't see why she can't read it. It's not like we're divulging secrets. And maybe it will serve to convince her of our need."

Ama's computer pinged and she scanned the message. "Our operative in Milwaukee says Chandra hasn't been there in about six months. Italy is nine hours ahead of us, so we'll have to wait until our person there is awake."

"Awake? Are they a pre-fader?" Alec asked, referring to those who had been about to fade, and so had taken jobs in the real world instead.

"Yes. One of the lesser Roman gods, he's a curator at a museum now." Ama closed her laptop and looked at Alec. "So, since we've got a few hours to wait, why don't you go home? Shower, relax for a while. Hell, maybe even sleep. Take some time for yourself. I promise I'll call you the moment I hear anything."

Alec considered her options. Selene needed some time on her own to think, so going to her was out of the question. Hanging around the office was just going to agitate her, since there was little she could do. She focused on Selene's energy and knew she was still on the train, and she was calm, maybe even asleep. She had a thought. "Hey, Ama, if we do head to Italy, do you think you could see where Tis is? If she's anywhere in the vicinity, maybe she could meet us there?" Alec's worry about Tis's state of mind hadn't abated at all, and it would be good to check on her if possible.

Ama made herself a note. "I'll look into it. I think she was farther east than that, but I'll see. I think Meg is home, if you wanted to go hang out with her?"

Alec shook her head. "No, you're right. I could use a break." She turned to Zed, who'd been uncharacteristically quiet. "Do me a favor? Have a talk with Osiris about Esh. I know it won't do much good, but he shouldn't be allowed to walk away from this without a sanction of some kind." Sanctioning a god had become the only way to deal with unruly gods in a business where they all had to play nicely together, and it usually involved some form of taking away a power or right, which only their own higher god could do.

"I'll do it the moment you leave. Your job is hard enough; we don't need people messing things up." He stared out the window thoughtfully. "Although, if we look at the oracle, his interference might be what leads you to the next step in the puzzle. Perhaps it was meant to be as well."

Alec felt a headache coming on. She hated being so powerless. "Whatever. So long as he doesn't do it again. Oh, and I've put in an inquiry with the researchers about someone Selene described to me. If anything comes back, I want to know right away. I'm going home."

Alec left in the Hummer. She'd considered flying home, had wanted to open her wings and feel the freedom of the air rather than the pull of gravity on her feet. But she was too tired even for that. It was an exhaustion of the soul, and she felt the enormity of the situation, the complexity of emotions, settle inside her like leaden scales. Tilted one way or the other, her life would change. And where did that leave Selene?

She headed home, ready for her dark room and soft pillow. There was only so much she could do in a day, but knowing the days could be numbered, time was a shackle around her ankle. She thought about Selene lying curled in her arms on the beach, and sighed. She'd love to have her there now. She hadn't realized just how lonely she'd been, but Selene's presence in her life made it markedly more interesting, and when they weren't together, she craved her company.

What does it all mean? And why does every damn thing have to mean something?

She shed her clothes as she walked through her apartment and fell into bed. Exhausted, she fell asleep with images of Selene's body arched in orgasm dancing before her.

Chapter Twenty-one

T he train car was nearly empty. Selene hadn't seen the other passenger get on two stops after hers, but when he had, she'd felt that strange nervousness again. Like she'd felt on the train before, and when she'd been followed onto the freeway. He got on and took a seat in the next row, several seats down, but facing her. She glanced at him and looked away, but she could feel his eyes on her, and when she looked again, he was staring at her intently. She looked to the sides of him and saw it—the same strange fuzziness she saw around Alec and the Hummer.

He's not human.

The thought sent cold chills through her and she started trying to figure out her options. *How many times have I been so close to one and not known?* No one Alec had introduced her to had been malevolent, but the things that had followed her on the freeway hadn't been part of Cupid's entourage. Alec had said she was looking into it, but with everything else going on, they hadn't gotten around to talking about it any further. The moment they got together, it was like everything else ceased to matter. But the guy staring holes into her didn't look like he wanted to talk about cheesecake recipes. There was something wrong with his eyes…but from where she sat, she couldn't quite make out what it was.

She couldn't breathe properly. She slid her cell phone from her bag, ready to punch in Alec's number. She wished to hell she'd had Alec drive her home in her winged vengeance machine.

Battery low flashed in red across her screen. And then it went black.

Shit shit shit. She might only have one chance to call, and she'd need to do it fast. She knew, without understanding why, the creature on the train was there for her.

She pressed herself against her seat when the creature got up and started to move toward her, flashing sharp yellow teeth in a grisly smile.

Whoosh.

The door between the cars slid open, and the conductor stepped in just as they pulled to a stop at another station. "Well, hey there, stranger. It's been ages. How's things?"

Selene thought she might very well wet herself, she was so relieved to have Mark there. He sat down in the chair opposite her, his legs stretched out and his big hands over his protruding belly. The creature moved back toward the far door, and with a soft hiss, slid it open and left the car.

"Mark, did you see that man, just now? The one who just left?"

He looked around the empty car, puzzled. "I didn't see anyone. You sure you weren't sleeping or something?"

She bit her lip and sat on her hands to keep them from trembling. "Yeah, I must have been. Sorry. Things are great. How are things with you?"

He started talking about his newest interest in meditative psychology and spiritualism, and she only half listened, constantly watching the door to see if the creature reappeared. When Mark said a name that caught her attention, she focused on what he was saying.

"I mean, he makes a lot of sense, you know? But even if he makes all kinds of sense, if you don't have faith, if you don't have anything to believe in, then what is there? I don't know about you, but believing in my fellow human beings doesn't seem like the greatest answer."

"You're talking about Frey Falconi, right? Where did you come across him, again?"

"Boy, you sure are distracted today. You feeling okay? You look kind of pale. Want me to go grab you some water?" He rose to leave and she held up her hand.

"No! Please, don't go. Tell me more. I'm okay, really."

He looked dubious but stretched out again and kept talking. "I was listening to one of those talk radio stations, and he was the guest speaker. He sounded all right, like a nice guy, good sense of humor. I've always thought there had to be more to life, something out there afterward, you know? But man, I couldn't stop listening. It was like being hypnotized, and I started to think, yeah…you know, maybe this amazing planet really is enough. I mean, I don't know if I'm ready to give up my faith, but he's given me a lot to think about."

Selene thought about it. Alec had said belief gave people hope, beyond what their daily lives offered them. Frey believed they'd be better stripped of the mythologies and focused on the here and now. Who was right?

And where did creatures like the one she was watching for come in?

The train slowed and the voice over the intercom announced her station. Mark stood and looked out the window. She was paralyzed with fear. Did she get off and pray the thing wasn't there, waiting? What if it was?

Pray. Would it work? Zed, or Alec? If she prayed to one, would the other hear her? Alec wasn't a god, so would prayer work?

She closed her eyes, put her hands together in her lap, and thought, "I don't know if you can hear me, Zed. God of thunder, eater of Hindu foods. I need you. I need Alec. I need help. Please."

She opened her eyes and shrugged internally. How did you know if your prayers had been answered?

The train stopped, and the doors opened. Mark looked down at her, his smile kind. "Good to see you, Selene. I don't know what's the matter, and I don't know if you were just praying, but if you were, I bet they answer you. I think they always answer the converted quicker than the jaded believers. Don't know why, but I think they do." He squeezed her shoulder and turned to get off the train. "Don't wait too long, or you'll miss your stop."

Shaking, her legs weak, she moved toward the exit. She stepped into the bright sunlight, blinded, able only to see an enormous shadow of a man standing in front of her. She stumbled back, fear making her mute, and her arm was caught in a strong grip, pulling her away from the departing train.

She looked up into Zed's marble-like face and nearly wept with relief. *It worked. Prayer worked.* She felt dizzy with wonder and shock.

He put his arm around her and led her to his convertible BMW. "So, want to tell me why a prayer from you set off alarms in the building that have never gone off before?"

She stopped and looked around, feeling far braver with him next to her. "There was a…thing. I don't know what it was. Nothing Alec has ever introduced me to. It was…evil. Whatever that term means, that's what it was."

He frowned, deep lines creasing his face. "Have you seen anything like it before?"

"A few days ago. I told Alec, and she said she was looking into it. These things followed me from my house and onto the freeway. I saw their faces when I got off the exit…I don't know what they were. Strange eyes. The one on the train today, his eyes were strange too, but I can't tell you why. And all of his teeth were sharp, yellow. And he hissed."

Selene stared at the sky, which was quickly turning from blue to thunder clouds. Zed seemed to grow and his voice hurt her ears. "Get in the car." He took out his phone, and within seconds was issuing orders. "Find Alec. And Ama. And find out where Aka Manah is holed up these days. I'm taking Selene to get some of her things, and then we'll be back at the office."

Rain began to fall, big, bullet-like drops, and Selene began to shiver. Zed glanced at her and put the roof up. He flipped on the heat and she quickly felt better.

"Zed? What's going on? What are those things? Who is Aka Manah?"

"I think it would be better if we answered your questions back at the office, and started looking at some things from a different angle. For now, I'd like you to pack a bag, with enough for at least a week. We can bring you back if you need something else, of course, but the campus might be the best place for you right now."

Anger, raw and ready, rose within her. "I don't want to be forced from my home. Can't you just make them go away?"

He sighed. "The problem with creating a world where we all live in one place, is that no one has the kind of power over their domain they once had. In Greece, in my day, no one dared defy me. Now, at Afterlife, I'm still in charge in a big way. But there are things, other beings, who don't answer to me, or to anyone. And alone, I'm not entirely sure I'd be able to keep you safe. So, grab your things and we'll get back to base." He gave her what she assumed was meant to be a sympathetic look, although with his sharply chiseled features it was hard to tell. "I'm sorry, Selene. Being a demigod isn't easy."

Demigod. Half. God. She rolled the words around in her mind, tried to think of the many fables and tales she'd heard about half-god, half-human people. Cozy nights in front of a fire didn't seem to apply to most of them. Suddenly, she really, really wanted a cozy night in front of the fire.

"The demi bit means you think my father is human. But Alec said no one knows who my father is."

He nodded. "We're assuming, because you're aging normally. Though, now that you've been introduced to your real world, that may change. Who knows? The simplest option is that he was human. But we have no idea."

They pulled up in front of her house, and she ran to the door to avoid the pouring rain, punctuated by sharp cracks of thunder and eyeball-bursting flashes of lightning. But when she went to put her key in the door, it swung open. She hated the craven whimper that came from her, but the knowledge that Zed might not be enough to protect her made her wish Alec were there too.

Zed put an arm around her shoulders and pulled her close. He pushed the door open and they peered inside together. He held up his free hand and she saw a wicked looking silver lightning bolt appear in it. They entered the house.

Everything looked normal. Nothing was out of place.

But the stench of rot and putrefaction nearly made her vomit.

Zed looked down at her. "Quickly. Get your things. We need to go."

He followed her into her bedroom and stood guard as she haphazardly threw things into a suitcase, paying little attention to what was there. Given the smell in the house, the clothing might be unwearable anyway. She ducked into the bathroom and half-stifled a scream. Red and black splotches covered the walls in long swipes, as though hideous fingers had trailed paint along every surface. Zed came up behind her.

"Are you ready?" he said, looking around the bathroom. Thunder shook the house.

She swiped the contents on the counter into her toiletries bag, threw it in the suitcase, and nodded. Her heart was pounding so hard she wondered at what point she'd have heart failure.

Zed grabbed her case and she locked the door behind them. *Because that's going to do a lot of good.* She got in the car and Zed pulled away.

"You might want to close your eyes. I'm going to get us back quickly, and that doesn't always work well for human equilibrium."

She thought back to the myths and what had happened to some of the women Zeus had an interest in. She not only closed her eyes, but covered them with her hands.

It seemed hardly any time passed before Zed said, "You're okay to look now."

They pulled into the parking lot at Afterlife, Inc. Selene said, "Will Alec be here?"

"I sent her home to rest hours ago. When she does that, she's usually dead to the world." He laughed and the clouds began to lift slightly. A ray of sunshine broke through like a finger pointing at the building. "Not literally, mind you. But I tried to wake her up once, when I was having one of my…tantrums, she called them. And I've never been more terrified. So, if she's asleep, we might just have to wait."

The thought made Selene ache. She'd had to flee her home, and the only person she truly trusted was a woman with wings and fangs. But that's exactly who she wanted with her now. "How is it my prayer got through so fast? I mean, I hoped like hell it would, but I didn't really think…"

He sighed. "You didn't really think it would, because you're not really a believer?"

She nodded, sad that he looked so downcast.

"It came through because I had our parameters set to the highest sensitivity with regard to you, so that if anything at all came through from you, it came straight to me. And boy, did it. You set off sensors all over the building, not just in my sector. If I hadn't come, someone else would have. You might not believe in us as religious beings, but you believe in us because you've been around us, you've talked to us. You believe in what you can see, and so when you prayed, you were praying to someone you believed in, even if it isn't in the traditional way."

Selene's head began to throb, and she felt a migraine imminent. She'd prayed, and had the prayer answered, because the person she was praying to was real. What did that mean for religion as a whole? She thought of Frey's arguments and wondered what he would make of all this.

"Come on. Let's get you inside and see who is where. Then we'll get an idea what to do next."

She followed Zed inside, and when the glass doors slid shut behind her, she took a deep breath. *Safe. For now.*

CHAPTER TWENTY-TWO

Selene kept the bag of ice pressed to her temple. Alone in what appeared to be a staff office space, she lay on the couch trying desperately to get the migraine to ease. She'd taken her medication, but it still felt like an ice pick was being shoved through her head. Although she knew not much time had passed, she wondered how much longer it would be before Alec came to the office. A soft touch on her arm made her jump slightly, and she winced as pain shot through her skull. She moved her arm off her eyes and squinted at the person in front of her.

"Hi. I'm sorry to bother you, but Zed said you had a migraine, and I think I can help." Ama squatted beside her, looking concerned.

"If you can do anything at all, I'd be incredibly grateful. I can't function when I'm like this, and sitting in a building full of gods when I'm being chased by…things…doesn't seem like a great time to be incapacitated."

Ama laughed softly and brushed hair from Selene's face. "You couldn't be much safer than you are here, but point taken. Can you sit up?"

Selene sat up slowly, willing her stomach not to react. It probably wouldn't be good to vomit in a goddess's lap. Once upright, she closed her eyes against the waves of pain.

"Good. I'm just going to touch your head and shoulders. Hopefully, you'll start to feel better soon."

Ama's hands were gentle on her forehead, and as her fingertips slid softly down the side of her face, over her jaw, to her neck and then across to her shoulders, Selene felt the tension in her neck and head begin to ease. Ama repeated the motion a few more times, and the pain became nothing more than a manageable ache. She opened her eyes.

"Thank you so much. That feels so much better. I wish you were around all the time!"

Ama shook her head. "I'm sorry it's not working as it should. You're special, we know that, and maybe that's why. It usually only takes a touch, maybe two, before all the pain is gone. May I try a different spot?"

Selene shrugged. "Anything you like."

Ama motioned her to turn to the side, and she moved to sit behind Selene. She placed the base of her hands against the bottom of Selene's neck, and the skin quickly grew warm. Selene could feel it tingling all the way down her arms, and the last vestiges of the headache finally left her.

"There. That's better. Just had to get to the source."

Selene turned to face her. "I can't thank you enough. Can I repay you, somehow?"

Ama laughed. "Believe me, it's in our best interest to keep you healthy." She looked serious and gave Selene a searching look. "How are you holding up? Really?"

Selene sat back on the sofa and looked at the ceiling, trying to organize her thoughts. "Really? I don't know. I'm scared, for one. And I'm confused. I feel like I don't know what's going on, and every time I turn around it's as though I'm part of a game no one has told me I'm playing." She felt tears well up and tried to force them back. "To be honest, it's quite frustrating."

Ama leaned back and put an arm around her. "It must all seem very surreal right now. How can I help?"

"Can you explain even a quarter of what's going on?"

Ama shook her head. "I'm sorry, but I can't tell you much, no. That's Alec's job, and we have to let her do it."

"Okay, fair enough, I guess. Can you tell me more about Alec, then?"

"That I can do. What do you want to know?"

"Anything. Everything. Have you known her long?" Alec had told her there wasn't anything between her and Ama, and yet, Selene wondered how Alec would resist such a beautiful, kind woman.

"Alec and I go way back. For a time there was some crossover in our religions, and we developed some beings similar to Alec and her sisters. But as we didn't have them to begin with, because we were far younger than the religion she came from, she and her sisters stepped in as guides for a while, until our religion settled and decided we had no need for avenging spirits after all. But Alec would still come by and visit occasionally, if she was on my side of the world."

"What was she like? When she was younger?" *You know, younger than the five thousand years she is now...*

Ama laughed, full and sweet. "Temperamental! She had the patience of a trapped wasp, and if anything got in her way, she simply moved it. Whether that meant mountains or ships, it didn't matter. She was truly stunning."

Selene could hear the admiration in Ama's voice, and her stomach fell slightly. Had Alec lied to her? "And you two? Were you ever..."

"Goodness, no. Alec is...well, she's always been..." Ama stopped, clearly searching for the right words. "Selective. She's always been very discerning in the women she beds, which I can tell you is most unusual in a world like ours." She tilted her head, her brow furrowed slightly. "But then, she's also very private. So we might not know as much about her as we think we do." She rose and gave Selene a smile. "But I can tell you this much. I've never seen her so attentive to a woman as she's been to you. Now that may be because of the situation, or it may be something else. But I like it."

"And you and Zeus? Have you been together long?" Selene didn't want Ama to leave. Her presence was so calming, and Selene felt as though she had someone to talk to other than Alec.

"We've been together off and on for centuries. His wife isn't a big admirer of mine, and truth be told, I don't care for her much either. Fortunately, she took an outside world position, and we don't have to deal with her much. But it makes sense, Zeus and I. We're both sky gods, both at the top, both responsible for large numbers of people. I keep him grounded and he gives me…Well, I suppose he gives me passion." She smiled and winked. "And with that, I should get back to work. Are you okay here on your own?"

Selene nodded, still exhausted. "I think I'll just go to sleep for a while. Thank you again."

Ama waved as she left, and Selene lay down, her head pillowed on her arm. She didn't have much more information on Alec than she'd had before, but somehow, talking to people who knew her made Selene feel that much closer to her. *I wish you were here.*

Selene closed her eyes and drifted into a dreamless sleep.

Alec woke from a deep sleep, the words reverberating in her head. *I wish you were here.* It was as though Selene had spoken right into her ear. She bolted from bed and grabbed her phone. Five missed calls and three missed texts.

Z: Need you in office now.

Z: I know I told you to rest. But problems with Selene.

Z: Wake up, you lazy old bat.

What the Hades? Alec hit the speed dial for Zed. "What's going on? What do you mean problems with Selene? Is she okay?"

"If you didn't sleep the way you do, you'd know. I've always told you to have Heph make you some kind of alarm that would wake—"

"Zed, is Selene safe? Don't irritate me."

He laughed and she held the phone away from her ear. She'd been fairly even-tempered for centuries, but she was finding that when it came to Selene, nothing was certain, not even her own patience.

"She's fine. But I did have to go to her place to get her. Alec, we think she's being followed by daevas."

Alec sat down, trying to work through what Zed had said. "Seriously? What makes you think that?"

"Well, apparently, she saw a few of them the other day, the things you asked the research team about. And when one was on the train with her today, the poor thing decided prayer was her only option. Fortunately, I heard her and got there in time. But the damn things left a nasty mess in her house."

"Where is she now?" Alec moved quickly through her place, pulling on clothes and transforming to her more human-like state.

"She's sleeping in the staff room, safe and sound. She had a migraine Ama took care of, and then she went back to sleep. But she's been asking for you."

Alec grabbed her keys and headed to the Hummer. "I'll be there in a few minutes." She hung up and headed for work. The thought that Selene had been in trouble, serious trouble, if it really was daevas, and she not only hadn't known, but hadn't been there for her, made Alec want to punch, or kill, something. She settled for pounding her fist on the steering wheel, which dented slightly but didn't bend.

When she pulled up outside Afterlife, she looked around. Although no one seemed to be there, she could feel a presence that wasn't one of theirs. She growled slightly before heading inside. Cerberus was in her true form, and Alec gave her a scratch behind her ears and smiled slightly when her back leg twitched. "Keep an eye out, okay? Something isn't right."

Cerberus gave her a lick from the middle head, while the right one tried to put her head out for another scratch. The third head stayed turned toward the front door.

Alec headed straight for Zed's office. When Selene woke, she'd want information, and Alec needed to be able to give it to her.

"Do we know anything more?"

"Hello to you too. I'm fine, thank you." Zed didn't look up from his computer. "And, yes. We've located Chandra. But we don't have any more information on Selene's new friends."

"That's something. Where's Chandra?"

"Lake Nemi, Italy."

"Trust her to go somewhere with a lake dedicated to her. Can you get me a specific location?"

"Already in your email." Zed looked at her. "Are you really going to take her there?"

Alec sighed and ran her hands through her hair. "I wasn't entirely sure before, but now I don't think I have a choice. Chandra might know more than we do, and I don't think she's going to tell anyone other than Selene if she does."

Zed looked thoughtful. "That's true. She never would tell me about her child, or why she gave her up rather than raise her among us. Had Selene grown up with us, surely it would have made everything simpler? Maybe Chandra got a different version of the oracle, I don't know. And obviously she doesn't have to answer to anyone, let alone me." He stood and came around the desk. Placing his hands on Alec's shoulders, he said, "You know we'll support you in any way you need. But be careful, Alec. We don't fully understand everything at play, and at the end of the day, she's a human. You know how unreliable they can be." He placed one hand over her heart. "Be careful with this. It takes a hell of a long time to heal."

She kissed his cheek, aware how insubstantial he felt. "I'll do what I can, and I'll be as careful as I can. I promise." She stepped back, needing a bit of physical space. Being that close to a god could be overwhelming, even for her. "Can you book us flights to Italy? The sooner the better, I think." She moved toward the doorway and said over her shoulder, "I'm going to check on Selene and make sure she's okay to go. If you hear glass breaking, come save me."

He laughed. "No way. If you piss her off, you're on your own. I've had my fill of angry women."

She smiled as she walked down the hall. Jesus and Mohammed were talking by the water cooler, and she gave them a wave as she passed. While the religions fought over who was right on the outside, inside the office, there were no such arguments. Everyone knew they needed believers, and trying to build a batch of believers that took away from the other religions only hurt everyone. When people started believing in gods other than the ones they followed originally, that faith was always just a little weaker, and eventually, it often faded altogether, leaving the deity in question weaker, or possibly, gone.

She entered the staff room and found a nymph staring at Selene, her head tilted like a confused dog's. The nymph gave Alec a licentious grin and moved so she could press her lithe body against Alec's.

"I saw you at the party the other day. I could take care of your needs better than this little meat bag could. All you have to do is ask."

Alec smiled politely. She desperately wanted the girl gone, but making a nymph angry could have badly bizarre results. The last person who had upset one had ended up with a strange case of VD, something gods couldn't actually contract. He'd had to beg the nymphs to take it away, publicly, before they gave him the cure.

"I don't doubt that for a second. But you see, this particular meat bag is important to the company, my own feelings aside. So I have to do what I have to do, right?"

The nymph pouted but moved out of Alec's personal space. "Well, when you're all done, come find me. I've heard good things…"

She waved as she headed off down the hall, her bark-like skin shimmering under the fluorescent office lights. Alec shook her head. Politics were the last area she'd wanted to get into, and yet, she was up to her feathers in them now. She sat gingerly on the edge of the couch next to Selene, who lay on her side, facing the window. She raised her hand to touch her, but before she did, she studied her profile.

Asleep, so relaxed and soft, she still had a slight frown line, as though even in sleep she was deep in thought. *She's so beautiful.* Alec's heart beat a little faster. She wanted to lie down beside her, pull her close, and keep her safe. But none of them were safe, and now Selene wasn't safe either. *It's my fault. I brought her into our world, and now she's got rabid dingoes after her.* But that wasn't completely true. Yes, Alec had brought Selene into their world, but it was foretold. Whether or not Alec had done it, Selene would have ended up in their world no matter what.

"I didn't look at the nymph because she creeped me out and gave me the willies. And now you're doing it."

Alec started. Selene's eyes were still closed, she hadn't moved...Then she saw her reflection in the window Selene lay facing. "Clever."

Selene turned over to face Alec. "I'm so glad you're here. Even if you do stalker-stare while I'm sleeping."

Alec caressed Selene's cheek. "I'm sorry I wasn't around. I should have driven you home. I should never have let you go alone."

Selene shook her head and placed her hand over Alec's. "There was no way to know, and it's not like you've had a ton of time to figure it out." She sat up and rubbed the sleep from her eyes. "Do you know anything new?"

Alec had to exert all her willpower not to pull Selene into her arms. She looked so sweet, so vulnerable. *So human.* "Not about your fan club."

"Then about what?"

Alec stood and moved away, needing a bit of distance in order to think clearly. "We found Chandra." Alec waited for the words to sink in. Selene closed her eyes and sat so still Alec briefly wondered if she'd fallen back asleep.

"Where?" she asked softly.

"Italy. We can get a flight tonight." Alec poured Selene a glass of water, not sure what else to do with her hands. "But I should warn you—"

"No. You've warned me enough. I want to see her."

"But—"

"Please. Alec, my whole life, I've been alone. I was a child sent from house to house like a regift no one wanted. And now I have the chance to learn why." She took Alec's hands in her own. "Please."

Alec rested her forehead against the top of Selene's head. "Okay. Let me find out our flight details."

Selene looked up at her. "Why do we need a plane? I thought you just zapped yourself wherever you wanted to go. Or flew, or something."

"I tend to take the Hummer, because it's less tiring, and it's like being zapped somewhere, as you say. But we can't drive to Italy, even in the Hummer, and although I could fly there, it would be a hell of a lot harder with a passenger in my arms."

Selene grinned, and then began to laugh. "The fact that I even asked the question makes me doubt my sanity, yet again. Thank you for explaining it to me, even though it was ludicrous."

Alec took her hand and led her from the staff room toward Zed's office. "When it comes to our world, ludicrous is often the theme of the day, so never hold back with the questions." She stepped into Zed's office and raised an eyebrow when he came around the desk to give Selene a hug.

"How are you feeling?"

"Much better, thank you. Ama has quite the touch."

He laughed and wiggled his eyebrows. "Oh, in more ways than you can imagine." He turned to Alec. "Your flights are booked. You'll arrive tomorrow afternoon, and one of our associates will meet you at the airport." He moved to the window and pointed. "See that house there, with the blue shutters? That's going to be Selene's until we figure this mess out and she can go back to her place." He turned around. "Will that suffice?"

Selene nodded. "I suppose it will have to. Thank you for setting it up for me."

Alec turned to Selene. "Let's grab your things, and I'll head over there with you. Then we'll get ready to head to the airport." She turned to Zed and said quietly, "I have Cerberus on alert. Something felt funny when I came in."

Zed cleared his throat and gave her a sharp nod. "I already had Selene's things taken over there. But let me know if there's anything else you need. I'll do a perimeter sweep."

Alec once again took Selene's hand and led her out of Zed's office. This time they headed down the back stairwell, which opened into the big open square outside the main building. She didn't let go of her hand as they walked. She needed to feel her solidity, to know she was okay.

"Alec?"

"Yeah?"

"Do you know what those things are? Or when I can go home?"

Alec opened the door to Selene's small, temporary cottage. Everything inside seemed to have been made for her. Big, comfy chairs, libraries of books lining the walls, and stacks of teas and coffees in the open plan kitchen suggested someone had taken the time to make it just right.

"Tea?" Selene nodded and Alec put the kettle on. "They're called daevas. We think that's what they are, anyway, based on your description as well as what Zed saw at your house. The research team came up with the same idea. They're a kind of demon, known for mischief and chaos. Their keeper is Aka Manah, a Zoroastrian demon with a lot of time on his hands and not much to do." She pulled together their tea while she talked, the task helping her concentrate on more than her desire to hold Selene. "Aka leads them, but they've been in existence for nearly as long as humans. They're manifestations of humans' petty sides. So, unfortunately, they don't require belief either. Aka simply took over managing them, a job no one else wanted. Satan has his own, but they're not daevas. Just standard demons, and he keeps a tight rein on them."

"But why are they after me?" Selene took a sip of tea, her eyes closed, and made a sound of appreciation.

Alec knew what other sounds Selene made, and tried not to think of them, and tried not to notice the way Selene's lips touched the mug. *So soft...* "That, we're definitely not sure about. But trust me when I say everyone available is trying to find out."

They drank their tea in silence. Alec could practically see the thoughts flying through Selene's mind, but she didn't want to push her. When she was done with her tea, she set it aside and leaned forward. "Selene? Are you sure? I mean, really, really certain? If she's not what you hope, or what you wanted her to be, or turns out to be something you don't like...can you handle that?"

Selene stared at Alec for a long moment, her gaze searching. "I don't have any preconceived notions. All I know is I spent my life thinking my mother and father were dead. Now, not only is that not true, but the truth itself is…unbelievable. So yes, I'm sure. And I'll deal with whatever we find."

Alec had no choice but to believe her, and there were too many possibilities for answers to deny that going might be beneficial on more than one level. "I'm going to leave you to pack, and I'm going to run home and grab a few things. I'll be back in about an hour." She grinned. "Let's go find your mother."

CHAPTER TWENTY-THREE

Selene stepped off the plane in Italy, stretching and yawning. Apparently, one of the benefits of living forever was the ability to save enough money to always fly first class. *What a perk.* When she'd finally managed to fall asleep, it was in a seat that turned into a fully reclined bed. The only downside was that she and Alec couldn't sleep next to each other, although Alec had offered to substitute as Selene's mattress. She was woken with warm towels to wash her face and hands, and plenty of orange juice and coffee. She felt like Little Orphan Annie thrown into the Warbucks mansion, if Annie were a mythological creature and the Warbucks mansion was Mount Olympus. Alec laughed at her constantly, but she didn't mind. She loved Alec's laugh, and seeing her smile made Selene feel like she'd won a prize.

She shivered when she felt Alec's hand on her back.

"Our guide should be waiting by baggage claim."

Selene nodded. The closer they'd gotten to landing, the more nervous she'd become. Sleep had included dreams where she was searching, running, and hiding, but she couldn't figure out to or from what. When she'd opened her eyes, Alec was right there beside her, her hand resting lightly on Selene's shoulder as she read a magazine. It was comforting, as well as scary, how right it felt. Even now, knowing what she did.

They headed for baggage claim, and her thoughts ran in circles. What would her mother look like? Would she be glad they'd come?

Would she turn them away? Would she be a white lump of rock imbued with human traits?

A short, swarthy man approached them with a wide smile and his hands out. "Alec. How lovely to see you again after all these years."

Alec gave him a hug and the requisite European kiss on both cheeks. "Picus. How have you been?"

He shrugged and laughed. "The real world isn't so bad. I get to taste everything, with no one looking over my shoulder and no one asking me for things they don't deserve. It's a trade-off, yes?" He turned to Selene and held open his arms. "And you! Welcome to Italia. I understand you have a specific reason for coming? Well, let's get your things and we'll talk about it in the car."

Selene liked him. She couldn't place his name, but his energy was happy, light, and endearing. *At least he isn't like Eshnu, or one of those oversexed female gods.* The thought of being in Italy and watching someone fawn over Alec brought on an instant case of irritation. She saw plenty of people, both men and women, look at Alec admiringly, but the way the female gods threw themselves at her was something else, and she sure as hell knew she didn't like the thought of Alec being with some curvy, bitchy nymph.

Picus grabbed her bag for her, and she followed them out to the little convertible waiting by the curb.

"Why do so many gods like convertibles?" she asked, thinking of Zed's car as well as others she'd seen outside Meg's house.

"Open skies, sweet lady. None of us like being closed in, especially those of us who are gods of the outdoors."

Alec held the door open for Selene. "Picus was the Roman god of farming, until the Christians took over and urbanization began."

"I faded faster than many of the gods, and so I took the chance to get out. And ah, the things I've seen! The women I've loved!" He grinned at Selene in the rearview mirror. "I've relished my existence among the humans."

She smiled at him, but she was too nervous to engage in the kind of conversation he was offering. Alec seemed to understand.

"So, how far is it to Nemi? I haven't been anywhere outside Rome and Venice in centuries."

"And shame on you for that, old friend. Nemi is only about an hour away. I've booked you into a hotel in the town, and after dinner, I'll take you where you want to go." His expression turned serious. "Are you sure that's where you want to go?"

"Yes. We're sure." Selene didn't want to risk losing out on her chance by there being any question.

He tilted his head slightly. "Okay. Just checking. She won't be available until evening, of course." He turned to Alec. "Now, tell me about life in Los Angeles. How are things at headquarters?"

Alec proceeded to give him a rundown of the different factions in the building, spending plenty of time on the Roman section. He asked questions about people Selene hadn't heard of, and they laughed about various old escapades. Selene zoned them out, paying attention to the beautiful countryside and thinking about the night to come. The afternoon air was warm but she still wrapped her arms around herself, chilled from within. Almost as soon as she'd done it, Alec was leaning back to place her jacket over Selene like a blanket. She gave Selene a wink and turned back to the conversation, and Selene snuggled up in the warmth of Alec's jacket. She pressed her face to the black material and breathed in Alec's scent. Instantly calmer, she continued taking in their surroundings. Soon, they pulled up in front of a charming terracotta colored building adorned with trailing vines and enormous pots of flowers.

"Here we are. They serve breakfast each morning, but I'm not sure how long you'll be here. More than tomorrow morning and you'll need to let them know."

They all got out, and Picus and Alec took the bags. Cool slate tiles led them into a large, airy reception area. The friendly receptionist checked them in and handed them a single key. Alec turned to Selene. "Do you mind sharing a room with me?"

Picus turned red. "I'm sorry. I thought I booked two rooms. I can look for another hotel."

Selene rolled her eyes. "Alec, is that a serious question?"

Alec laughed. "It doesn't hurt to check. I wouldn't want to make assumptions."

Picus looked relieved. "Okay. I'll let you get settled in. I suggest a walk along the lake. About half a mile away there is a lovely bistro with good wine and a beautiful view. You must try their strawberry pie. I'll pick you up around six for dinner."

They waved him off and Selene asked Alec, "Why do we have to wait until after dinner to see my mother?"

Alec picked up their bags and Selene followed her to their room. "Chandra is mostly nocturnal. She's often up during the day, but she's not at her best."

Of course. Naturally. Selene sighed and wondered when this new world would begin to make sense.

Selene came out of the bathroom, toweling her hair. She'd stood under the hot water and let it soothe the knots in her shoulders and the migraine pulsing at the base of her neck. She'd tried to meditate, to clear her mind and just feel the spray on her skin. If she was going to get clarity, she had to make room in her mind, clear a space to think rationally. *About a completely irrational situation.* She'd finally managed to get a sliver of peace, but when she focused on her body, and the hot water, she became aware of her aching nipples and the tingle between her thighs. The feel of Alec's hands on her, in her, the way the feathers felt beneath her…she'd taken the shower head off the wall and aimed it where she needed it most, while thinking of Alec making love to her on the beach. She came silently, her head thrown back and her thighs shaking.

She looked at Alec, lying on the bed, her eyes closed and her enormous wings spread across the white sheets. *A dark angel. No. Not an angel at all. Something else entirely.* Selene moved to the bed and slowly drew her fingertips from the top of Alec's foot over her shin, up her thigh, and softly over the crease between her soft, dark mound to the top of her leg. Then over her taut, tight stomach, between her breasts and along her collarbone. Selene met her eyes, which were dark with lust and dancing with a soft blue light.

"Can I make love to you?" Selene asked softly.

"Of course you can. But you know I love touching you—"

"No. I mean, to you. The real you. Not the one you show me on a daily basis. The you without the magic stuff. I want to take my mind off everything and concentrate on you."

Alec frowned and pulled Selene to her. "Why would you want that, baby? It's all me, just a different outfit, so to speak."

"But it's not, is it? It's a pretense. I want the real thing."

Alec stared at her for a long time, searching her expression. Finally, she nodded slightly. "If you're sure. But if you get freaked out, or change your mind, just say so. Or hell, just stop, and I'll get the message."

Selene gave her a long, lingering kiss, starting slightly when she felt Alec's fangs at the sides of her lips. When she opened her eyes, Alec's eyes were the color of the ocean at sunset, blues mixed with blacks and reds. Her pupils were oblong, like a cat's, and her look was decidedly feral. Selene found the desire emanating from her intoxicating.

She crawled onto the bed and lay against Alec's body, tracing her contours. She was all muscle, with no discernible body fat. Her skin wasn't soft and mushy like a human's, but rather firm, like a dolphin's. Her hands, the ones Selene often thought about, looked the same, except for the deadly sharp, blackish-gray nails. Her six-pack trembled under Selene's touch. It was then Selene felt powerful. This beautiful, deadly creature actually wanted, *needed*, her touch. She slid lower, exploring slowly. Her thighs were rock hard, like marble, as were her shins and feet. Her toes were slightly long, again tipped with lethal looking nails, and as Selene drew her fingertips over each toe individually, she gave Alec a questioning look.

"There were several early centuries we lived in trees and caves. We needed to be able to hang on properly."

Selene nodded but kept exploring. She made her way up the inside of Alec's thighs and stopped at the apex. She breathed in her musky, spicy scent, one she could almost taste. Heat radiated from her, and as Selene carefully parted her, she knew it was one area Alec was all woman.

She flicked Alec's clit while keeping eye contact, and couldn't help but smile when Alec groaned and let her head fall back. *So beautiful. So astonishing.* She tasted hot, if heat had a taste. Smooth, almost alcoholic. Selene reveled in it and licked, sucked, and swirled her tongue over Alec's quickly engorging clit. Alec's hands tangled in her hair, holding her still as she rode Selene's mouth. Just as she was about to come, she looked down at Selene, who met her gaze with an expression she hoped conveyed just how sexy she found her.

Alec exploded with a cry, arching her back, her wings folding toward the ceiling, her tongue darting out, her nails raking Selene's scalp. Selene swallowed and held on until Alec's body relaxed again. She rested her head against Alec's thigh as they both came down. She would need to ponder how it felt, making love to something not human, but for now, she just wanted to sink into the afterglow of the moment.

"Come here."

She scooted up the bed to lay in Alec's arms. When she looked up, Alec had returned to her more human looking self.

"Why did you change back?"

Alec kissed the top of her head. "I suppose I really only use my true form when I'm working now. Being in it with you during sex is hot, but I'm actually more comfortable in this form when I'm just relaxing. Is that okay?"

Selene laughed. "Okay? You're the sexiest woman I've ever laid eyes on, in either form. Yes, I'm good with it."

Alec wrapped her arms and wings around Selene. "You okay?"

Selene could hear the vulnerability in Alec's question. "I'm more than okay. You're breathtaking. Thank you for letting me."

They lay quietly for a long time before Alec said softly, "I haven't let anyone touch me that way in a long time. Since…well, a long time. I'm usually fine with giving. Thank you for wanting me." She placed a gentle kiss on Selene's head and held her a bit tighter.

Selene held tight but wasn't sure what to say. *What do you say to comfort a fury?* Instead, she kissed Alec's shoulder and snuggled in closer. *Sometimes words aren't necessary.* She fell asleep, grateful for the respite from her overwhelming life.

CHAPTER TWENTY-FOUR

Selene looked around the lovely café. With oddly matched wooden tables and rustic chairs, the canopied outside allowed for a perfect view over the lake, as Picus had promised. The vodka and orange juice relaxed her somewhat, and she dipped her bread in a beautiful tasting olive oil mixture.

"So, how far away does my mother live?" Selene asked.

Picus grinned slightly and motioned across the lake. "You can see her house from here."

Selene scanned the area but saw only a ruined castle... "The castle? She lives in a ruin?"

He laughed. "That's not a ruin, child. It might look a little run-down from here, but believe me when I say it's fully functional. She's renting it from the family who owns it. They're away for the winter, because they like to go to the Caribbean this time of year. They won't be back until June, and by then she will have moved on, as she does."

Selene stared at the castle, trying to imagine what was beyond the forbidding stone walls. *So close. She's so close.* She started when Alec put a hand over hers.

"Just a little while longer, okay? Let's have dinner, and then we'll head over."

Picus turned to Alec. "Oh, I have a message from your sister, Tisera. She wanted to join us, but she's working on a case in Syria and can't make it over. She said she'd catch you when she gets back to the States."

Alec thanked him, and Selene saw the flash of disappointment in her eyes before she covered it with a joke. *I wonder what that would be like. To have siblings to miss?* Selene turned her attention back to the conversation at hand, but her stomach was doing backflips, and she didn't think she could eat anything. She picked at her pasta, but when the strawberry dessert came, she moaned at the sweetness of the strawberries. Alec grinned and held one up after dipping it in cream.

"Want it?" She placed the stem end between her teeth and wiggled her eyebrows suggestively.

Selene gladly went for it, closing her mouth slowly around it while keeping her eyes on Alec's. She watched the desire flare in them as she bit through the strawberry and leaned back.

Picus gave a low laugh and pretended to fan himself. "I have an entirely new appreciation for strawberries."

"Me too," Alec said, chewing the rest of the strawberry while gazing at Selene.

They finished their dessert and coffee, and Selene's stomach backflips turned into swan dives. She wasn't sure her legs would support her.

Alec slipped her hand under Selene's elbow as they walked to the car. "You can do this. And I'll be right beside you the whole time. If you want to leave, all you have to do is say so."

Selene nodded, unable to speak her mouth was so dry.

They made the short drive around the lake, and Picus parked at the bottom of the ramp leading into the castle. "I'll wait for you here, ladies. I have the greatest respect for Chandra, but I also have a healthy dose of fear." He blew Selene a kiss. "Good luck, bella."

They got out, and Selene's legs felt like they'd collapse. *I can do this. I can do this.*

They got to the main gate and Alec used the enormous metal ring to knock, creating a resounding thudding sound that echoed all around them. She closed her eyes and her brow furrowed.

"What are you doing? What's going on?" Selene whispered.

"I'm trying to let her know it's us, not some people who want to tour the castle."

"What, you're trying to mind-meld with her? Now you've got telepathy?" Selene's nerves were getting the best of her, and she found herself wanting to shake Alec.

Alec opened one eye and looked at her. "Would you shush? I can explain later, but for now—"

"It's rude to tell someone not to speak."

Selene spun around to face the woman speaking, and if it hadn't been for Alec's arm around her waist, she might have collapsed to her knees.

She was staring at a spitting image of herself. *If I glowed, I'd look just like her. And if I looked...harder.* The woman was unmistakably her mother, and the strange halo around her told the truth of what Alec and Zed had told her. There was nothing earthly about her.

"It's not rude if they're interrupting a conversation in progress," Alec said. She slowly withdrew her arm from around Selene's waist and moved toward Chandra. She held open her arms. "It's nice to see you again."

Chandra's glow dimmed slightly and she smiled. She stepped into Alec's embrace and held her tightly. Her eyes were closed, and her face softened. Selene thought she looked genuinely happy to see Alec, and she was glad. It would have been a difficult visit if she'd turned them away.

They pulled apart and Chandra looked over Alec's shoulder at Selene. Her chin went up and her glow increased. "Selene."

Selene stepped forward, trembling. "Mother."

Chandra's head tilted slightly, and the moment seemed to stretch unbearably. Slowly, her glow dimmed so Selene could see her properly again, and she began to smile. "I knew I'd see you again one day. I'm so glad that day has come." She opened her arms.

Selene couldn't move. Her hands twitched, and although she wanted to move, desperately wanted to go to her mother, the shock of the moment, the surreal feeling, all became overwhelming. Fortunately, her mother took the initiative and came to her instead.

She enfolded Selene in her embrace, and Selene began to cry. She let the tears come, let the sobs tear through her. "I can't believe...I just don't..." There were no words for what she was feeling.

Her mother left an arm around her shoulders and motioned to Alec. "Let's go inside." She waved at the door and it opened in front of them, and after they'd entered, it closed loudly behind them.

Selene stopped crying long enough to look around. There were thick, sumptuous rugs lining the long, wide hallway. Arched doorways led to rooms off to the left and right, but they headed for the largest archway ahead of them and into an enormous, ornately decorated living room. Heavy draperies covered the stone walls, with depictions of Roman myths beautifully worked into the fabric. Overstuffed sofas sat before a huge fireplace with a roaring fire already burning brightly. Chandra sat beside Selene on one of the sofas, and Alec sat across from them on another.

"Would you like a drink? Something to eat?"

Selene sniffed, hoping there wasn't snot running down her face. "Tea, if you have it?"

Chandra rang a small bell next to her, and a stunning young woman appeared in the doorway, wearing a sheer, flowing white gown. "Bring some green tea, please." She looked at Alec. "For you, my dark friend?"

Alec shook her head. "I'm good, thanks."

Chandra turned to Selene. "You must have so many questions."

"You have no idea."

"No, I probably don't. But why don't you start with the most important ones to you at the moment, and we'll go from there?"

Selene thought for a moment, trying to gather herself. *What do you ask your goddess mother?* "Why did you give me up? I suppose that's the one that has haunted me all my life."

Chandra sighed and her face hardened. "The most complicated question first." She stood and moved toward the fireplace. She looked at Alec. "You know about the oracle, I assume, or she wouldn't be here with you?"

Alec nodded.

Chandra turned back to Selene. "How much have you been told about the oracle?"

"Not much. Nothing I truly understand."

"Then it's fitting you hear it from me."

The young woman in the beautiful dress entered with a tray and set the tea items down in front of them. Selene was no expert, but they looked like they might have come with the original castle. They were heavy, ornate, and probably irreplaceable. *Please don't let me drop them.*

Chandra laughed softly. "They're just things, Selene. Nothing more. Items are meant to be used, and they eventually disappear. As do all things." Her cold gaze slid over Alec, who moved to pour the tea.

"The oracle?" Selene studied her mother, trying to take her in. She was tall, but not as tall as Alec. Slim, but somehow solid. Her cheekbones were high, her face sharp angles and shadows. She was attractive, beautiful, perhaps, but distant and cold. *Is that how people see me?*

"Yes." Chandra stared into the flames. "Do you know, there have been very few female demigods, the most famous of whom is Helen, daughter of Zeus and Leda. Achilles, Hercules, Perseus... names you know. But rarely do you know the women." She took a cup of tea from Alec and inclined her head in thanks. "I was on one of my many jaunts here. I watched the people around me in a dance club, swaying, making connections through the music and intoxicants of various kinds, and I realized how alone I was. Granted, I don't often desire anyone near me, and I usually stay in the heavens where I'm most comfortable, but on that occasion...I wanted a companion."

Selene sat gripping her tea, fascinated. *Lonely. I know that feeling.*

"I found one. I knew at the time he wasn't human, not entirely. But he was human enough. We went to a nearby woodland and had sex. It was good." Chandra's smile was wistful. "Very good. In the morning, he kissed my forehead and went on his way. It wasn't meant to be anything more than what it was." She sat on a straight-backed chair near the fireplace, the flames lighting up the wall behind her. "You can imagine my surprise when you came along shortly after."

"Shortly after? Was I premature?"

Chandra's laugh was hollow, eerie. "No, child. We don't have the need to carry a child as long as humans do. What surprised me, however, was the guests who arrived at the time of your birth." She held out her mug and Alec quickly refilled it. "The Fates showed up in my room, all three of them. I hadn't seen the Sisters in many, many years, and I admit I wasn't happy they showed up that night. Like Death, they're rarely bearers of good news. They told me—"

She stopped and stared off, seemingly lost in her thoughts.

"Yes?"

She looked at Selene, and Selene shivered slightly under the cold, distant stare.

"In their usual infuriatingly vague way, they told me you were going to be a savior. A bridge between worlds, to keep both from destroying each other and themselves. But to be that bridge, you had to be hidden away, kept safe from those who would harm you when the time came for you to act. Without you, the world as we know it, human and god, would cease to exist. They wrote most of it down in the version of the oracle you have in California, but the other information they imparted only to me. Apparently, your father, as a being of both your world and mine, was important somehow. That way you had enough of my world to belong in it, but enough of your world to exist there as well." She gave a strangely stiff shrug. "The Fates know, and to disbelieve the oracles they pass down is to be reckless, no matter what kind of being you are. So I brought you to the orphanage, so they could find a proper family to bring you up. Of course, I kept an eye on you, always. I knew what you were doing, where you were, and what you'd made of yourself, despite the oafish humans you ended up with. I knew, however, that I couldn't come to you and risk showing your enemies where you were." She looked at Selene and her gaze softened so much that she looked almost real. "I'm sorry, daughter. I had to do what was best."

Once again, words failed her. Alec came and wrapped an arm around her, and she leaned thankfully into the embrace. "I won't pretend to understand. What does that mean? A bridge?" She turned to Alec. "And where do you fit in?"

"The oracle only gives us pieces, never the full picture. The Fates figure that if people knew exactly what was coming, they'd stop doing other things, or do stupid things, because they knew there wouldn't be consequences. So we each only get a piece of the

FURY'S BRIDGE

puzzle." She looked at Chandra. "For instance, I didn't know what your mother just told us about your father." She sighed and shook her head. "Chandra's right, the Fates are infuriating that way. They alone know the whole story, but they'll never just tell you the whole damn thing and save everyone a lot of headaches and frustration. They've dictated people's lives in their weaving, and the rest of us abide by what they say. Truthfully, they're more powerful than any of us. And it's true, we're fading at an alarming rate these days. Something needs to be done to stop it, or everything at Afterlife will fade away. You know, except those few of us who exist without believers. But I don't know about the part where the human world falls apart too. Maybe because they need the gods after all? I don't know."

Selene felt like she was going to be sick, but the idea of vomiting on the ancient carpet kept her mouth shut. "You're saying I'm responsible for saving all those people you've introduced me to? People I didn't believe in." She looked at her mother. "And you're telling me bad people are out to get me, because I'm supposed to be a bridge of some kind, although we don't know what kind, to save the planet." She could feel the hysteria rising, but didn't bother to keep it down. "Great. Excellent. That sounds just fucking fabulous. No problem, let's go save the world, Alec. Or worlds, as the case may be. That should be nice and simple." The room started to spin, and Alec pulled her over so her head was between her knees.

"Breathe, baby. Come on, Selene. I know it's a lot to take in. But you can't fall apart."

"Can't I?" Selene pulled away from Alec and stood. She started pacing, gesticulating at the air violently. "I think I can, thank you very much. I think I can completely fall apart. You know why?" She pointed at them both in turn. "Because evidently, it won't matter. The oracle says I'm the one, which means I can fall apart, have a breakdown, if I'm not already having one, become a heroin addict, get involved in gang wars, eat peanut butter and banana sandwiches on the toilet, and have unprotected sex with a ton of people, and it won't matter. Because the *Fates* say so."

Chandra watched her impassively, while Alec looked at her helplessly.

She turned to her mother. "So, you have no idea who my father is. Does he know I exist?"

Chandra's smile was thin. "I do, and he did."

Selene waited, but no more was forthcoming. "So, did you want to let me in on this little secret too?"

Chandra was silent, her stare focused and unwavering as she watched Selene pace. "He was a demi-demon named Clark."

Alec straightened and looked sharply at Chandra. "A demi-demon? Who was his maker?"

Chandra's expression didn't change. She flicked a glance at Alec before returning her attention to Selene. "I don't know. I never found out, and he was killed by a rabid monkey in India before I could ever speak to him again. But yes, he did know about you. I told him to stay away from you, and he did so. As a demon, he wasn't terribly interested in childrearing, but as a human, he could be rather sentimental."

Selene clutched her arms around herself and closed her eyes. *If I click my heels three times. If I pinch myself, or drink an elixir, or wave a wand...something must be able to get me out of this nightmare.* But when she opened her eyes, the world was the same as when she'd closed them. Her mother, goddess of the moon, and her lover, a winged fury out of some people's nightmares, were staring back at her.

Her mother moved toward her, and the closer she came, the calmer Selene felt. By the time her mother grasped her hands in her own, Selene felt like she could breathe. Her mother's expression had softened again, and Selene was struck by the ephemeral nature of her mother's expressions and reactions. The moon was solid, immovable. And that's how her mother seemed, at a distance. But now, standing in front of her, was a soft woman with kind, strangely navy colored eyes. There were specks in them, white ones, and Selene realized she was looking at stars in her mother's eyes.

"Selene, my daughter. My child. I'm sorry this burden has fallen on you. I'm sorry you grew up so alone, and that I couldn't be there for you. If you'll have me now, I'll try to be what you wanted when you were young." She looked at Alec and smiled. "Alec will tell you I'm not always easy to be around, and it's true. But I can try, and maybe we can meet in the middle. If nothing else, I can be another person on your side as you face your destiny."

"But what if I don't want this destiny? What if I want to make my own fate?" Selene whispered.

Chandra shook her head sadly. "I'm afraid none of us are able to escape our fates, child. That's the one constant. Even I was subject to a fate I didn't know about, by having you."

Selene looked at Alec, who got up and came to her right away. "What can I do?"

Selene took her hands from her mother's and turned to Alec. "I need to process. I need to breathe." She looked at her mother. "Can we talk more tomorrow? I don't even know what questions I've got left at the moment."

Chandra stepped back, her cold visage back in place. "Of course. My priestess will show you to your room, and we can discuss the next steps at breakfast tomorrow." Her mask slipped briefly when she said, "Sleep well, daughter. I'll be watching over you."

Selene took Alec's hand, and they followed the beautiful priestess down a maze of halls to a sumptuous bedroom with a bed big enough for an orgy.

Alec grinned. "I can sleep with my wings free, if you don't mind. It's nice to have a bed this big."

Selene looked at her and allowed the confusion, hurt, and bafflement she'd been feeling show. Instantly, Alec had her in a tight hug, her wings wrapped around her. "I'm here. And I'll be here right to the end of this. I promise."

Selene let Alec take her clothes off and help her into bed. Alec crawled in beside her and wrapped Selene in her wings. She thought it would take forever to get to sleep, but safe in the warmth of Alec's soft, silky embrace, pulled tight against her hard body, she felt sleep claiming her quickly.

Tomorrow. I can deal with all of this...insanity, tomorrow. Tonight, this is all I need.

Chapter Twenty-five

Anger. No, not anger. Rage. That's what Alec felt radiating from Selene from the moment she woke up.

"When can I see her?"

Alec sat up in bed, letting the sheet fall to her waist. She appreciated that even in her current state of mind, Selene took a moment to look her over like she wanted to eat her.

"It's morning. She might be awake soon, but she'll be muddled. We can see if she eats breakfast."

"Does she need to eat?" Selene was riffling through her clothing and pulling it on haphazardly.

Alec was afraid to tell her she'd put her top on inside out. *Better she takes her wrath out on Chandra.* "No. None of us do, technically. But we do get hungry, and it's a nice ritual to have." She got out of bed and stretched out the kinks in her wings from keeping Selene held close all night.

Selene had stopped moving and was watching her. "I want you again. Tonight." She turned to pull on her sweatshirt and then stopped. "Oh my God! Picus! I totally forgot about him last night. He didn't wait, did he?"

Alec laughed and pulled on her jeans. "I let him know we were staying the night. He'll come back when I call him to pick us up." She took a chance and gently turned Selene to face her. "Baby, what has you riled?"

"I'll tell you and my mother at the same time, if that's okay? Do you think she's got coffee?" Selene threw open the door and headed down the hallway.

Alec sighed. There had to be consequences to what Selene had learned. She knew that. But she hoped like hell those consequences wouldn't include her turning away from them altogether. She hurriedly hopped into her boots as she tried to follow Selene out of the room.

They followed the delicious smells down the hallway to the kitchen. Coffee was ready, and various breakfast foods lined the counter, along with more luscious strawberries. Chandra sat at the large wooden table, a mug clasped in her hands. She looked tired.

"I wasn't sure what you might want, so I had a variety made." Her smile was slight, her eyes unfocused.

"Thank you." Selene grabbed a mug and poured herself a cup, and the intensity coming off her was palpable. She went to the table and sat facing Chandra.

"Who the hell do they think they are? Who the hell do any of you think you are?"

Alec raised an eyebrow. *This is new.*

"I'm sorry. What do you mean?" Chandra was clearly trying hard to focus.

"They ruined my life. I could have had a mother. Maybe not a father, but a mother. I don't know you. Maybe you would've been a shit mother. But you would have been better than anything I had as I was shoved from house to house. And why? All because someone, somewhere, decided I needed to save people. Why the hell does someone else get to decide my fate to the point I get no say in it?"

She spun to face Alec. "And this bridge between worlds business—saving your kind from fading, saving humans from chaos. I care about you, deeply. I think we have something special, sure as hell unique. But my life was taken from me, the life I could have had, because some old women on the fifth floor of your building decided I was some kind of Tolkien style ring bearer." She stood up, shaking. "And I think that's pretty fucked up."

Alec winced. She'd considered aspects of what Selene was saying, but watching her hurt, seeing her righteous anger, made

Alec ache for her. "You're right. I'm sorry. I wish I could say more, but—"

"No. Don't you dare tell me the Fates have decided or some such bullshit. The truth is, I have a say in this. I can decide, based on my own beliefs, my own ideologies and practices, what to do. And I'm going to do that."

Chandra stared at Selene as though trying to see her properly, but from a long distance. "You're mistletoe."

Selene stopped pacing and stared at her. "What?"

"Mistletoe. It doesn't root in the ground, and it doesn't live in the air. It takes root on a tree, above ground, in between. Like mistletoe, you're not of one world, but two."

"I'm a parasitic plant. Excellent. Thank you, Mom. That's helpful."

"The point is you need both to live, to be happy. The tree of the earth, and the air of the ether. Without both, you will wither."

"You're saying I need the gods? I need the belief system I never had a use for growing up?"

Chandra frowned and her face grew shadowed. "You are a god, Selene. A demigod, yes. But our world, the one you don't wish to believe in, is your world, just as the one you live in is. Like mistletoe."

Selene paced, drinking her coffee, pouring herself another cup and drinking it quickly. Alec stood to the side, watching. Selene was on a roll, working toward understanding, and Alec needed to give her the space to do it, even if the direction she was taking was terrifying.

"So let me make sure I understand. I'm a bridge of some kind. I'm a demigod, who is supposed to help keep the gods from fading. And I'm also supposed to help humanity, and keep them from descending into chaos. And Alec, a five-thousand-year-old fury, is supposed to help me. But we don't know how, and we don't know against who. Nor do we know why there are creepy, smelly, ugly things trying to get me. Is that about the sum of it?"

Chandra and Alec stayed silent. The question was clearly rhetorical, and there wasn't really anything to say that would make

Selene feel better, given her perception of things. *Which is pretty much dead-on.*

Selene slumped into a chair and rested her head in her hands. The sounds of the house creaking, the wind blowing outside, and the occasional chime of the clock filled the room to bursting, so thick was the silence between them. Finally, Selene looked up at Alec.

"When we met, you knew who I was. You knew everything about me, didn't you? It wasn't random."

Alec shook her head. "No. I'm sorry. I wasn't sure how to meet you, and showing up at your house in the woods to show you what I am didn't seem like the best way to do it."

"So you lied to me. And manipulated me." She turned to Chandra. "And you gave me up because three old women told you to. You got rid of me, so I could save other people one day. Without thinking about what my life would be without you."

She stood up slowly, gripping the table. Alec moved to help her but stopped when Selene threw her a warning look. "Don't. I need space. I need time." She made her way to the doorway, looking almost like she might faint. "Because the truth is, I don't know if the gods need saving. The truth is, even knowing what I know, I still need to decide if the world, humanity, would be better off without religion as a crutch or a club. And I can't do that when I'm surrounded by people who need me to choose one way or the other." She looked at Alec with tears in her eyes. "You said you'll be here no matter what, because you don't need people to believe in you. I hope that's true. And I hope you're still around when I make my decision, whatever that may be." She turned to her mother. "I don't know how I feel about you. I don't understand what you are, really, and I don't understand what I am. I thought I did. I clawed my way out of the mire. I became a professor. I had a relationship. I was happy, kind of. And now, I have no idea who I am, or what I am. I'm more lost…" She hugged herself and let the tears fall. "More lost than I've ever been, now that I've found you."

She turned away. "Can you have Picus take me to the airport, please?"

"I'll call him now. Do you want me to come with you?" Alec desperately wanted her to say yes, to say she still wanted her by her side.

"No. I'm sorry. I'll call you."

She walked away, and Alec felt the heart she'd forgotten she had, splinter.

Chandra came to stand beside her. "Follow her. She might not want you near her while she works things out, but she needs your protection. Are the daevas after her?"

Alec nodded, still staring at the empty doorway, willing Selene to come back, to change her mind.

"Then she needs you more than you can imagine. I'll keep a closer eye on her as well. I don't know what her father might have to do with this, but if there are daevas after her, then it must be to do with Selene's demon side. The oracle says it will be the child of night's light, which is me, and the dark, which was her father. It's the daevas who own the dark when they walk among the humans." She lightly touched Alec's shoulder, and her hand was cold.

"I'll keep her safe, no matter what she decides. She won't know I'm on the plane with her, and I'll make sure she's safe when she's back home." She called Picus, and he was there to pick up Selene within ten minutes. Alec heard the door open and close as Selene went out to meet him. She got into the car, and Alec could see Picus prattling away at her, but Selene's expression was blank, empty. Alec called Zed and told him they were on their way back, but hung up before he started asking more questions.

She didn't have any answers. Selene had walked away from her, and she wondered if a fury could fade after all.

Chapter Twenty-six

Selene lay curled on her side, hugging a pillow as her tears wet another pillow beneath her head. When she and Mika had split up, she'd felt awful, unloved and unwanted. In the miniscule amount of time since then, she'd found out the world she'd known, the one she walked through every day believing she understood more than the average person, due to her study of philosophy and her rejection of religion...it was all wrong.

And not only that, but somehow she was supposed to save that world from disintegrating. Because people weren't believing anymore. It was exactly what she had wanted, what Frey wanted. The cessation of unwarranted belief so people and governments stopped hiding behind religion and had to be more honest about the lies they told and the truths they kept hidden.

She thought about the people she'd met at Afterlife. According to their oracle, she now had the power of life and death. *Over gods. What does that make me?*

The trees outside were making their beautiful music as they danced in the wind, and she let it soothe her. She drifted to sleep but was quickly overrun by dreams where she needed to do something but couldn't find a way to do it, all with a sense of impending failure. Sweat soaked her T-shirt when she woke, trembling once again. Dusk had fallen, and she figured food was in order, although it was the last thing she wanted. *Maybe a rice cake with some peanut butter.* In the kitchen, she startled at her reflection in the window, before she realized there was another noise, one she didn't recognize. She listened harder and froze near a wall, thinking of the mess made of her bathroom. Afterlife had taken care of the cleanup, and she'd wondered at the time if they had assigned lowly, displaced gods to do the painting.

Although she was still afraid of the creepy bastards coming for her, somehow, she knew someone, or something, would be watching out for her. Given that she was supposed to save their sorry asses, she knew there'd be some kind of guard detail near her cabin. She was happy to accept that, if it meant she could sleep in her own bed, away from the crushing pressure of expectation, where she could process the whirling dervish her life had become.

The noise grew louder, and her heart hammered against her ribs. She closed her eyes and forced away any thoughts of Zed or the others. Not unless I really need them... *Isn't that always the way?*

A long, low scratching sound came from her back door. It started near the top and went slowly, terrifyingly slowly, to the bottom. She could hear the wood splintering and choked back a sob.

And then she heard a sound she knew. The sound of a baby bear snuffling. *Bears. It's bears.* Shaking so hard she could barely stand, she slid open the window next to her and grabbed the air horn from next to the door, where she always kept it. Living in a forest full of large, hungry animals meant keeping deterrents handy. She aimed the horn at the open window and depressed the lever, letting out an awful screeching sound. She heard the momma bear growl loudly, and Selene could hear them lumber off. She slid to the floor and wrapped her arms around her knees.

This is my life now. Wondering if a bear is a ghoul sent to get me. Trying not to think of gods, because they just might answer my prayers.

The phone rang, and she gasped at the loud noise in her quiet house. She crawled across the floor to the phone, not trusting her legs to hold her up.

"Yes?"

"Selene? Are you okay?"

"Frey. Yes, I'm fine, thank you."

"You sound a bit funny. Are you sure?"

Selene took a steadying breath. "I'm sure, thank you. I just had some bears at my door, that's all. They're gone now."

"Wow, bears. I can't say I've ever had that problem! Look, I won't keep you. I was wondering if we could have dinner and see where things stand? My work is going great, but I need something special, something more, and I still think you're it. After tonight, if you still don't want to do it, I'll stop pestering you. What do you say?"

The last thing on earth Selene wanted to do was leave the house, especially to talk about a career in public philosophy. But then again, maybe Frey was exactly the type of person she needed to talk to right now.

"Sure. Same place as before? I can be there in about an hour."

They hung up, and she pulled herself to her feet. Since she'd been back from Italy, she'd done nothing but think. And miss Alec. She missed Alec ferociously, and part of her wondered if she was holding Alec responsible for turning her world upside down, even though Alec, too, was just doing as she was told. *Following orders, like any good fury would.*

She got dressed slowly, praying things would start to make some kind of sense soon.

❖

"So, you see, that's where things stand right now. I could use you on my team. I've quoted plenty of your essays in my video talks and conferences, so my followers are already interested in you. Now all they need is a face to go with the brilliance."

He was laying it on thick, and she couldn't get any sense of whether there was anything genuine to what he was saying. She leaned forward, keeping her focus on the fork she kept moving a millimeter to the right, and then back to the left. "Frey, what if we're wrong? What if God, or any of the gods, exists? What if they're out there, answering prayers and doing what gods do? What if..." She swallowed. *How much can I say without sounding like I've just been released from a locked unit?* "What if religion is real, and hell is real, and there really are rules based on belief systems?"

He stared at her, clearly bewildered. He wiped his mouth with his napkin and sat back in the chair. He looked contemplative for a long moment. "I don't think we'll convert the true believers. The ones who need faith in order to get up every day. But they're rarely the ones making massive decisions about life on this planet. The more non-believers and undecided we can convince, the more that will spread. I had a phone call from an important head of state recently. He said he'd been following my talks and had his kids watch them. He's teaching his kids to think philosophically, logically. And those kids will be decision makers one day, making decisions based on truth rather than superstition." He took a sip of his wine, not taking his eyes from her. "And if these supernatural beings really do exist, I imagine they'll put a stop to it, somehow. A plague, or flood, or something like that. To let us peons know they're still up there. Although, we'd probably discount that as a change in climate."

Frey's words hit home. *That's me. I'm the way they're trying to stop it.* The idea that she was being used rankled. And yet, it also made them more...real. They weren't sending plagues or floods. They needed someone to plug the dam, and instead of using old-school tactics, they sought out help in the unlikeliest of places. Their vulnerability made Selene pause. It wasn't their fault they had humanity's flaws, when they'd been created in man's image, was it? They stayed quiet for a while before Selene said softly, "And who are we to tell people what to think? What to believe?"

"We're the ones who are right. We're the ones who know better and have to step up and lead. If we don't, who will? Those who can, lead. Those who can't, follow. We can teach more to lead, and teach even more to follow. We can make the world a place of sound reasoning rather than ill conceived, faith based entitlement."

He placed his hand over hers, making her shiver. "Can't you feel it? Can't you feel the potential for greatness? For people to look up at you, adoring you, hanging on your every word? Imagine, Selene. Imagine the control we could have, to make the world better."

She shrank from him, pulling her hand from beneath his. "That sounds…frightening. More than frightening, actually." In that moment, she saw beyond the great philosopher, the beach boy façade. She saw something flutter around him, a darkness she'd never noticed before. "Is that why you're in this? For fame and power?"

He tilted his head. "Of course not. I want to make the world a better place. But if fame and power come with it, is that a bad thing? Plenty of corrupt religious and political people have power, and they ruin the world with it. If we have it, we can use it for good. Why not?"

"Power corrupts, Frey. And what you're saying sounds a lot like things said by people you wouldn't want to be compared to." Her chair scraped loudly as she pushed away from the table, causing a few of the diners to look their way. Frey smiled at them uneasily. "I've made my decision. You can keep your job, your TV appearances, your radio talks and blogs. I'm not sure what I believe in anymore, if anything, but I know damn well I don't want to be part of some power grab." She picked up her purse and coat. "I believed in you. I really thought you were one of the good guys." She sighed and looked away so he wouldn't see her eyes welling up. "Please don't call me anymore."

Patrons stared as she walked from the room, but she didn't care. She'd finally made one decision, and she felt the burden weighing her down ease slightly. She still had to figure out what she wanted, what she believed, and what to do next, but it certainly wasn't going to be with a glory hound like Frey Falconi, even if she agreed, or had agreed, with some of his ideals. *And what was that surrounding him?* It wasn't like the strange shimmer she saw when she was looking at Alec. It was more like a barely perceptible mist of some kind. But she hadn't seen it the other times she'd been with him.

Out on the street, she looked at the promenade of shops and decided she didn't feel like going home just yet. She wandered aimlessly, looking in shop windows but not really seeing anything. *Okay, break it down. Look at it logically. 1. God, and lots of other gods, exist. This is a fact. 2. People believing in them keeps them alive. When people stop believing, the gods fade away. Or get real jobs. 3. Religion gives people hope, a reason to continue on in the face of entropy. 4. Religion gives people a crutch to lean on, and a reason for war. 5. People will always have a reason for war. Is fighting for gods who do, actually, exist less worthy because I don't agree with it? 6. Do I have the right to tell people what to think or believe? Especially when I know that the people they're praying to are listening?*

She stopped and stared into a shop window, unseeing. That was it. Yes, she could tell people to think logically. She could tell people to be rational. But she could no longer suggest that religion was a myth, an antiquated mythology intended to keep people compliant. Because she knew it wasn't strictly true. *Is there a middle ground? Can there be both?*

She finally looked at the glass, at the shop. It was empty. But what she saw standing behind her made her knees buckle.

It was the…the things, that had been behind her on the freeway that day, like the one on the train. They grinned at her, their yellow, pointed teeth catching the last light of the day. She spun to face them, placing the window at her back. People walked along in both directions, totally oblivious to her terror and their malicious stares. They came toward her, people parting around them, as though they knew something was there to be avoided, but not aware they were even trying to avoid something.

"You're coming to meet our master," one of them hissed, and his breath smelled of sour fish and smoke.

"I'm not going anywhere." Selene swallowed, fighting every instinct to mentally beg for help. *I'm not helpless. I don't need gods to save me.*

"You are, pretty flesh sack. And when he's done with you, he's promised us we can have you as our toy." He stroked her face, his nails raking her cheek. "Don't you want to be our toy?"

Selene screamed. Not out loud. She screamed in her head. She screamed for Zed, for Alec, for anyone listening.

Thunder suddenly boomed above them, and both creatures cowered slightly. "Take her now. If we don't bring her back, Master will be angry with us."

The other creature's breath smelled of rot, decay, and death. Selene gagged but managed to speak. "Do you think I'd be out without guards? I think you'd better run, you maggot ridden filth trenches."

Thunder crashed again, this time rattling the windows. A shadow fell over the three of them, and Alec was there in all her terrifying glory, her wings spread, her eyes black-cherry red, her fangs looking razor sharp. The snake tattoos on her arms raised their heads and hissed, swaying back and forth as they moved toward their prey. The creatures fell into a crouch and scuttled, crab-like, backward. "You'll regret this, fury. Our Master wants your head next to Medusa's. He said to tell you to come see him for some fun."

She let out a roar that made Selene's eyes water as she moved protectively in front of her. "Tell your master I'll be waiting for him. When he's ready to come himself and stop sending toadies, we'll talk."

The creatures disappeared into the crowd and the clouds cleared. Alec turned to Selene and folded her wings. "Are you okay?"

"I think so. Alec, I don't understand why those things are after me. What master were they talking about?"

Alec sighed. Or, at least Selene thought she sighed. It was hard to tell under the fangs and feathers what the emotion was.

"We're trying to find him, and once we have him, I'll find out."

Alec's fangs retracted and her tattoos became, once again, incredibly lifelike ink. Her pupils rounded and she stood before Selene as the woman she'd met on campus. *It feels like a million years ago now.*

"You're safe now. Want to grab a drink?"

Selene nodded and hooked her arm through Alec's. She needed the physical contact to know she was safe. They headed toward the Coffee Bean in silence, though Alec covered Selene's hand with her own.

Once seated, Selene gratefully sipped the hot drink, feeling like she'd been frozen inside. Alec simply sipped her own drink and watched her impassively.

"Did you hear me call?"

"Every non-human in the Milky Way heard you call. Zed was keeping an eye on you from a distance, but I've been around, making sure the daevas didn't come after you."

"You've been following me?"

"From a distance. We know you're in danger. And I'm sure as hell not going to let anything happen to you." She looked down at her coffee and said softly, "I promised."

"I had a feeling someone was watching, but I wasn't sure if it would be you."

"I gave you space. I stayed far enough away not to bother you, but close enough to keep you safe. Like a bodyguard."

Selene snorted. "A five-thousand-year-old bodyguard with fangs. I'm a lucky girl."

Alec gave her a sad smile. "I would've hoped you thought so, once." She shrugged. "But life goes on, right? Have you given any thought about what you want to do?"

Selene thought about the epiphany she'd had just before the daevas had shown up. "I think so. I need to decide on a plan, but I think there's a way to meet in the middle. To get people thinking critically, but without asking them to stop believing in whatever faith they have."

Alec looked so surprised, so relieved, Selene wanted to reach across and hug her. Instead, she held her mug tighter. "When I've got more than a germ of an idea, I'll let you know."

Alec's smile could have lit up the room. "I can't tell you how happy I am to hear it. I mean, you know what it means to me. To us. The Fates are always right. I shouldn't have doubted."

Selene frowned. "I'm not doing this because some old hags with control issues in your office said some magic words and sent you an email. I'm going to do this my way, so it works for all of us."

"Speaking of us..." Alec looked at her searchingly.

"I don't know. You lied to me. Right from the beginning, you lied to me, even if you did eventually tell me the truth. But that was only because you had to. How will I know you're telling me everything in the future?" She let the tears roll down her cheeks unchecked. "How can I trust you?"

Alec shook her head. "I don't know. I lied because it's not the kind of thing you tell someone when you first meet them. 'By the way, I need you to believe in things you don't believe in, and save a world you know nothing about.' It doesn't exactly scream second date, does it? But you're right, I could have come clean sooner, and I didn't. I didn't want to rush it. I wanted to give you time…"

They sat silently, lost in their own thoughts. Finally, Alec said, "If you give me a chance, Selene, I'll never give you reason to doubt again. I swear it, on what I stand for as a fury."

The words were clear, sharp, undeniable. Selene swallowed and came around to Alec's side of the table. She sat in her lap and wrapped her arms around her neck, feeling secure when Alec wrapped her arms around Selene's waist. She was tired of being alone, and this woman, this fury…wanted her. And she wanted her in return, whatever she was.

"Okay. We can talk about it. I miss you, and I'm going crazy without you."

Alec lifted her face and kissed Selene softly, sweetly, making promises of a future they couldn't be sure existed yet. "I hate watching you from afar, not close enough to take away your pain."

They sat cuddled like that for some time before Alec sighed. "We'd better let Zed and the others know what's going on. You shouldn't stay alone at your place until we know what the hell is going on. Are you okay staying at Afterlife? I could stay at your place with you, instead of in the trees outside, but I think it would be better if we were closer to backup if we needed it."

"Can I stay with you?" Selene bit her lip, unused to being so forward, but not wanting to spend another second without Alec at her side.

"We could, but my place isn't nearly as secure as the company grounds, and I'll feel better if I know you're in a secure area. So I'll stay there with you. Just for now, okay?"

"You won't leave me?"

Alec kissed Selene's knuckles while looking up at her. "Never."

They untangled and walked down the promenade back to Selene's car. Selene stopped to dig around in her purse for her keys.

"I call it the magic bag. I'm always finding things in it I'd forgotten about—"

She cried out as she was flung to her knees. Pain flared through her wrists as she caught herself on the ground, and a weight on her back pushed her cheek to the pavement. She heard Alec roar and swear, and as the toxic odors of fish and smoke assailed her, a rag was placed over her mouth. She tried to scream and breathed in whatever chemical was on the cloth, making her cough. Nails gouged her cheek, the car tires in front of her spun, and the world faded into fog.

Alec...

Chapter Twenty-seven

A lec groaned. The pain was excruciating, constantly dragging her under. Her toes only just touched the ground, and her wrists were attached to thick, heavy chains above her. Worse, her wings had been attached to the chains as well, spread open and impaled with rings to attach the chains to. It felt as though every nerve in her wings was on fire, and she couldn't feel her hands, which were also bound in chains, keeping her from motioning with them. Her shoulders ached unbearably and her toes kept cramping as she tried to get some purchase to take the weight from her arms.

None of that was as agonizing as watching Selene and knowing she couldn't do a damn thing.

Selene lay unconscious on the cold cement. Chains bound her wrists and ankles to a large bolt in the floor, but she hadn't woken up yet, and it had been several hours. The need to get to her, to make sure she was okay, was tearing Alec's mind apart. Once she got free, she'd shred every breathing body responsible for this.

Selene moaned softly and stirred, and Alec took a breath of relief, which made her ribs ache even more. "Selene? Baby, please wake up. Please, sweetheart. I need you to wake up."

Selene blinked and coughed. When she spoke, her voice was a harsh wheeze. "What happened? Where are we?" She struggled to an upright position, but just as quickly scooted away to vomit, going to the end of her chain length. When she was done, she collapsed back in her original position and finally looked at Alec. Horror and fear appeared instantly.

"Oh my God. Alec…Jesus. What have they done to you?" She tried to get closer, but her chains kept her a couple of feet from where Alec hung.

"That bad, huh? I managed a few good punches, I think, before they hit me with some kind of Taser thing and dropped me. I'm so sorry, Selene. I was unfocused, paying attention to you instead of our surroundings. I knew they were around; I should have been more aware. I just figured they'd scuttled back to their nest. Are you hurt?"

Selene flexed her limbs. "My left wrist hurts and it's swollen. Everything else seems to be okay." She touched her face and grimaced as she traced lines down her cheek. "That thing got me with its nails. Now I need a rabies shot."

"Probably tetanus too. I think their nails may be partially metal." Alec tried to make light of it, but the fact that they were trapped there was very, very bad news. "Selene, can you try praying? Like you did when you screamed earlier. I have a feeling nothing will get through, but can you try?"

Selene nodded and closed her eyes. Alec could feel her energy pulsing, and she caught a kind of echo of the prayer, but it was as faint as mist.

"What do you think?" Selene asked.

Before Alec could respond, the door to their cell opened, letting in bright light. Selene stood in front of Alec protectively, making Alec's heart swell. *Sweet, sweet woman.* She didn't seem at all fazed by the fact that the being who had just entered had ram's horns and hooves, as well as a snake-like tail.

"I'm so sorry for our inhospitable welcome. I'm afraid my lackeys can be rather overzealous. However, we also need to talk uninterrupted, and this seemed the best way to do so."

"Who are you? And why have you done this? Take Alec down right now."

The man laughed and tilted his head at Alec. "Aren't you going to introduce us, old friend?"

"We were never friends. Selene, this is Aka Manah. He's a demon—"

"No. Not *a* demon. *The* demon. And I'm hurt by that friends comment." He turned back to Selene. "You can call me Adam. It's easier in this era, and I fit in a bit better."

She lifted her chin. "How does something like you fit in anywhere?"

He laughed again, a cruel, grating sound. "The same way a creature like your girl Alec here fits in. We blend, hiding who we truly are, taking humans unaware, forcing ourselves on them, watching them wither and die under our power." He gave Selene a wide berth as he moved toward Alec. He looked up at her, his head tilted slightly. "But then, sometimes something happens, and we forget which mask is the true one." He drew back and punched Alec solidly in the stomach, making her body swing and her wings and arms take her weight. She gritted her teeth against a scream, unwilling to give him the pleasure, and not wanting to scare Selene, who screamed for him to stop. She caught her breath again when her toes touched the ground.

"Why are you doing this? What could you possibly want with us?"

He moved away from them and sat on a filthy, sagging sofa against the wall, as primly as if he were in a restaurant. He sighed dramatically. "I didn't want it to be this way. I really didn't. I tried it the business way, the way Afterlife would do it. I read the oracle, I figured out who it was referring to and I put together a damn fine plan. One that was working beautifully. Until our flying rat there stepped in." He waved vaguely Alec's direction. "If it hadn't been for her, you'd be doing exactly what I intended you to do, and I'd be so much further along with my plan."

He stood and brushed dirt from his jeans. "But that's okay. You'll both rot here, and I'll continue on. Sure, it will be a bit slower with just Frey doing it, and Selene would have turned more followers by delving into her demon side, but in the end, I'll get what I want."

Alec glanced at Selene, who looked stunned. "And what is it you want, Aka? Better food? An office in the building? You burned down the last one we gave you."

"Nothing as base as that, Alec." He ran his hand down Selene's cheek and laughed when she jerked away. "No. I want the world. And by being so vocal about why people shouldn't believe in your antiquated gods, Selene and Frey allowed my workers to go among people and sow the seeds of chaos. True, level playing field, chaos. When more people believe in Frey and his…well, *my* mission, the scales will tip, and I'll gain control. Especially with the splendid powers of rhetoric I've invested in him. Your silly, ethnically diverse gods will fade away, leaving me in charge." He opened his mouth, and a long, split tongue emerged. He licked Selene's face, and although she put up her hands to deflect him, it was too late. Brown slime slid down her cheek and dripped onto her shirt.

"And you think we'll be content to hang around down here while you do all this? You don't think they'll be searching for the bridge?"

He shrugged and headed for the door. "They can search all they want. This building is sealed. The outside is stone, the inside is mostly glass, and you're in a concrete bunker below it. And there's never been any religion in it, so there's no line for you to connect to." He opened the door and grinned at them. "So, yes. I think you'll hang around down here until I decide to use you as my playthings when it suits me. I'll be sure to keep the human alive long enough to enjoy her at least once. And I'll make certain to do it in front of you, Alec, so you don't feel like you've missed out." He stepped through the open doorway and laughed. "And now, I must go meet with Frey to see how things are progressing. He was, of course, devastated at your refusal, so clearly did I make it known I wanted you there. He's so easily led, good man. He really believes this is for the best, and that the powers I've given him to convince people to come to our cause are meant for the greater good. Ah, well. He has his uses. Good night. Don't let the daevas bite."

He closed the door behind him and they stayed silent for some time.

"Is it true?" Selene asked. "Can there really be a place prayer can't get through?"

"Yeah. Science type places, government buildings, some schools. Places where the separation of church and state are taken seriously, and places where logic and reason are prized above spiritual belief. And being underground won't help."

Selene sighed. "Then I guess it's a good thing that nasty-ass spitball slimed me." She held up one hand, uncuffed and covered in the slime he'd dripped on her face. "That stuff is really slippery." She wiped it on her other hand and worked it around the cuff, grimacing as the metal rubbed her skin raw. Soon, the other cuff was off. "Now what? I can't slide a cuff over my foot."

Alec thought about it. "If you can get to my left pocket, I've got a tiny pocketknife on my keys. I feel like they're still in there. It might be enough to work the lock on your cuffs."

Selene got as close as she could and leaned forward. She stretched until she was off balance several times, missing Alec's body by centimeters. "I'm afraid that if I fall on you, I'll pull on your arms and wings. I don't want to hurt you any more than you already are."

"We're going to hurt a hell of a lot more if we don't get out of here quickly. I'm betting Aka hasn't given his minions orders to leave us alone."

Selene bit her lip. "Then this might hurt. I'm sorry." She leaned forward again, this time stretching until she fell forward and caught herself on Alec's pockets.

Alec swallowed a scream, but she couldn't keep her eyes from watering. Selene quickly found the keys and used a combination of her stomach muscles and Alec's body to heave herself back again. Alec let out a shaky breath, fearing the possibility of blacking out again.

"Talk to me. Stay with me, Alec. Breathe, baby. Tell me about Aka. Adam…do you think he sees himself as the father to a new world? Is he clever like that?"

"Clever…maybe. Devious, certainly. Demonic, obviously." Alec fought the waves of dizzying pain. She allowed herself to fully shift to her real form as a way to conserve energy. It also made her slightly taller, and she was able to take more weight off her arms.

"I worked for him for a while, when it was believed furies were a kind of flying demon. He's twisted and creates havoc for no other reason than to make himself laugh. He's been a low-level player for a long time. Looks like he wants to come out to play again, and using daevas was a good way to do it."

One cuff slid free, and Selene went to work on the other. Alec could see her fingertips bleeding as the pocketknife slid in and out of the tiny lock.

"Why does his plan sound plausible? Because it does, and I really hate that it does."

"I agree. But the oracle says if you come to our side, we'll win. It doesn't say we'll die in a smelly basement next to a nasty old sofa."

"Proof that the Fates can be wrong?"

"If you'd gone to their side, the oracle said we'd all fade, and a new era, one of darkness, would take place. So as usual, the oracle had a built-in safety net, so no matter which way you went, it would be right. The Fates are good like that."

"The ultimate politicians. Excellent. Lucky us." The other cuff slid open, and Selene pushed them way. "How do I get you down?"

Alec looked at the winch system holding her in place. "I don't know that you can actually undo me. But I think you can let me down. Take the chain off that wall over there, and, hand over hand, bring it down so I can at least stand properly."

Selene quickly did as Alec asked, the sound of the chain catapulting off the walls around them.

Alec lowered her arms and gasped as her shoulders were relieved of their burden. Her wings ached, but the lessened pressure relieved them too. "God, that feels good. Thank you. How far will it go?"

Selene kept going until the chain stuck, leaving Alec's hands at chest level and her wings nearly folded.

"That slime must be gone now, right?"

Selene held up her hands. Only brown flakes were left.

Alec thought, and couldn't find any other solution than one Selene would hate. "The cuffs they've used on me aren't like the ones they've used on you. They're stronger, harder, and wider. That little knife isn't going to open them." She sighed and closed her eyes. "Baby, you're going to have to leave me here. The moment you get outside this building you can start calling for help, and it will arrive within minutes. But you have to get away from the building, Selene. You have to. If they keep you hostage, the world is going to go to hell, literally, very quickly."

"If you think I'm leaving you here, you're insane. More so than I am, and that's saying something." Selene went to the couch and ripped off a section of the cover. She reached in and started yanking and pulling at the ancient springs. She fell back when one snapped free and landed on her already sore wrist.

The snapping sound was almost louder than the chain had been.

She lay on her side, cradling her wrist against her chest. Alec could see her taking deep breaths, and once again, her helplessness made her rage inside. "Selene? Baby?"

Selene rolled back to her feet slowly. She picked up the spring, her wrist held protectively against her. "Let's see if this works on your cuffs."

She tried, but with one hand, it was nearly impossible, and although Alec tried to help, the thick cuffs meant she had almost no dexterity. "Baby, listen to me. I bet if you fold it over and twist it, you can get the door open. You'll have to be stealthy, silent, and super-aware, but I bet you can get out of here. If not, they'll bring you back, and we'll be together."

Selene was shaking her head vehemently, tears rolling down her face.

"Yes, baby. You have to do this. You can do this. You've got to try."

Selene rested her head against Alec's chest and sobbed. Alec rested her cheek on Selene's head. Sending her out on her own was terrifying, but that was the only game in play. She had to believe in the Fates, and she had to believe in Selene. *Everyone has to believe in something.*

"Okay." Selene sniffed and stepped back. She cradled Alec's bruised face in her hands. "I'll do it your way. But once this is over,

I call the shots once in a while, okay? No more of this 'Selene, save the world' crap, understand?"

Alec gave her a tired grin. "It's a deal."

Selene went to the door and worked the wire in. Twenty infuriating, frustrating minutes later, they heard the telltale click, and when Selene turned the handle, the door cracked open.

"Go, baby. Go get help. Call for backup when you're away from the building, and get somewhere safe until it comes. I'll be right here when you get back. I promise."

Selene ran over and gave Alec a hard, desperate kiss, ignoring her fangs completely. "You'd better be ready when I get back. I hate waiting around."

After one more hard kiss, she turned and went to the door. She looked over her shoulder at Alec, staring at her as though to memorize her, and then slipped silently from the room, closing the door behind her.

Alec closed her eyes again, alone in the dark room, powerless for the first time in her existence, with more at stake than ever before. *Please, please let her make it through.* No one answered, and she swayed there, alone in her chains, letting her home, darkness, take her away.

Chapter Twenty-eight

Selene crept silently through the labyrinthine facility. Half-glass walls leading to a maze of offices and abandoned laboratory spaces made it hard to stay out of sight. Most of the glass was cracked or broken, and many of the walls were smeared with the kind of stuff that had been in her bathroom. Swear words and filthy suggestions were scrawled across doors and even on the ceilings. Cruel, inhuman laughter echoed distantly through the empty halls, and Selene's skin crawled. *Alec. Think of Alec. I have to save Alec.* The thought of Alec's pain steadied her and she continued her slow creep forward, following the dusty green arrows for the emergency exit.

She turned left at the end of a hallway and froze. Voices came clearly from one of the rooms on the right, a room she had to pass to make it to the exit door. *So close.* She prayed, not sure it would get through yet, but willing to try. She crept close to the door and realized she recognized both voices.

"I told you. I don't like it. The lady-bat, sure. That makes sense. But Selene is a good person with the right ideas. She just needed a bit more convincing and time. I could have gotten her to turn on the bat and the old man, and she'd have been on our side. She shouldn't be down there."

She gritted her teeth. *Falconi is one of them.* She thought of the strange darkness attached to him, and now she knew where it had come from.

"Which of us knows better? The one with thousands of years of experience, or the putrefying mass of flesh with a lifespan akin to a fly? A 'good person' isn't going to be of any use. We needed to reach her dark side, her father's side. That's why I increased your powers of persuasion the last time you spoke with her. But instead, they got to her first, and now she's useless to us. This is the only way. Don't turn weak now."

"I'm not weak. I actually still believe in what I'm doing. I think rational, logical, philosophical thought is better than religion. I still believe religion is the root of the problem. I'm not a fan of yours, but I'll do what I need to do to make the world better."

There was a scuffle, and Selene heard an awful gurgling noise. She took a chance and peered around the corner of the doorway.

Aka Manah held Frey off the ground by his throat, looking as irritated as one would if bothered by an insect. He said, "Very soon, I won't need you. You're nothing more than a puppet." As though to illustrate his point, he swung Frey from side to side. "You believe in whatever the hell you want to; I don't care. When I've got what I want, you can join Selene at my feet and discuss how religion is a letdown. In the meantime, you'll continue to use the powers I've given you to convince the world they don't need the gods. And when those spineless oafs at Afterlife go away, I'll make the world my dark playground."

He dropped Frey to the floor, who lay there gasping and holding his throat. Aka turned away and walked toward a desk. Selene knew it might be her only chance.

She scuttled past the doorway.

Frey looked her in the eye.

Time slowed.

He looked back at the floor and she half-crawled, half-ran the rest of the way to the door, waiting for Frey to yell, for Aka to come stalking out of the office.

Instead, only the strange laughter continued to echo, and as she made her way to the door marked Exit, though added below it was "to Hell," she quietly pushed it open and stepped into the sunshine.

❖

"I don't know why. I can't understand it. He knows about you, about the others. He knows what Alec is. I don't know why he let me go. But I heard him defending me. He said I was a good person, that I didn't belong down there."

Selene was so tired of explaining. The moment she'd made it outside, she'd made a run for the trees, and once in them, had kept running until she found a tiny village with a small café. She'd found a place in the corner and closed her eyes. She hadn't wanted to start calling until she had some distance from the daevas nest, just in case they could hear her too. With everything she had, she prayed. She called to Zed, to Meg, even to Death. And when she opened her eyes, they walked into the café, a triad of destruction, vengeance, and hope. And then a guest she hadn't asked for arrived: her mother, looking dazed and muted. Still, she went straight to Selene's side and sat, stone-like, beside her. Selene blurted out a condensed version of what had happened. "And Alec…she's chained up by her wings." She finally let the tears fall.

"Did you see how many there are working for him?"

"I didn't see anyone. I heard weird, screeching laughter the whole time, but never saw any of those walking nightmares, and he didn't say."

Zed and Meg both pulled out their phones and started dialing. Dani put her hand over Selene's. "How are you holding up?"

She squeezed her cold hand. "I'm okay, mostly. Tired and pretty bruised. My wrist hurts like a bitch. But more than anything, I'm terrified about Alec's safety. Her poor wings…"

Dani grimaced. "They know a lot of her power resides in her wings. If they were free, she could probably break the chains, and her snakes would wake up. But bound by metal like that, unable to use her wings, they've effectively paralyzed her."

Selene's mom reached for her injured wrist and Selene instinctively pulled away, but Chandra gave her a stern look and she capitulated.

Her touch was icy, and although her hands felt like granite, they were gentle. She wrapped her hands around Selene's wrist and stared at them intently.

Selene whimpered as she felt a bone shift under her skin. It wasn't from the pain, because there was none, but the creepy feel of it mending turned her stomach slightly. Her mother removed her hands and turned back so she was once again facing forward, just her arm touching Selene's slightly. She was there, but not there. *Like the moon during the day. And blindingly bright at night. And dad is a demon. Being a foster kid wasn't so bad after all.*

Chandra's lips twitched in a kind of smile, and Selene wondered just how transparent her thoughts were. She quickly tried to wall them off and turned to Dani. "What's going to happen now?"

"Well, my guess is Zed and a few of the other old-timers are going to go in and have a talk with Aka, and get Alec out. After that, we'll have to see."

Zed and Meg returned to the table. "Dani, can you stay with Selene? Get her out of here—take her to the compound, and let Cerberus know we're on lockdown. When we've settled things here, we'll bring Alec there. Love heals and all that garbage." Zed glanced at Chandra, but clearly didn't feel the need to address her. He waited for Dani's response.

Dani smiled her usual sad smile. "Of course I will. I don't have any pickups to handle personally today, so I'm all yours."

"I can't go with you?" Selene asked, knowing full well the answer.

"And risk getting you caught and used as a hostage? Not a chance. We're going in to rescue one; we don't want to make it two. And no offense, but there's not much you can do that a contingent of gods can't."

Cars of every kind began pulling up outside, and even a few vehicles that looked more like electric clouds than cars. Many of the deities Selene had seen at Meg's dinner party showed up, as did more she didn't recognize. One of them, though—

"Is that God? Like, the Christian one?" she whispered to Dani.

She grinned. "Like I said, they got the big guns in. No one gets to decide on mass chaos without the express consent of the rest of the heads of faith. Certainly not world chaos, that was just stupid and greedy. But that's Aka for you, no boundaries."

The powerful looking, dark-skinned man with a dark gray beard and fathomless eyes looked briefly at her, but she didn't think he'd actually seen her. And she was glad. She was on personal terms with enough gods already. That one had a reputation for turning people into spices and throwing pests at them.

They all left and disappeared down the path leading into the woods, talking and pushing one another like a group of teenagers getting ready for a night out.

"I wouldn't want to be Aka right now." Dani rose from the booth and held her hands out to Selene and Chandra. "Let's head to Afterlife, shall we?"

Alec moaned softly. Her wings were on fire. From the base to the tips, it felt as though someone was holding a torch to them. If Selene hadn't lowered the chains, Alec knew she wouldn't have been able to withstand the pain. The fact that Selene wasn't a mass of wounded flesh in the cell beside her gave Alec hope that she'd somehow made it out.

She let her head drop forward and tried to breathe the way Selene had asked her to. Slow and steady.

The door opened and dread filled her when she saw the female silhouette. But the figure came closer, and she'd never been as happy to see anyone in her life. "Ama. Thank every god ever born."

Ama quickly gave her a kiss on the cheek and then began inspecting the chains. "I'll need Zed to get the ones off your wrists, but I think I can get the ones from your wings." She looked at Alec calmly. "This is going to hurt, Alec. Do you want something to bite down on?"

Alec shook her head. There sure as hell wasn't anything she'd put in her mouth in that cell. Especially with Selene gone.

"Okay. Breathe deep. You can scream; we've got them surrounded and Selene is headed back to the office." Ama reached up and took the ring in Alec's wing in both hands. With a fierce yell, she pulled the ring in two, taking some of Alec's wing with it.

Alec didn't scream. She blacked out.

When she came to, the other ring was out of her wing and Zed was standing in front of her, lightning bolt in hand. He tapped it to the metal cuff and the jolt ran through her body before the cuff fell into pieces at her feet. Ama stood behind her, her arms around Alec's waist to brace her, and when the second jolt of electricity slammed her body back, but allowed her wrist to drop free, she let Ama take her weight as she fought to stay conscious.

"Aka?" she asked.

"With the board. His little minions have all slithered back into the nooks and crannies they came from. Except one, the human involved with Selene."

Alec slowly pulled herself from Ama's embrace and stood, though she swayed with the effort. "I want to see him."

"You're not in any shape—"

"Now, Zed."

He frowned at her but shrugged and led the way out. She leaned on Ama for support, glad for her strength. Zed led her to a conference room, where Frey Falconi sat huddled against a wall, his hands over his ears and his eyes tightly shut, as though that would make all of them go away.

"Did you know?" Alec asked.

He glanced at her, then shut his eyes again. "I knew he wanted the gods gone, but he was only saying what I thought anyway. That the world is better off without religion. I didn't know he wanted to be some kind of maniac world dictator, no. At least, not at first. And I didn't know he was going to hurt Selene. When he suggested we work together, I really did think it was a great idea. She's amazing, and a hell of a philosopher. When he told me about the gods later, and about Selene joining them, I was disappointed. I did my best to convince her, yes. I didn't believe what he said about her father, because if there was anyone who didn't seem to have a dark side, it was her. But I never, ever would have hurt her. That's why I let her escape."

Alec listened, her snakes at the ready. But they stayed in place. He was telling the truth, and he was genuine.

"Fine. I believe you. But don't think about trying to run. The others are going to want to talk to you."

He nodded vigorously, and had just begun to lower his hands from his head when an awful screeching sound filled the room, and a tiny gremlin-like creature leapt from the light fixture and onto Frey's shoulder.

He rammed a razor sharp letter opener through Frey's neck and then laughed as he was sprayed with blood. The gremlin lapped at it with his tongue before leaping from Frey's shoulder onto the table, then scrabbling along the wall to the doorway, and out onto the ceiling, where he disappeared through a hole in the tiles.

Alec and Ama watched as Frey gurgled his last breath. *He was right. Religion was a bad thing for him.*

Alec turned to Ama. "I think we'd better get back to the office." Somehow, the gremlin had been given orders to end Frey Falconi's life. That meant Selene might still be in danger after all. *And I really, really want to be in her arms right now.* Alec sighed at the thought. *Some big bad fury I am.*

Chapter Twenty-nine

The enormous meeting hall was crammed full. Gods, underling gods, personal assistants to gods, entourages, and even some ex-gods talked to and over one another, a cacophony of languages and sounds.

Selene stood next to Alec, so exhausted she could barely stay upright. Although none of her cloud-based, magical cohort needed food or sleep, her own body felt like she'd been run over by a 747. Zed, Ama, the main Christian and Jewish Gods, and Allah all stood at the front, waiting for any latecomers. Finally, Zed, as the oldest among them, aside from Alec, raised his voice so it bounced off the walls like thunder.

"Attention, please. Thank you for coming. As you can see, the oracle has come about in our favor, for the moment. The Bridge is safe, and the threat to our worlds has been curtailed." There was a smattering of applause, but gods didn't often feel the need to pat others on the back. "Aka Manah, a demon from the Zoroastrian department, has been taken into custody and given to Orcus and Nemesis, who will see to his punishment."

"What did he actually do, Zed? Was he the reason for the mass fades?"

Zed held up a hand as other questions started to be shouted out. "Perhaps I should allow our fury to explain, as she was there." He motioned to Alec, who stepped forward with Selene still safely under her arm.

There hadn't been any more attacks, and the perimeter sweep was clear. Still, Selene wanted to stay as close to her as possible.

"Aka had determined that it was time for chaos to reign. He decided to use the human need for understanding and knowledge against them by using a mortal named Frey Falconi. He used Falconi's belief in philosophy and logic, along with his natural charisma enhanced by Aka's powers of persuasion, to reach beyond religious belief, giving humanity an option other than religion for hope and meaning. He did so only to provide an opening he could manipulate to the detriment of both gods and humans. That was the reason for the mass fades."

Selene listened half-heartedly, not wanting to think of the horrible demon or his daevas. *Or my father. What does that make me?* She didn't have the energy to pursue the thought and focused on Alec instead.

"When enough humans had stopped believing in us, and therefore diminished our power and ability to interfere, he was going to let the daevas loose on the world, and place himself in a ruling position. Too few in number, we wouldn't have been able to stop him. And when he showed himself to the people, they'd have no choice but to believe in him, which means he'd never fade. He would have ruled without consequence. Fortunately, we managed to keep that from happening." Alec turned and smiled at Selene. "We're still figuring out the next step, but with Falconi dead and Aka in custody, we might have a better chance than we had before."

"Selene, are you still going to be helping us?"

Alec tried to wave the comment off, but Selene stepped forward, not letting go of Alec's hand. "We've only just come back, and we have things to discuss. I don't know if I play any further part in this extremely unexpected journey, however, I do have some things to discuss with your…department heads."

Alec gently pulled her back under her arm as Ama stepped forward. "There will be a company-wide email shortly, detailing what you've heard here today as well as any other relevant aspects, so that nothing is taken out of context, and no rumors are started. If you have questions, please bring them to your department head, instead of starting an internal mess of coups and mutinies. Thank you."

They left the stage as a group, and were surrounded by followers, asking various questions. The fears of fading, while diminished, hadn't completely receded. Alec opened a wing and put it around Selene, effectively blocking off those who wanted a word with her. As soon as they were out of the crowd, Alec scooped her up in her arms and carried her to the Hummer. Had Selene not been so tired, she might have protested. But at the moment, she was so glad to be off her feet, she hoped Alec wouldn't ever set her down again.

"Where are we going?" Selene asked, her eyes already closed as she leaned her head against the window.

"My place, if that's okay with you? Zed okayed it, and we've had someone move your things from the cottage to my place already. Too many people would bother you on site, so it makes sense to give you some privacy."

Selene meant to say thank you, but before she could, she fell asleep.

Selene woke when Alec gently placed her in the softest bed she'd ever been on. She sank into the black comforter and pillows and sighed happily. When Alec turned to go, she grabbed her hand.

"Please stay with me?"

"Baby, I'm not going anywhere, ever. I need to change the bandages on my wings, and then I'll come join you. I promise." She kissed Selene's hand and headed from the room.

Selene closed her eyes, but as jarringly, nauseatingly exhausted as she was, her mind was crowded with questions and few answers.

Alec came back in and lay beside her. Selene curled next to her and relaxed completely when she laid her head on Alec's chest and was enfolded in her wings. Ama had carefully sewn the gaping holes shut and applied her healing magic, but the wounds were too deep and too jagged, so they'd need time to heal on their own.

Fortunately, Alec said she didn't feel any numbness anywhere, and would be able to fly again without issue.

"What's on your mind, beautiful?"

Selene felt the tears well in her eyes. "Where do I start? What does it make me, that I'm part demon? Does that mean I'm evil too? I don't feel like I'll ever really know my mother, and having gotten to know her even a tiny bit, I'm not sure I want to. Although, there's something in there, something nice, sometimes. And what does that say about me? I feel like people are still looking for answers from me, but why? The big evil villain plot to destroy the world has been foiled. Isn't that enough? Why did they ask if I'm still helping?" She let the tears go, frustration, fear, and fatigue falling with them. "And us? Where does all of this leave us?"

"Whoa, there. Let's take on one thing at a time, okay?"

Selene nodded and waited. She needed reason right now. She needed logic and a plan. *Please give me that rather than more wise-woman words on old paper.*

"First of all, your parents. There are a lot of people, both gods and humans, who don't like their parents. Biology doesn't necessitate likability. Your mother is a good woman, and when she's in her prime every month, she's amazing. But she'll never sit and bake pies with you, Selene. And your father…who cares? He was DNA, and nothing more. Sure, maybe you'll find out something about yourself you can blame him for. Or maybe not. God knows, I don't mind a bit of dark in my light, if that's the case. You're the amazing woman you are because you decided who you wanted to be and made it happen."

Selene considered that perspective for a moment. What role did genetics play in personality, particularly when the people related hadn't been around one another? She'd need to look into the research, get answers based on more than supposition. But Alec was right. With no help, she had made it to the top. She'd consider the rest later, but she felt easier about it now. "Okay. Next?"

"Next. You're right. People are still looking to you. In fact, I would venture to say people are looking to you in both our worlds. Zed called you the Bridge because that's what the oracle refers to you as. A bridge between our worlds. We don't know exactly what that means yet, but we'll figure it out. Together."

Alec stroked away some of Selene's tears and her wing tips caressed Selene's back. "And that leads me to the next question." She tilted Selene's chin so she could look into her eyes. "I'm making it my life's work to take care of you, and to make you the happiest you've ever been. I can't fathom a day without you, and if you're willing to let me, I'll show you what a love for the ages really is."

Selene's tears began again, and she buried her face in Alec's chest. "But I'll die. You'll have to watch me get wrinkly, and warty, and get liver spots and gray hair. What if I get sick? Clearly, I can't pray it away…And that's a whole other can of worms I still need to swallow. I need answers to religions limitations, and why and—"

"Stop, baby. Shh." Alec placed her fingertip on Selene's lips. "You're right. I'll have to watch you get older. But the more time you spend with me, or at Afterlife, the slower time will go for you. It's kind of a between-time place, Limbo, if you will. You'll age far slower than normal, which gives us more time together. And then…"

"And then?" Selene looked up at Alec, confused by her sudden silence.

"Well, then we can talk about the options. You're a demigod, baby, remember? Think back to the tales and what happens to demigods."

Selene thought of the various stories from different cultures. "Well, they all have harrowing, difficult lives full of monsters and terror, and then they die, usually at a young age."

Alec laughed and Selene's tummy flipped at the delicious sound.

"Okay, yeah, that's mostly true. And proving to be accurate so far, don't you think? But what happens after they die?"

Selene's eyes grew wide. "That's true? They die and go to where the gods are, often becoming gods themselves."

"Kind of true. They don't become gods, certainly not anymore, but they can come to live at Afterlife, and usually get jobs among us. They don't die in the sense Dani takes them, generally."

"And I've got more questions about that, too, by the way." Selene sat up and stared at Alec. "So, when I die, I'll still be here. With you."

Alec gently pulled her back down so Selene was lying on top of her. "If that's what you want. I'm in love with you, Selene. I have been since the moment I saw you, I think. Forever is a long time in our world, baby, and you may not want me that long. But I'll be here for as long as you do."

Selene took Alec's face in her hands and kissed her, putting every ounce of love and desire she could into it. "I want you. I don't fully understand what's going on, and I'm not happy about being some heroine pawn told what to do by some bizarre, matriarchal top management. But I do know I want you more than I ever thought it possible to desire another person. I crave you, and no matter what, I want to show you how much I love you with every breath I have, from now until I join you on your side of the time warp."

Alec lifted her and gently flipped them over so she was lying on top of Selene. Her kisses were deep, passionate, filled with promises she knew, now, could be kept. She slipped Selene's shirt off, then quickly pulled off the rest of her clothes before sitting back on her heels to look at her.

Selene flushed, unused to someone's scrutiny of her body. But the way Alec was looking at her, as though she were both too precious to touch and yet something to be fully devoured, made her feel sexy in a way she'd never known. Alec moved between Selene's legs, her wings fanning out over her to drape down either side of the bed. *An angel. My own dark, avenging, dangerous angel.* When Alec's tongue slid softly, so, so softly, over her clit, every thought fled, replaced by nothing but the feel of Alec's touch.

She buried one hand in Alec's feathers and held on to her muscular shoulder with the other. Soft and hard. A perfect contrast, a perfect balance. As Alec licked her slowly, circling her clit, building the physical release while breaking through the emotional dam, Selene gave herself over and watched Alec between her legs. Alec looked up at her, and her pupils had elongated, making her look dangerous…Selene's orgasm drew closer, and she pulled Alec's head down. "Please, baby. Please suck harder."

Alec complied, sucking her clit into her mouth, pressing her tongue hard against it, then releasing it to suck it in again. Selene bucked and shook, and when Alec slid two fingers inside her, she exploded, coming hard, glad Alec had wrapped one arm around her thigh to hold her in place.

Alec moved back up beside her after they'd both caught their breath, and Selene snuggled in close. Held in Alec's arms, she drifted to sleep, safer and more sated than she'd ever been.

Chapter Thirty

That's the most absurd idea I've ever heard. I thought you were supposed to help us, not make us laughing stocks. Or get us killed. These bodies aren't entirely indestructible, you know. They can take ages to repair if you really mess them up."

Zed paced his office, but Jesus was looking at Selene contemplatively, as was Ama. God was inscrutable, but she'd expected that. Allah, like Zed, looked perturbed. Fin, whom Alec had introduced as a Celtic god and longtime friend, sat at the table eating a cronut. He winked at Alec as he licked his fingers. Alec had explained to Selene that as a primary god, even a pre-fader, he had a say in this conversation. Selene decided she liked him, even before she knew he preferred Guinness.

"You said it yourself. I'm supposed to be the bridge. I think that means I'm supposed to bring our worlds together, not keep them as opposing forces that can be used against each other. I really, really believe this is the way." Selene held her ground.

Jesus grinned. "I think she might be right. I mean, some of us are already doing it, right? We just have to figure out how to make an appearance, get noticed without getting lynched. Or crucified." He shot a glare at his father. "I like it."

Allah shook his head. "They believe because it's faith. Faith must be tested by the absence of proof. If proof is suddenly there, faith is no longer necessary, and all that the gods do is taken for granted."

Selene frowned. "With all due respect, you don't do much. Have you seen the state of the world? It's not exactly a shining example of your abilities as a group. You're a creation of human belief, so you can't really ever be stronger than a human can conceive of. And you've got their limitations too. You have to show them what's possible, so they believe it, and then you can make it happen."

At this, Selene felt the room darken and the energy shift. "Get pissed off if you want to. Go ahead, let your egos take over. But you know it's true. You're just as jealous, petty, spiteful, and egotistical as the humans who keep you alive by believing in you." She looked around the room, meeting their eyes. Now that she knew what came after death, she had no fear whatsoever of their reactions. "But you can also be exactly what they need, what they believe you to be. Do it my way and prove you deserve their adoration and prayers."

They all stayed quiet, but Jesus was practically vibrating with excitement, his smile wide.

Finally, it was God who broke the silence, and the high pitch of his voice made Selene think of Mickey Mouse. "I think we try. I did it once, with my son. It didn't go exactly as planned—"

Jesus snorted and crossed his arms over his chest.

"But it did work, for a while. It certainly got people's attention." He looked at Zed. "You and your family used to do it all the time, before I came along. And people behaved better, or worse, because of it."

Zed sighed. "We'll take it to an emergency board meeting and put it to a vote." He looked at Selene, and she was glad to see how solid he appeared. "You know this could backfire?"

"And what? People stop believing in you because of it? You don't have much to lose. And Alec and I will do our best to make the transition easier."

Ama had been typing away in the background, and she stood up to get their attention. "No need for a board meeting. I've been updating them via a live feed." She looked at them each in turn, solemn and unsure. "The board has voted. The majority wins—we go with Selene's plan."

The silence was heavy until Jesus got up with a shout and wrapped Selene in a hug.

She laughed and felt Alec squeeze her hand. Selene had needed to do the talking, as the one designated as the bridge, but Alec had insisted on being there to support her. *Because that's who we are together.* The thought warmed her and she smiled at Zed.

"Then it's settled. The gods are coming out of the closet."

About the Author

Brey Willows is a longtime editor and writer. Her passion is literature and the classics, and she has published a large handful of short stories and several articles and reviews. When she's not running a social enterprise working with marginalized communities on writing projects, she's editing other people's writing or doing her own. She lives in the middle of England with her partner and fellow author and spends entirely too much time exploring castles and ancient ruins while bemoaning the rain.

Books Available from Bold Strokes Books

Divided Nation, United Hearts by Yolanda Wallace. In a nation torn in two by a most uncivil war, can love conquer the divide? (978-1-62639-847-4)

Fury's Bridge by Brey Willows. What if your life depended on someone who didn't believe in your existence? (978-1-62639-841-2)

Lightning Strikes by Cass Sellars. When Parker Duncan and Sydney Hyatt's one-night stand turns to more, both women must fight demons past and present to cling to the relationship neither of them thought she wanted. (978-1-62639-956-3)

Love in Disaster by Charlotte Greene. A professor and a celebrity chef are drawn together by chance, but can their attraction survive a natural disaster? (978-1-62639-885-6)

Secret Hearts by Radclyffe. Can two women from different worlds find common ground while fighting their secret desires? (978-1-62639-932-7)

Sins of Our Fathers by A. Rose Mathieu. Solving gruesome murder cases is only one of Elizabeth Campbell's challenges; another is her growing attraction to the female detective who is hell-bent on keeping her client in prison. (978-1-62639-873-3)

The Sniper's Kiss by Justine Saracen. The power of a kiss: it can swell your heart with splendor, declare abject submission, and sometimes blow your brains out. (978-1-62639-839-9)

Troop 18 by Jessica L. Webb. Charged with uncovering the destructive secret that a troop of RCMP cadets has been hiding, Andy must put aside her worries about Kate and uncover the conspiracy before it's too late. (978-1-62639-934-1)

Worthy of Trust and Confidence by Kara A. McLeod. FBI Special Agent Ryan O'Connor is about to discover the hard way that when you can only handle one type of answer to a question, it really is better not to ask. (978-1-62639-889-4)

Amounting to Nothing by Karis Walsh. When mounted police officer Billie Mitchell steps in to save beautiful murder witness Merissa Karr, worlds collide on the rough city streets of Tacoma, Washington. (978-1-62639-728-6)

Becoming You by Michelle Grubb. Airlie Porter has a secret. A deep, dark, destructive secret that threatens to engulf her if she can't find the courage to face who she really is and who she really wants to be with. (978-1-62639-811-5)

Birthright by Missouri Vaun. When spies bring news that a swordswoman imprisoned in a neighboring kingdom bears the Royal mark, Princess Kathryn sets out to rescue Aiden, true heir to the Belstaff throne. (978-1-62639-485-8)

Crescent City Confidential by Aurora Rey. When romance and danger are in the air, writer Sam Torres learns the Big Easy is anything but. (978-1-62639-764-4)

Love Down Under by MJ Williamz. Wylie loves Amarina, but if Amarina isn't out, can their relationship last? (978-1-62639-726-2)

Privacy Glass by Missouri Vaun. Things heat up when Nash Wiley commandeers a limo and her best friend for a late drive out to the beach: Champagne on ice, seat belts optional, and privacy glass a must. (978-1-62639-705-7)

The Impasse by Franci McMahon. A horse packing excursion into the Montana Wilderness becomes an adventure of terrifying proportions for Miles and ten women on an outfitter led trip. (978-1-62639-781-1)

The Right Kind of Wrong by PJ Trebelhorn. Bartender Quinn Burke is happy with her life as a playgirl until she realizes she can't fight her feelings any longer for her best friend, bookstore owner Grace Everett. (978-1-62639-771-2)

Wishing on a Dream by Julie Cannon. Can two women change everything for the chance at love? (978-1-62639-762-0)

A Quiet Death by Cari Hunter. When the body of a young Pakistani girl is found out on the moors, the investigation leaves Detective Sanne Jensen facing an ordeal she may not survive. (978-1-62639-815-3)

Buried Heart by Laydin Michaels. When Drew Chambliss meets Cicely Jones, her buried past finds its way to the surface—will they survive its discovery or will their chance at love turn to dust? (978-1-62639-801-6)

Escape: Exodus Book Three by Gun Brooke. Aboard the Exodus ship *Pathfinder*, President Thea Tylio still holds Caya Lindemay, a clairvoyant changer, in protective custody, which has devastating consequences endangering their relationship and the entire Exodus mission. (978-1-62639-635-7)

Genuine Gold by Ann Aptaker. New York, 1952. Outlaw Cantor Gold is thrown back into her honky-tonk Coney Island past, where crime and passion simmer in a neon glare. (978-1-62639-730-9)

Into Thin Air by Jeannie Levig. When her girlfriend disappears, Hannah Lewis discovers her world isn't as orderly as she thought it was. (978-1-62639-722-4)

Night Voice by CF Frizzell. When talk show host Sable finally acknowledges her risqué radio relationship with a mysterious caller, she welcomes a *real* relationship with local tradeswoman Riley Burke. (978-1-62639-813-9)

Raging at the Stars by Lesley Davis. When the unbelievable theories start revealing themselves as truths, can you trust in the ones who have conspired against you from the start? (978-1-62639-720-0)

She Wolf by Sheri Lewis Wohl. When the hunter becomes the hunted, more than love might be lost. (978-1-62639-741-5)

Smothered and Covered by Missouri Vaun. The last person Nash Wiley expects to bump into over a two a.m. breakfast at Waffle House is her college crush, decked out in a curve-hugging law enforcement uniform. (978-1-62639-704-0)

The Butterfly Whisperer by Lisa Moreau. Reunited after ten years, can Jordan and Sophie heal the past and rediscover love or will differing desires keep them apart? (978-1-62639-791-0)

The Devil's Due by Ali Vali. Cain and Emma Casey are awaiting the birth of their third child, but as always in Cain's world, there are new and old enemies to face in post Katrina-ravaged New Orleans. (978-1-62639-591-6)

Widows of the Sun-Moon by Barbara Ann Wright. With immortality now out of their grasp, the gods of Calamity fight amongst themselves, egged on by the mad goddess they thought they'd left behind. (978-1-62639-777-4)

18 Months by Samantha Boyette. Alissa Reeves has only had two girlfriends and they've both gone missing. Now it's up to her to find out why. (978-1-62639-804-7)

Arrested Hearts by Holly Stratimore. A reckless cop with a secret death wish and a health nut who is afraid to die might be a perfect combination for love. (978-1-62639-809-2)

Capturing Jessica by Jane Hardee. Hyperrealist sculptor Michael tries desperately to conceal the love she holds for best friend, Jess, unaware Jess's feelings for her are changing. (978-1-62639-836-8)

Counting to Zero by AJ Quinn. NSA agent Emma Thorpe and computer hacker Paxton James must learn to trust each other as they work to stop a threat clock that's rapidly counting down to zero. (978-1-62639-783-5)

Courageous Love by KC Richardson. Two women fight a devastating disease, and their own demons, while trying to fall in love. (978-1-62639-797-2)

Pathogen by Jessica L. Webb. Can Dr. Kate Morrison navigate a deadly virus and the threat of bioterrorism, as well as her new relationship with Sergeant Andy Wyles and her own troubled past? (978-1-62639-833-7)

Rainbow Gap by Lee Lynch. Jaudon Vickers and Berry Garland, polar opposites, dream and love in this tale of lesbian lives set in Central Florida against the tapestry of societal change and the Vietnam War. (978-1-62639-799-6)

Steel and Promise by Alexa Black. Lady Nivrai's cruel desires and modified body make most of the galaxy fear her, but courtesan Cailyn Derys soon discovers the real monsters are the ones without the claws. (978-1-62639-805-4)

Swelter by D. Jackson Leigh. Teal Giovanni's mistake shines an unwanted spotlight on a small Texas ranch where August Reese is secluded until she can testify against a powerful drug kingpin. (978-1-62639-795-8)

Without Justice by Carsen Taite. Cade Kelly and Emily Sinclair must battle each other in the pursuit of justice, but can they fight their undeniable attraction outside the walls of the courtroom? (978-1-62639-560-2)